RULES TO LIVE BY

THE LODGE #1

QUINN WARD

1

———

Fuck. My. Life. I tangled my fingers through my hair as I blinked a few times before looking at the computer screen again. There had to be some sort of mistake. No way in hell was my bank account balance that low. I hadn't expected to log in and see millions accumulating interest, but there should have been more. I scrolled through the recent transactions, letting out a frustrated scream when everything added up. Except, apparently, my ability to do simple math.

I shoved away from the rickety dining room table, kicking an empty beer can on my way to the thermostat. Turning it down a few more degrees wasn't likely to do much, other than possibly land me in the emergency room with pneumonia, but I would pretend, at least for a little while, that I was being all adulty and responsible.

Yeah right, the little voice inside my head scoffed. *If you were responsible, you would grow the hell up and get a real job.*

Oddly enough, my conscience sounded almost identical to my dad. He'd be so pissed if he realized I was living like this. Not as upset as he'd be about the fact that I had completely blown my inheritance in less than four years, but he definitely wouldn't be happy.

I took a detour to the bedroom on my way back to the kitchen/dining room combo in my apartment. Who in the hell was I kidding? Pretending like this shit hole was sophisticated enough for separate rooms. Hell, one drunken stumble the wrong way and I would probably crash through the few walls I did have.

If you weren't such an idiot, you wouldn't have to stay in this dump, that damn voice scolded me.

"Well no shit," I responded out loud. Yes, I was talking to myself. Probably made me less than mentally stable, but at least when I was holding conversations with myself, I didn't have to look at the faces of the few friends I'd managed to hang onto. I didn't want to see their pity or their disappointment, or whatever the fuck else they couldn't school in their features.

The front of one of my dresser drawers fell off in my hand when I tried getting a sweatshirt. I threw the broken piece of wood at the wall. "Fuck!"

This was it. The end. This was one of those turning-point moments I'd heard on the psychobabble talk shows my mom used to watch all the time. I had reached a crossroads, and I could either make a choice or one would be made for me.

As I sat there wallowing in self-pity, I heard my phone ringing from somewhere out in the main area of the apartment. If I didn't come up with some cash, my service would get shut off in a couple of weeks. Then what the fuck was I supposed to do? Not many places were eager to hire a dude who couldn't even keep his phone bill paid so they could call him back for an interview.

I let the damn thing ring. I wasn't in the mood to talk to

anyone. I didn't want to come up with a believable lie when the two guys I still talked to from the band called, asking me if I wanted to head out and grab drinks with them. Did I want to? Fuck yes. Unfortunately, little things like eating and drinking cost money. Money I apparently didn't fucking have.

The phone stopped ringing.

And then it started again.

I fell back on the bed, covering my head with a pillow. I didn't give a shit who it was. Eventually, they'd give up. Everyone always did. Now that the band had split, there was no reason for people to push me to be sociable. No one wanted to hang out with the emo-rock-star-wannabe with a serious case of Peter Pan syndrome. They all had their own lives. Obviously, since that was one of the main reasons After Effect split up. We had never been the type of band who could rake in the dough, but at least when we were playing gigs regularly, I didn't have to sit around the apartment trying to figure out how low I could turn thermostat before getting sick or how many times it was actually necessary to eat in a given day.

I missed it. I hated them for moving on and leaving me in their dust. And most of all, I hated the fact that my dad was right.

He always told me I'd never get anywhere with music, but I had been determined to prove him wrong. He was one of those pretentious assholes who thought you were only worth as much as the college degrees hanging on your wall. I thought he was about to have a coronary when I told him I wasn't going to college. He'd tried guilting me, reminding me that I wouldn't see a penny of the inheritance my grandfather left me until I turned twenty-one if I chose to forfeit college. At the time, I'd been young and oh so naïve. Three years hadn't seemed like that long to eventually have freedom. Freedom to chase that lottery known as a lucky break.

Lucky breaks didn't happen for people like me. Once the money came in, I was able to hang on a few more years, but now I was quickly coming to the end of that money, and it was time to figure out who in the hell I was without music.

The fucking phone started ringing again. Whoever it was, wasn't going to stop trying to annoy me enough that I picked up. I stomped out of the bedroom, tripping over a hamper full of laundry in the hall. Clean? Dirty? Who the fuck knew anymore. I had become a huge fan of the sniff test, because dragging all my shit to the laundromat was both a pain and another added expense.

"What?" I answered without bothering to look at the caller ID. If they wanted to annoy the fuck out of me by calling repeatedly, then they didn't deserve a pleasant greeting. Whoever the fuck they were.

"Someone woke up on the wrong side of the bed," Jordan teased. Of course, it was Jordan. He'd been my best friend since we were kids and he was the only person I trusted to never turn their back on me. But if he knew what was going on, he would try to fix my problems because that was the type of guy he was. He was the one who caught a lucky break. When he hit what he thought was his rock bottom, the love of his boss's life literally picked him up and carried him to a whole new world. Now, he had two men who'd kill for him. He'd found his happy little life with Doug and Eli, and he wanted everyone he knew to be as stupidly happy as he was.

Well, I had bad news for him. Sometimes, life sucked.

You're not being fair, the voice lectured me. *You know damn well how much Jordan suffered to get to where he is now.*

I did. And that's why I had sworn off relationships. No

amount of dick on hand was worth the pain he had gone through with all the men he swore were the one before realizing that he wasn't looking for one, he needed two. That was Jordan; my lovable, sometimes high maintenance, best friend.

"Sorry. I was trying to get some shit done," I lied. To assuage my guilt, I started straightening the kitchen counter. I flipped open the lid on the garbage can and shoveled all the junk mail into it. Jordan wouldn't have believed me if I told him I was cleaning. He always gave me a hard time about being such a slob. I wasn't. Not really. But looking around this place, I seriously thought the clutter gave it some much-needed character.

"What are you doing next Tuesday night?"

I paused, debating how to answer. If it was anyone else, I would've made a sarcastic quip about needing to check my jam-packed social calendar, but this was Jordan. I didn't want to piss him off. "Same thing I do every night. Sit around the house trying to figure out where in the fuck my life went wrong."

"Is everything okay?" Ugh. He had that super sweet, worried tone in his voice.

"Yup," I responded with a pop of my lips for emphasis. "Life's just peachy."

Jordan knew better but he didn't call me out on the lie. I'd been a mess since the band split up and I knew Jordan was genuinely worried about me.

"Any luck finding a new job yet?"

"A new job would imply having an old job," I pointed out. "And as my dad would be all too eager to explain, the band wasn't a job. It was an avoidance tactic."

"Knock it the hell off," Jordan scolded me. If he was standing in front of me, I had no doubt he would've cuffed the back of my head. "Self-pity isn't your style, Slade. And fuck what your old man says. He's an asshole."

"Tell me something I don't know," I quipped. I opened the fridge door out of habit, slamming it closed when I saw the bottom shelf was as empty now as it had been for the past week. No money equaled no beer. I really, *really* wanted a drink.

"Okay," Jordan said cheerfully. "Since you're not doing anything, we're having a housewarming party next Tuesday and you're coming."

"I am, huh?" I settled for a glass of water. Of course, that meant having to clean a fucking glass first. I listened as Jordan rattled off the details. Apparently, the guys had insisted on hosting a party, something about symbolic bullshit to welcome Jordan to his new home.

It was so sweet it made me want to fucking puke. I set my glass of water down on the milk crate that doubled as an end table, flopped onto the couch, and kicked my legs up on the coffee table. It gave a wobbly warning. One of these times, that thing was going to collapse, sending even more shit to the floor.

I didn't want to go to their happy little homemaking party. I wasn't in the mood to plaster on a smile I didn't feel, and pretend I was over the moon happy for my best friend and the two men he was now shacking up with.

Quit being a prissy little bitch. Alcohol would be really fucking nice. At least when I was blitzed, I didn't have to listen to that damn voice. And, if there was one thing I could count on, it was that Jordan's boss/partner wouldn't skimp on the booze.

Fine, I was happy for Jordan. I was also jealous as fuck of how everything seemed to be working out for him. And I wasn't so self-absorbed that I didn't realize what an asshole that made me. A good friend would be happy without all the residual bullshit.

"Did I lose you?" I shook my head a couple of times to clear the cobwebs. If I didn't get my shit together, Jordan was going to figure out how screwed in the head I was and he'd be over here, dragging me down to The Dandy Ginger.

That was the last fucking place I wanted to go. Rusty, the owner, had made all sorts of offers when I called to let him know that we needed to bail on all the dates he had booked us to play at the bar. I didn't want Rusty's charity. There were several things I *did* want from him, like just one night of him putting aside his stupid fucking moral compass so he would bend me over and fuck me so hard I'd forgot every man who had been inside of me before him.

Rusty was a big guy. Bulging muscles, matted with thick, coarse hair and absolutely everything I looked for when I went out. He also had enough baggage in his past to fill the lost and found room at an international airport. He kept telling me I didn't want him whenever I made a pass at him, but he was wrong.

Maybe I should head down there and try again. I could probably get Rusty to throw me a few free drinks. Not enough to get hammered, just enough to quiet the voices in my head.

"You're doing it again," Jordan pointed out. His words were slow and drawn out.

"Sorry, trying to figure something out over here," I told him. That wasn't a lie. I was trying to figure out how in the hell I was going to keep myself alive.

"So you'll be there?" he asked hopefully. "I'm not taking no for an answer Slade. I know you've been a bit of a hermit and that worries me. You are a beautiful little social butterfly and staying cooped up in that shithole you call home is bad for your soul."

There are a lot of things that are bad for my soul. I bit my tongue to keep from letting that inner thought escape.

"Yeah, I'll be there. Let me know what time."

"You really weren't listening to a word I said, were you?"

I let out a long sigh and bumped my head against the back of the couch a few times.

"No worries man, I was just giving you shit." He chuckled, and I pulled the phone away from my ear to scowl at it. His perkiness annoyed the fuck out of me.

"Eight o'clock, Tuesday night, at our place. You know how to get there?"

"Oh, fuck off," I scoffed.

"Just checking," he responded.

It was on the tip of my tongue to ask Jordan what he was doing tonight. He could come and hang out with me, help me take my mind off shit for a while. And if I asked, he would pick up a six-pack, no questions asked. But I wouldn't do that. Because even if he thought he was just doing me a favor by stopping at the store since he was out, I would know. And I wasn't a charity case, even when the other person had no clue they were donating to the keep Slade sane fund.

Apparently, I was quiet long enough for Jordan to notice. "Slade, is everything good? Really? Don't try to bullshit me."

"Just trying to figure shit out," I told him. Great. Now my head was throbbing. Within an hour, I'd be curled up on the couch with my eyes clenched shut, trying to will the pain away. I rubbed my forehead, desperate for any slight relief.

"No luck on the job front yet?"

"I have some feelers out," I lied. I wasn't about to tell Jordan I had barely started looking for a job. In the back of my mind, I still had at least six months before I had to worry about it.

Haha. Joke's on me.

"Well, if you don't get something soon, let me know," Jordan suggested. "We have a few openings down at the bar. You know I'd put in a good word for you."

Yeah, I did. And that was exactly why I hadn't even considered talking to Eli about a job. Things were already strained between us. I didn't need to add being a lowlife to the list of faults Eli saw in me. Fine, so maybe I had brought his negative assumptions on myself. Probably had something to do with that night he caught me blowing some dude in the back hall. I didn't see what his problem was; he ran a gay bar for fuck's sake. But apparently, according to Jordan, he'd had a close call in the past and wanted to at least pretend like he was keeping things on the up and up. He wasn't naïve; he knew that guys were getting off in his bar every night.

"I'll keep you posted," I responded.

"Make sure you do." There was silence across the line, then soft breathing. The silence dragged on for a beat. Two. Three. "Slade, I know you have issues with taking handouts but you gotta let it go, man. Stop believing all the bullshit your dad put in your head. Letting your friends help you when you're down isn't a weakness. Hell, how many times have you let me crash at your place when I was going through a bad spell with whatever guy I was dating?"

"So, your place Tuesday at eight?" Confirming that I'd attend their little get together was a good way to get Jordan off the topic of my dismal career opportunities.

"Yeah," he confirmed. "Don't worry if something comes up and you're not able to make it. I'd completely understand."

The sad tone in his voice said otherwise. He struggled a bit with figuring out his place in his new relationship. He had vented to me a few times about not wanting to take on all of Doug and Eli's friends as his own. He had done that when he was with Tyson, and when the two of them split, most of their so-called mutual friends did, too.

"Jordan, I'll be there."

"But if you get a job between now and then…"

"Then I'll tell them I had already made plans for that night." Not like that would be an issue since my phone wasn't ringing off the hook to interview for jobs I hadn't applied for. "It sounds like this is a big deal to you. Don't worry, I'll be there so you have someone to talk to."

"That's not the only reason I invited you," Jordan scoffed.

"But it is one of them?"

"You know damn well it is."

"For a guy who has everything he's ever wanted, you seem to have a hard time believing you're where you're supposed to be."

"Yeah, and for a guy who doesn't understand the attraction to being in a committed relationship that lasts longer than one round of orgasms, you sound a bit jealous of my relationship," Jordan shot back.

If he only knew the half of it. There were some things that I had never told anyone, including Jordan. While I would feel bad keeping most secrets from him, no good would've come from telling him this one and now it was too little, too late.

I swallowed around the lump in my throat and blinked my eyes a few times. I wasn't going to get all mopey and weepy.

"Hey man, I hate to do this, but I really gotta run," I told him. I prayed he wouldn't ask me where I was going. I didn't want to admit my only destination was my bed.

"Yeah, cool. Okay." I heard him let out another long sigh as if he was tempted to say something else. He must have decided against it. "Okay, well, I will see you Tuesday night."

"Yeah, sounds good. Anything I need to know? Any sort of dress code?"

"No, man, just come as you are. Not like you'd listen if there was a dress code anyway, but this is just a chill get together with our friends. Call it a way for everyone to get to know one another better."

Oh joy. Just what I needed. More people trying to get to know the basket case who was standing at the dead-end of his life. I tossed my phone to the other end of the couch after Jordan and I said goodbye. It would die soon if I didn't plug it in but that was okay by me. If my phone was dead, it couldn't ring. If it didn't ring, no one could interrupt me while I was trying to sleep.

Such an exciting life I led, sleeping away my Friday night instead of rocking it out on stage.

2

JACK

"I don't understand." Doug had probably explained himself while I was attempting to multitask. Most of the time I was pretty damn good at it, but my baby brother wasn't making any sense. He was talking about having a housewarming party. I wasn't sure that really applied when he was moving back in with the guy he'd been with for over a decade.

"Eli is worried about Jordan," Doug explained. That was nothing new. Eli was usually pretty easy-going about most things, but it seemed his indifference didn't extend to their boy. "He hasn't invited anyone to the apartment since he moved in. And he keeps calling it our place, as in mine and Eli's, not his."

"So, the two of you decided you were going to put on this charade of a party as a way to... What exactly?" I closed the lid of my laptop so I could give Doug my complete attention.

"We're hoping that he won't feel as out of place if everyone is getting together."

"Eventually, the two of you are going to have to find a way to make him understand he isn't a guest in your home."

Far be it for me to tell anyone else how they should deal with the boy, but the two of them coddled Jordan far too much. It wasn't good. If they didn't curb his bad behavior, eventually, he was going to start lashing out. At that point, it would be nearly impossible for them to regain the upper hand. Doug had enough of that from Eli, who'd kill him if he found out Doug and I had been talking about their predicament as well.

"I know." Doug let out a ragged sigh. "It's just so damn hard sometimes, Jack. He gets this pouty look on his face and his eyes go all sad like a puppy dog, and I can't bring myself to discipline him."

"Well, maybe it's time for you to put your own shit aside and..." Okay, so maybe I was going to tell him where I thought he was going wrong. It was a hazard of the job, I supposed. I had seen enough bratty little subs who didn't take their D/s relationships seriously. But this wasn't just anyone. It was Doug, and I had over forty years of bossing him around. It became second nature to me.

"Have you ever considered that when he plays all sad and mopey, he's testing the two of you?"

"I've considered that," Doug admitted. "But I don't know. I think more of it is him still trying to get used to being in a healthy relationship. He's never been with anyone who didn't treat him like crap."

"From what you told me, his ex was a pretty decent guy," I argued. There was a knock on my door before Sam, one of my assistant managers at The Lodge, walked into the office. I held up a finger to acknowledge he was there and let him know I would be a minute.

"If you can't make it, we all understand." And here was the beginning of the guilt trip. If I didn't nip this in the bud, Doug would launch into a lecture about how I needed to trust my employees and step away from time to time.

"Never said I wouldn't be there just because I don't understand why you're going through all this trouble." Eli had to *hate* the idea of a bunch of people in their home. He was one of the most private people I knew when it came to his personal space. That spoke to how much both of them loved Jordan.

"Do you seriously not understand? Can you honestly tell me that you wouldn't do the same if it was your boy who was struggling to settle in?"

That would require having a boy, and it'd been a few years since I found myself in that position. The last relationship I'd been in had ended because Colin accused me of being married to my work and said he was tired of feeling like the mistress. When I realized he hadn't been totally wrong about that, I stepped back from pursuing anything with anyone.

"Fine. Maybe I do understand a little bit," I conceded. "But don't expect me to bring you a housewarming gift. You got everything you're getting from me when the two of you originally moved into that place."

When Doug and Eli initially approached me about the dilapidated building down in the district, I thought they were nuts. But when Eli came to me with a solid business plan and a set of crudely assembled numbers, it didn't take too long before I began to see what drew Eli to the property. Eli knew that my weakness was potential. I had offered to buy into Club 83 as a silent partner. I wasn't keen to make my interest in the bar public knowledge since I owned another club nearby—albeit one that had fewer bands, a hell of a lot less clothing, and a series of private, semi-private, and public rooms. Eli's was the club where everyone turned a blind eye to the sexy hijinks that went on. The Lodge was a place where everyone would gather around to watch.

"I'm just warning you to be careful so he doesn't develop any bad habits. I see how much the three of you love each other, and I'd hate for anyone to get frustrated because expectations aren't being met."

"Jesus, Jack." I flinched at the unexpected outburst from Doug. Okay, so maybe I could've been a bit more tactful in what I said, a bit more tender in my delivery, but that wasn't me. I was straight to the point with my employees, anyone I played with, and always with my friends and family. "You do realize that not every relationship is a business transaction? We don't have benchmarks we're hoping to meet."

"I do." But I was woefully out of practice with any interaction that was more than a simple transaction. "I'm sorry, Doug. I didn't mean to come across crass, but I worry about you. You were a wreck when you and Eli split up. You can't really blame me for doing whatever is necessary to keep you from going through that sort of pain again."

"I know, and I appreciate it. But don't let Jordan hear you saying shit like that. He's finally starting to sink into his role outside the bedroom, and I'd really like to keep it that way."

"Good. I'm happy for you, Dougie."

"Don't call me that," he grumbled.

"I've been calling you Dougie for forty-three years. What makes you think I'm going to change now?"

"Well, it would be nice if you could respect that's a nickname that would've been better left in our childhood," Doug complained. "Remember when Eli and I first got together, and he heard you call me that? It took me almost a month to make him understand I didn't find anything amusing about him wandering around the club calling out for me by that ridiculous name."

"Yeah," I laughed. "That was great."

The two of us chatted a bit longer about what was going on in our lives—nothing, because Doug was still lost in his new boy, and trying to plan an exit strategy to get out of the job he currently had crunching numbers. I was proud of him for finally deciding he didn't need to have a traditional job in order to be successful. He had taken a lot of shit for his art when we were younger, but the truth was, he was way too talented to do nothing with it.

Eventually, Doug told me he had to get going because it was almost time for Jordan and Eli to go to work and he wanted to spend some time with them. "Good. Send both of them downstairs with sore asses."

"Oh, I intend to." Doug chuckled and I grimaced. There were some things you simply didn't need to know about your brother's sex life, and since he was *not* a disciplinarian unless he had to be... "Anyway, if you can make it out to our place next week, we'd love to see you. Otherwise, we need to figure out a time for the four of us to get together for dinner or something."

Yeah, right. I couldn't remember the last time I had had a nice relaxing dinner with everyone. By three o'clock every day, I was pulling into the parking lot behind The Lodge, getting ready to open the doors. I liked to tell myself I wasn't as bad as Eli, because I had no problem letting my staff do their thing while I did mine. But I felt better being on site. God forbid anything went sideways. It was much easier for me to take control of the situation when I was just down the hall, rather than having to drive in from the outskirts of town.

Speaking of... I looked up to find Sam sitting on the

couch across the room, fiddling with his phone. He was such an asset to The Lodge because it was easy for him to tune out when told he didn't need to be part of a conversation. Other times, he would hang back and observe, never stepping in unless his intuition made the hairs on the back of his neck rise.

"Sorry about that," I apologized. "What can I help you with, Sam?"

Sam held up a manila folder and cautiously stepped forward. "I probably should have asked your permission ahead of time..." Well, that was one way to get my attention. Sam wasn't the type to do anything without being given the green light.

I motioned for him to move closer. "Go on."

"So, in one of my classes, we had to put together a business proposal. I raised more than a few eyebrows when I decided to base my fictional business on this place, but I figured it would be easier if I was working with an environment that I was familiar with already." Sam practically collapsed into the chair on the opposite side of my desk.

"That was a smart move." Sam sat up a bit straighter and his eyes shone, dimples forming at the sides of his mouth when he smiled under the praise. "What makes you think you should have asked my permission?"

"Well, I went into it honestly thinking it was just going to be a goofy little project, but then I did really well with it. I wanted to show you what I worked on because I think there are some things that we could bring to the club." He paused, hedging, squirming around in his seat.

"Relax, Sam. I'm not going to promise you we can make any big, sweeping changes, but if there's something in there that seems doable, I am more than open to suggestions."

Sam rested the folder on his lap, placed his hands on top

of it, and gazed at a spot on the floor in front of him. It couldn't be easy for him to put himself out there like this.

"Sam," I said, digging deep for the low-pitched voice I used when I was in Daddy mode.

His gaze glittered up to mine, and it crushed me that his earlier excitement had been replaced by uncertainty.

"It was brave of you to approach me. A lot of men wouldn't have had that sort of strength." I held out my hand. "May I see what you came up with?"

He remained so still I wasn't certain he'd heard me.

"Sam, let me look," I said, a bit more forcefully this time.

His hand shook as he obeyed me. "I'm not saying I think I know better than you or anything, but maybe a fresh perspective would help us bring in more business."

"More business is always good, Sam," I praised him. "And I like having innovative people on my team. It will be a shame when you eventually graduate and move on to a real job."

Sam's eyes widened and his mouth fell open, but no words came out. Why did he look like the idea of going out and making his own mark on the world was a punishment rather than the huge accomplishment it was?

"I mean it, Sam. And do not take that as me trying to shove you out the door. I would be damn lucky to keep you around, but there are so many other things waiting for you out there."

"I know, it's just..." his voice trailed off again.

"It's just, what?" I slid the folder off to the side and leaned forward, resting on my forearms on the desk. "Talk to me, Sam. What's really bugging you today?"

"It's nothing you need to worry yourself with."

"I'll be the judge of that," I insisted. There was little I liked less than people assuming I was too busy to worry about their problems. I wasn't some sort of self-absorbed asshole whose sole focus was on the businesses I ran or invested in.

But you are a bit obsessed with the bottom line. Isn't that the whole reason you're single now?

"Let me see what you've got." Sam was silent as I scanned over the business plan he had put together. It was easy to see the bits he had lifted from The Lodge but, at the same time, there were all these fresh ideas I had never even considered. After a cursory glance, I closed the folder and pushed it to the center of the desk.

"I'm impressed," I told him.

"Seriously?" He gaped at me, sitting on his hands to keep from fidgeting. There was something about this entire exchange that toed the line between professional and far too enticingly personal.

"Definitely. There are a few of the ideas you came up with that I'd like to work on implementing if you're game."

Sam practically bounced in his seat. "You're serious?"

"Absolutely." It was times like this I hated the formality of having a desk in between the two of us. Sam was the type of man who needed tenderness. He thrived on innocent touches and the simplest displays of affection.

He deserves a boss who isn't wishing he could pull him onto his lap and hold him.

I cleared my throat. "Sam, you have a bright future ahead of you. Please don't think my earlier comment about you graduating college and moving on had anything to do with me not understanding your value to everyone here at The Lodge."

I wanted some time to sit down with his proposal and figure out which ideas to implement and which to pass on. Once that was completed, I intended to reward Sam for his ingenuity. Maybe that would help him stick around for a while.

"I would love to work with you on it, sir." Now, he *was* bouncing in his seat. He pulled out his phone, startling when he noticed the time. "Damn. I need to get out there and get the floor set up for tonight."

"Relax. I'm pretty sure your boss understands what's keeping you back here."

Sam shrugged. "Sure, but that doesn't mean I'm going to piss him off now. He just made me a pretty sweet offer when I expected him to laugh in my face."

"I'm not that bad, am I?" It stung to know that one of my employees was intimidated by me. Sure, I could be a demanding boss, but I was always fair to everyone.

"Let's just say you have a very set way you like things to be done," he clarified before he rose from his seat and held out a hand. Most of the time, Sam was incredibly quiet and timid, but his handshake was firm and steady. I liked that. It proved that he would do well with whatever dreams he decided to chase.

Once the door closed behind him, I opened my laptop and started entering this month's invoices, yet again. Boring, menial work, but it allowed me to keep tabs on every penny that was going in and out of the club. Just the way I liked it. I hadn't gotten this far with my own ventures, or my investments, by sitting back and letting other people take the lead.

3

SLADE

My stomach growled as I stood in front of the private entrance to Jordan's place. I could do this. Before everything went to shit, I had no problem standing on a stage, entertaining hundreds of people at a time. And once our sets were done, it wasn't unusual for me to spend the rest of the evening bouncing from one group to the next. I shouldn't be freaked out by a small party hosted by one of my best friends and his men. Everyone here was safe.

"You look as though walking through that door will lead to imminent death," a deep voice boomed behind me. I flinched, stepping to the left and allowing him to pass. "I assume you are here for the housewarming party."

I gaped at the man before me. He looked far more out of place than I did in his three-piece suit and tie. I hadn't been aware people actually dressed like that anymore. Every stitch of clothing was tailored to perfection, hugging the lines of his body. He reminded me of my dad's business colleagues. I hated him a little bit at first sight for that reason alone.

"Answer me," he demanded.

I was tempted to tell him to fuck off just on principle. I didn't owe this person anything. I sure as shit didn't have to answer to him. But for some reason, I did. The longer he stared at me, the more compelled I felt to respond. "Yes, sir."

"Then, don't you think you should head inside? You're going to miss the entire party if you stand out here second-guessing yourself." He reached around me and turned the doorknob. We were close enough I could smell the blend of woods and citrus of his cologne. My dick took notice too, hardening instantly, as I forced myself not to inhale as deeply as possible, imprinting this man's scent to my memory. He pushed the door open and waved me inside.

Again, I wanted to resist, solely based on principle. And, once again, I found myself incapable.

"What's your name, boy?" He placed a broad, strong hand at the small of the back, steadying me as we ascended the staircase. I wanted to step away from him, walk just a little bit faster—anything—to get outside of the black hole he was sucking me into, but I didn't. I couldn't. Not when I felt so unsteady. If nothing else, I had faith this stranger would keep me from tumbling to my death.

"Slade," I responded quietly.

"That's quite a unique name," he remarked. "Is it a nickname?"

"No," I lied. I didn't owe him anything I wasn't comfortable sharing. "It's what everyone calls me."

My legal name was one steeped in generations of family tradition. When I had moved out on my own to forge my own path, I had chosen a name—one that wouldn't remind me of how much I was letting down all the men who came before me when I fell flat on my face.

He didn't offer me his name and I didn't ask.

There wasn't time for proper introductions once we got into the apartment. As soon as the door opened, the stranger was whisked off and Jordan tackled me with a huge hug.

"You made it!"

"I told you I'd be here, didn't I?" The hug was, both, comforting and uncomfortable. Soothing and unsettling. I hated how good it felt to be wrapped in Jordan's arms. If I wasn't such a stubborn ass, I might have broken down right there in the entryway to the apartment.

"You did, but I wasn't sure you'd actually follow through."

My gut clenched. I might be flighty from time to time, but I couldn't think of any occasion when I had literally bailed on Jordan. Even in the worst of my depression, his was the one friendship I went out of my way to protect at all costs.

Jordan took a step back, resting his hands on my shoulders while he looked me over from head to toe. I squirmed under the scrutiny, imagining he could see every ounce I had lost recently. He dragged the pad of his thumb over my cheekbones.

"Are you having trouble sleeping again?"

Again. That word stuck out. I couldn't remember having ever told him about my issues with sleep, but he knew. Of course, he did. This was Jordan, the man who knew more about me than I knew about myself most of the time.

I shrugged. "It's been tough, but I'm getting through."

"Anything we can do to help?"

We. No, there was nothing they could collectively do for me. I hated that everything in Jordan's life had shifted from singular to plural. I felt like anything I said to him would immediately get back to Doug and Eli, and for that reason, I chose to keep everything to myself.

"I'll get through. I always do."

"But that doesn't mean you *have* to get through it on your own," Jordan argued. He slipped his hand into mine and pulled me deeper into the apartment. In the kitchen, there was a huge spread of food. He waved a hand over it. "Help yourself. I might have gone overboard with the menu for tonight. Couldn't help myself; this is the first time I really had a chance to try out a bunch of recipes without worrying we would wind up throwing out the leftovers."

"So, what you're telling me is, you really held this party as a way for all of us to be your guinea pigs?" I teased. Jordan's cheeks brightened and the corner of his mouth turned up in a shy smile. It was the first time I realized just how good he looked. Happy, when he hadn't been for so long. For that split second, everything in the world was right. My problems didn't exist. Jordan's adoring partners didn't agitate me. It was just Jordan and me.

"Jordan." All it took to burst my bubble of momentary happiness was the sound of Eli's voice behind us. Jordan narrowed his eyes, silently warning me that this conversation would be picked up at a later point. "Could you help Jack for a minute?"

Jordan's brow furrowed in confusion. The protective side of me wanted to lash out, asking Eli why he didn't help whoever it was himself, but I kept my mouth shut. Jordan was happy here. I wasn't going to do anything to cause him stress, and if the three of them were in it for the long haul, then I wanted to try to repair Eli's view of me.

"Yeah, sure..." His voice trailed off as if he'd been about to say something else. He cocked his head to the side and smiled at Eli. I held my breath, waiting for Jordan to stand up to him, but he never did. He simply walked away, leaving me alone with one of his partners.

I braced myself, waiting for Eli's lecture. It had to be coming. What other reason was there for him to dismiss Jordan, other than wanting a minute alone with me to warn me what he'd do if I upset Jordan.

"Look, I know you don't like me," I said before he could get a word in. "And I know I've earned part of that reputation, but you don't know anything about me other than what you've seen."

Eli held up his hands in surrender.

"You are absolutely right about that," he agreed. "I'm not going to give you any sort of lecture or tell you that I think Jordan would be better off if you didn't come around, because that's not true. I actually came over here for the exact opposite."

Now I was the one who was confused. I pressed my lips together to keep from making an even bigger ass of myself.

"I wanted to thank you for coming tonight," Eli explained. "Jordan has been worried about you. He said something about the band that you used to play with breaking up?"

"It happens." I shrugged. "Being in the club business, I'm sure you've seen other bands decide it was time to give up on their dreams and get real jobs."

"It's a damn shame," Eli remarked, and my eyes grew wide. Had Eli actually just given me a compliment? I thought I had. "It's never easy to let go of something you want. And, even though it's not exactly my type of music, I can admit that you have a hell of a lot of talent. Have you ever thought about going solo?"

"I'm not sure how well that would work," I admitted. What I didn't say was that I needed the guys behind me to support me when I was so fucking scared, I wasn't sure I could take those first steps onto the stage. Slade was a persona—a mask. To everyone who saw us play, I was this cocky, confident, talented singer who could pack any bar in the district. None of them understood how hard it was for me to silence my father's objections. Every single fucking time. It was only once the music began that I was able to close my eyes and feel the beat, hear the melody, and turn off everything other than the set.

"Just think about it," Eli encouraged me. "If you want to give it a go, come talk to me. I'll pencil you in whenever you want. If you're worried about how it will go, we can set you up on one of the slower nights when the crowd isn't as rowdy or vocal."

"Yeah. Okay. I'll think about it," I promised him. Unfortunately, I would do more than just think about it. I would obsess about it—tell myself all the reasons it was the worst idea ever and convince myself I was nothing without a band playing behind me. I held out my hand, which Eli shook firmly. "Thank you, Eli. It means a lot to know that you have faith in me. I don't want to make any rash decisions though."

"I can respect that. Now, here comes Jordan. If you don't mind, do you think it would be possible for you to keep this between the two of us?" His cheeks flushed and he looked... Embarrassed? He glanced past me again. "Jordan's worried about you, Slade. If it was up to him, I would have come over here and insisted that you take a job at the club. I refused to do that because I'm pretty sure that's not what you want. You strike me as fiercely independent; the type of man who needs to know that he can make it on his own."

"I am," I responded, shocked that Eli had picked up so much about me. "And please don't think I don't appreciate the offer. I absolutely do. It's just... Everything's changed, and sometimes I wake up feeling like the world is this vicious cyclone, spinning everything around and I don't know which way is up. I'm going to take some time, maybe play around a little, and figure out if I am even any good on my own."

"You are," Jordan interrupted. He draped an arm over my shoulder, pulling me into a side hug and kissing my temple. Such a simple display of affection he didn't understand affected me so deeply. "Maybe this is a good thing."

My fucking bank account said otherwise. I didn't want to be on the receiving end of a silver linings lecture. Jordan pressed his palms to my cheeks, forcing me to look at him. "I mean it, Slade. You used to be so damn confident. Back when we were kids, there was nothing stopping you from getting up and commanding the entire room's attention. What happened to that guy?"

My dad happened.

Every time he told me that music was a dead-end road, another chip of my dream broke off. I simply shrugged, not wanting to reveal that level of vulnerability to Eli. "Listen, I don't have to go in tomorrow night. Why don't I come over and you can play around for me? It'll be just like old times."

Yeah, exactly like old times. Me singing to Jordan, him thinking I was just screwing around when every note and lyric conveyed a message to him that I couldn't put into words.

Somebody mentioned free booze. I needed to find that. Stat.

"I'm going to get myself a drink," I told him. "Can you point me in the right direction?"

Instead, Jordan pointed to the kitchen counter. "Not until you eat."

Drinking on an empty stomach sounded like a damn

good plan to me. That way, the first drink would leave me tipsy and fuzzy enough it wouldn't bother me that there so many happy couples around the apartment. But Jordan was looking out for me when I was too reckless to take care of myself. Without another word, he began piling appetizers I couldn't even begin to name onto a plate.

"That's way too much food," I protested. With as little as I'd been eating lately, I would be sick to my stomach if I cleaned my plate.

"Are you kidding me? I've seen you pile three times as much on a plate, scarf it down, and then head back for more." It was true. Before everything came crashing to the ground, Jordan, and pretty much everyone else we knew, gave me a hard time for, what they called, my hollow leg. I had a never-ending appetite, at least partly caused by my inability to stop moving anytime I was awake. Now, I barely left my bed or the couch, and I was down to eating one meal most days. Some days, I couldn't be bothered to eat at all.

"Yeah, well, stress tends to do that to a person."

There was a grunt of disapproval behind me. I whipped around and found my face less than an inch away from the expensive silk tie resting on the chest of the stranger from the stairwell. I focused on the small diamond pattern, resisting the urge to reach out and feel the material to see if it was as soft as it looked. My libido nudged its way to the front of my mind, imagining that silk wrapped around my wrists, restraining me, keeping me from doing anything other than what this man demanded of me.

"Something funny?" I spat out. The part of me that wasn't disgruntled because it had been too long since I'd gotten off with anyone else, remembered we didn't like this guy. He was everything I steered clear of.

The stranger reached up, brushing the hair away from

my face. I should have pulled it back into a ponytail, but I couldn't be bothered. "Just trying to figure out what has a pretty boy like you so worked up he can't eat," he replied.

I held my breath as his gaze roamed over my body. I shouldn't have been so affected by the way his tongue peeked out between his lips. "As beautiful as you are, it seems you could stand to put on five or ten pounds."

"Oh, and do you make a point of handing out medical advice everywhere you go?" I crossed my arms tightly over my chest. My shirt hung looser than it had before. I fucking hated that this dude was right. "And, for that matter, where do you think you get off saying a damn thing about how I look?"

The stranger didn't back down. He stood straighter, squared his shoulders, and leaned in slightly. Despite the fact that he was only a few inches taller than me, I felt tiny under his judgmental gaze. Frozen, I couldn't do a damn thing. "Do you always have such a hard time taking a compliment?"

"The last time I checked, I wasn't aware that being told you're too skinny was a compliment." I hugged myself tighter, curling in my shoulders and lowering my chin.

I took the plate of food from Jordan. Most of it would be wasted, but that was easier than continuing to argue with someone I didn't know and shouldn't give a shit what he thought about me. Besides, knowing Jordan, he would absolutely withhold alcohol from me until he was satisfied that I had some food in my stomach. He obviously didn't understand the financial benefit of not having anything to absorb the alcohol.

I wandered around the living area, trying to find a place to sit, but everywhere I looked there were groups of friends talking, making me feel every bit the outsider that I was. I finally settled for a spot on the spiral staircase. The twisted wrought iron banister dug into my back and the stair tread was too narrow, even for my unhealthily skinny ass, but it was better than being forced into a conversation I didn't feel like having.

As I nibbled on the food, which was actually quite good, I watched Jordan. He flitted from one group to the next, as if these had been his people for years rather than months. I hadn't understood how the three of them made their relationship work, but the longer I watched, the more I realized I didn't have to understand. Maybe there was no logic to it; the three of them simply fit together.

When Doug stepped up behind Jordan, wrapping his arms around Jordan's torso and placing his hands on his stomach, my chest tightened. It wasn't the regret of not telling Jordan how I felt about him sooner that had me pressing my fist against my ribcage, it was this intense longing to have what he had.

And then, I looked at Doug. I checked him out as more than my friend's boyfriend. He was pretty damn fine for his age, and there was something familiar about his gaze when he looked over at me.

Holy shit. That was the connection. The stranger was somehow related to Doug. He had to be. The two of them weren't carbon copies, but the similarities were undeniable.

"You look absolutely miserable." I rolled my eyes, not surprised when I glanced up and saw the stranger looking down at me.

"You know, as much as you enjoy picking me apart, I feel like I should know your name at the very least." Not that it truly mattered. At the end of the night, I would head back to my place and he'd return to his fancy house, in his fancy car, and go on with his fancy life that was in a completely different league than my own. But I needed to know. It wasn't optional at this point.

"Fair enough," the man conceded. He jerked his head to the side, and, without any conscious thought, I scooted even closer to the edge of the step. He moved past me and sat on the tread above mine. I felt the heat from his body when his calf pressed against my arm, then he held out a hand. "I'm Jack."

It looked as though he debated saying something else but stopped himself. Probably wise, because the man wasn't nearly as funny as he thought. In fact, so far, he'd managed to somehow insult me with every interaction. After staring at his hand for a few seconds, I pressed my palm against his and shook. "It's nice to meet you, Jack."

"Is it though?" He didn't release me from his grip, and I didn't try to get away. "Every time you so much as see me, you look like you've stepped in something that smells bad."

"Shit," I corrected him.

"What?" Jack cocked his head to the side as if he was trying to figure me out.

"The word you're looking for is shit," I clarified. "I know it's probably beneath a man such as yourself to curse, but we are all adults here. You can do it. Trying to figure out a way to say what you mean without cussing just makes you seem like even more of an arrogant prick."

"You make an awful lot of assumptions for barely knowing me."

I smirked, then chuckled. "Well then, now you know how it feels." Putting an abrupt end to the conversation, I stood and walked away. I was proud of myself for not letting Jack act like he was better than me. He might be able to afford designer, custom-tailored suits, and probably drove a fancy sports car, but that didn't mean he was better than me.

And from the way he acted, it was long overdue for someone to knock him down a peg or two.

After tossing my plate into the garbage—upside down so no one would see how little I had eaten—I made a beeline for the area along the perimeter of the room that they had set up as a bar. I knew better than to open any of the hard liquor bottles, but I had come here determined to have a good time. That meant opening one of those fancy bottles.

Further proving how different my life was compared to Jordan's now, there were no plastic cups in sight. It looked as though they had borrowed glassware from the bar down-stairs. I scooped a bit of ice into a glass and began pouring myself a drink. I wasn't as good at coming up with tasty concoctions as Jordan was, but I did all right.

Still not in the mood for socializing, I grabbed my glass off the table and headed toward the windows that over-looked the district. There were so many people milling around, heading to the various bars for a night out. It was strange to see so many people out on a weeknight, but I had never been one to go out other than on the weekends. Weeknights had always been for band practice.

The chatter behind me was annoying. I should have stayed home tonight. When I turned around, I felt drawn to the staircase. Jordan had told me a bit about the renovations they'd been doing to create a semi-private living area in the space that wasn't used as Doug's pottery studio. I knew better than to go beyond the space they had deemed as open for the evening, but curiosity got the better of me. I just needed a little time alone. Time to clear my head, so I could come downstairs and be sociable, instead of wallowing in my own misery.

4

JACK

That damn boy was under my skin like a giant sliver. No matter how much I tried to push him out of my mind and enjoy my brother's party, I couldn't stop myself from watching him. By the third time he disappeared into the loft, I debated following him to see what he was up to. Last I knew, the third floor was Doug's space and I didn't want anybody screwing with his art.

"You good tonight?" Doug slapped a hand on my shoulder.

"Yeah. It's a nice, low-key party. Do you think you achieved what you hoped it would?" I cringed, hoping the question didn't sound as sarcastic as it had to my own ears. I still didn't understand why they coddled Jordan the way they did, but it wasn't my place to question. What they had going seemed to work for them. And, really, who was I to doubt them when I was so focused on work that I hadn't even played with a boy in over a year?

"I think so," Doug responded. He scratched at his jaw as he searched the room. There was no missing when he found the man in question; his eyes lit up.

I followed the direction of his gaze. Like me, Jordan was looking toward the loft, his eyes sad and brow furrowed.

"You sure about that? Jordan doesn't look like he's having very much fun," I pointed out. "In fact, he looks like he'd be more entertained if he was in the middle of a root canal."

"He's worried about Slade. The kid is one of his only friends, and he's been going through a run of bad luck lately," Doug explained. It wasn't any of my business, but I wanted Doug to keep going. I had assumed Slade's attitude was a front—a way to keep everyone at a distance so they couldn't judge him.

And what had I done? I'd judged him hard, from the moment I laid eyes on him. No wonder he was so stand-offish toward me.

"How so?" I pried when Doug didn't offer any further information.

"I don't know Slade all that well, but from what Jordan has told us, he put all of his eggs into one basket. Now, that basket has been dumped out and he's been left trying to pick up the pieces. Between you and me, I'm not sure how much longer the kid's going to be able to go on, but he's almost as stubborn as Eli and won't accept what he sees as a handout."

"So, you've tried to help him?" Of course, he had. Doug had a bigger heart than most people I knew. He hated seeing anyone in trouble. When we were kids, he would beg our parents to give him money for anyone who was down on their luck. More than once, he got in trouble for feeding his lunch to animals in the park. I used to tease him mercilessly about it, when, in reality, I envied his innate nurturing streak.

"Jordan keeps telling him to talk to Eli, but he hasn't so far. He's got it stuck in his head that Eli thinks he's a deadbeat, and he'd rather starve himself to death than prove Eli right."

"That's ridiculous," I scoffed. "Someone needs to teach that boy that, eventually, you have to set your pride aside and do whatever is necessary to keep moving forward."

"You offering to take on that job?" Creases formed at the corners of Doug's eyes. Both of us seemed to be imagining how I would knock some sense into Slade. I was certain Doug's idea was all puppies and bunny rabbits, while mine included tossing Slade over my lap, his bare ass sticking high in the air. I would spank him until he cried out, begging me to stop, then I would cradle him in my arms as he fell apart. By the time his sobs quieted, he'd be more receptive to accepting help.

I swallowed hard and tried adjusting myself as discreetly as possible. There was no logical reason as to why this boy had gotten under my skin the way he had. And damn Doug for putting ideas into my head. He knew damn well that stubborn little boys were my kryptonite.

When I glanced past Doug to see Slade stumbling down the steps again, my brother pursed his lips to keep from laughing out loud. "Look at him, Jack. Think how proud you'd be of him when he finally broke. He's exactly the type of challenge you need."

"Even if that was an option, and it's not, because he'd need far more time than I can offer him," I pointed out. "How do you know he would even be into someone else telling him what to do?"

And why in the hell was I considering this? I didn't need my brother and his partners playing matchmaker. Doug checked over his shoulder, shaking his head and sighing. When Slade bumped into the edge of the island countertop in the kitchen, he looked back at me and smirked. "I suppose it's a good sign that he's finally eating, but I'm pretty sure it's too little, too late. Just look at him, Jack, he needs you. Almost as bad as you need him."

"I don't need a boy to be complete, Doug," I stated. "I understand why it's hard for you to understand. You are a natural-born caretaker, and when you don't have anyone to watch over and nurture, you feel lost. I am not that way."

"Whatever you say, Jack." Doug tossed his hands in the air. "I swear, sometimes it's like you and Eli are the same person. If it wasn't for the fact that you and I look so much alike, people would assume that the two of you are brothers, not us."

"I'm nothing like him," I argued. Doug quirked an eyebrow and I paused, rethinking what I had said. "It's not that there's anything wrong with Eli, but we are totally different."

"No, you're really not. If you'd like, I can ask Jordan over. I'm sure he'd agree with me."

"Of course, he would. Your boy isn't going to dispute you."

"And that just goes to show how little you know about him." Doug laughed and shook his head. "Jordan is more and more outspoken every day. He has completely lost the ability to tell anyone what they want to hear. The only person he still holds back with is Slade. And that's only because Slade is skittish, and Jordan is afraid of running him off."

So much for steering the conversation away from the more than tipsy boy, with the messy long brown hair that I'd love to tangle my hands in and use to drag him somewhere more private. The boy who was, once again, attempting to climb the spiral staircase to the third floor. When he stumbled, nearly falling backward, I jumped into action without a second thought. No one else in the room existed as I darted over, steadying him with a hand against his back.

Slade spun around, draping his arms over my shoulders. And then, I felt the moment he realized what was happening. His entire body tensed, and he pushed away. "I don't need a knight in shining armor or my own personal superhero coming to rescue me."

I took a step backward, biting back my laughter when Slade bobbled again. I quirked my head to the side, as if to silently ask him if he was sure about that, then I took the bottle of beer out of his hand. If there was one thing Slade absolutely did not need tonight, it was more alcohol.

When Slade tried swiping it back, I held it out of reach. "Give it back, you pompous prick."

"You'll thank me for this tomorrow. Why don't we get some water, and possibly a little more food in you?" Cautiously, I slid my hand around Slade's back. He jerked away, then grumbled when he tripped over his own feet. He never fully relaxed, but he did finally let me steer him into the kitchen.

I pulled out one of the barstools and steadied him as he sat. He rested his elbows on the granite counter, burying his face in his hands. He said something I couldn't make out.

"What was that, boy?" Rather than focusing on him, I worked to put together a small plate of food for him. I'd sampled enough of Jordan's creations to know which were least likely to mix badly with the alcohol sloshing around in his stomach.

After sliding the plate in front of him, I grabbed a bottle

of water out of the fridge, uncapping it and placing that in front of him as well. Slade pushed it away.

"I don't want it," he slurred.

"I wasn't aware I had asked if you *wanted* it." My entire body tingled, instantly recognizing the way I had pitched my voice. My palms practically itched with the desire to sting against his bare skin. Slade glared up at me, his eyes unfocused and droopy. He was quickly losing the battle, and the alcohol was winning. "Drink it, Slade."

"You're awfully damn pushy. Arrogant prick," he mumbled, but picked up the water and took a sip. Someday, the boy would learn what happened to bratty little shits who talked back.

Someday, but not today. Not with you. You have no business acting like this boy owes you his obedience. I wasn't a fan of logic trying to creep in and crush this budding fantasy of mine. I knew it would likely go nowhere, but a man could dream, couldn't he?

"You're awfully mouthy for someone who doesn't know a damn thing about me."

Slade waved his hand erratically in the air. "Don't need to know you. Know your type."

"And what type is that, boy?" A wiser man would have walked away. Not me. I pulled out the stool next to Slade, sat down, then turned to face him with my forearm resting on the counter.

"Just... Fuck man, I don't know what I'm saying. But look at you. You're *that* type."

"The older and wiser type, you mean?" I glanced down, trying to figure out what he was getting at. Since the moment he laid eyes on me, Slade had seemed on edge. Now that I had a bit clearer picture of who he was and what he needed, it felt imperative that I understand where he was coming from as well.

Slade giggled as if I just told a hilarious joke. I reached up and pressed a hand to his shoulder, and he immediately stilled and went silent.

He looked up at me, eyes wide. He seemed ready to jerk away again but stopped himself this time. Interesting.

"Tell me, boy," I repeated. "What do you mean by people like me?"

"You're the fancy suit guy." He gaped at me; his confusion evident all over his face. I began to wonder exactly how much he'd had to drink. "You like showing everyone how rich you are, and you think you can fix everything for everyone, but you can't and that pisses you off. Stupid suits."

His rant trailed off and his eyes drifted shut. Slade's body tilted to the side, and he'd have crashed to the floor if I hadn't been there to catch him. It was well past last call for him.

"Let's get you home, Slade." I capped the bottled water and slid it into my pocket. Slade hooked his feet around the rungs of the barstool when I tried helping him up. "Don't fuck with me, boy. It's time for you to go home."

"You can't tell me what to do," he spat out. "You're not my Daddy."

"It's a damn good thing, too." I didn't release him. I hoped like hell Jordan could tell me where Slade lived so I could get him out of here before he caused a scene. Doug and Eli had gone out of their way to help Jordan have a good time, and I'd be damned if his wasted friend was going to ruin the end of the night.

"What would you do to me if you were my Daddy?" Slade pressed when I said nothing more.

"First of all, you wouldn't be getting sloppy drunk if you were my boy. It's not an attractive quality," I informed him.

Slade's gaze dipped to the floor and he lifted his shoulders slightly, as if he wanted to argue but couldn't. He curled in on himself, and the part of me that hated seeing boys beat themselves up for disappointing me, wanted to hold him—reassure him that he could fix this situation if he truly wanted to. I pushed that urge away. Slade wasn't my boy, and he needed a firm hand more than he needed to be loved on.

"And second, I don't put up with boys who act out when they don't get what they want," I continued. "There is a fine line between being a brat and a disrespectful little shit, and you seem to be dancing all over it."

"Well then, it's a good thing you aren't my Daddy," Slade snapped back. "Because this is the real me, and you obviously wouldn't be able to handle it."

I didn't believe any of that for a second. I wondered how much of the attitude Slade gave off was an act. Part of me thought it possible that Slade had slipped on a mask so long ago, he barely recognized the man underneath. And I shouldn't want to be the one to unmask him. I shouldn't wish for things that couldn't happen...like watching Slade blossom as he realized he didn't have to hide from himself or the world.

"Slade, come on." I tugged on his elbow, and this time he stood.

"I'm not fucking you tonight," he informed me.

I couldn't help myself. I leaned in close enough that he shivered every time I exhaled. My hand slid around to the small of his back, holding him close but not quite touching. "Let's get one thing straight, boy. If anyone is going to be doing the fucking, it would be me. But you're right, I'm not fucking you tonight, either. I like my boys to remember every graphic detail the morning after. I'm not a fan of blackout sex."

Slade's body twitched and he let out a noise somewhere between a whine and a groan. He wasn't at all subtle when he reached down and palmed his dick. I snatched his hand, pulling it to the side. Slade inhaled sharply; his breathing ragged as he glared up at me.

I chuckled. Jordan noticed us and quickly excused himself from the conversation he was having. "Everything okay?"

"Tell this jerk he's not my Daddy, Jordan," Slade blurted out.

"Huh?" Jordan cocked his head to the side and narrowed his eyes. "What in the hell have I missed?"

"It seems that while you've been busy taking care of your guests, your friend here has been keeping the alcohol stash company. I'm going to run him home." Jordan's gaze flitted from me to Slade and back again. He hummed quietly, a small smile forming. I didn't dare ask him what he thought he'd figured out, because I was scared of the answer.

"You don't have to do that," Jordan insisted. "He lives in the opposite direction of your place. I wouldn't want to put you out. He can crash on the couch."

"It's not a problem, Jordan. And I know how Eli feels about people spending the night. It'll be better for everyone this way. Besides, I'm pretty sure Slade would prefer dealing with tomorrow morning's hangover at his own place." The boy was going to hurt, and Eli wouldn't have mercy on him. Given the little bits I'd learned about Slade tonight, that would only make things worse for him.

Jordan snorted, and Slade's head whipped around to glare at him. "Hey man, don't blame me. I can't imagine anyone being that desperate."

"It was good enough for you when you needed a place to crash," Slade argued.

With every passing minute, Slade's eyes drifted further closed, and his body sagged against mine. If I didn't get him to the car soon, I would have to carry him down the stairs. I pulled out my phone and handed it to Jordan. "Enter his address into the GPS."

Then to Slade, I said, "Where are your keys?"

He patted his front pocket. "Right here, *Daddy*. You going to dig them out for me?"

God help me. Part of me hoped this was all a drunken act, but I wasn't so sure it was. Slade would be a handful, and I wasn't sure I was up for meeting his level of need. I held out my hand and cleared my throat. "Keys, Slade. Now."

He pouted as he pulled out a plain key ring with two keys, dropping them into my palm. "Happy now, *Daddy*?"

Not by a long shot. Tonight was supposed to be just a quick stop so Jordan didn't think I was shunning them before heading off to The Lodge. I needed to check in with Sam and see how things were going there, but that would have to wait. Slade needed me more right now.

I gave Slade and Jordan a moment alone to say goodbye, while I found Doug and Eli to thank them for inviting me. Doug bit down on his lips to keep from laughing as I explained that I was going to give their very drunken guest a ride home.

"Play safe," he reminded me as I gave him a quick hug. I flipped him off, then he pulled me in again. This time whispering in my ear, "Don't fight whatever you're feeling. He'd be a good reason for you to stop devoting every minute of your life to work. You've busted your ass for years, now it's time to enjoy life a little bit."

"Shut up, Dougie," I hissed. If Eli found out Doug had been trying to play matchmaker, he'd join in, and the two of them would be relentless. Much better to allow Eli to think this was just a ride home. Because that's what it was. Even if I wanted to give in to these urges, Slade was in no shape tonight.

5

SLADE

Sneaking a bottle of Fireball up to the third floor might not have been one of the smartest things I had done all night. Or maybe it was losing track of how many beers I drank that did me in. It wasn't the food I ate that had me feeling like I was ready to hurl all over the warm leather seats of Jack's car, because I'd barely touched what I'd been given. And screw both, Jordan and Jack, for thinking they needed to take care of me. I was more than— okay, so I sucked at taking care of myself, but I wasn't any better at accepting help.

"You still with me, boy?" Jack's fingertips dug into the back of my neck, and he began kneading away the tension while we sat at a red light. I jerked away, regretting it instantly when the world around me started spinning.

"Already told you, you're not my fucking Daddy." The words tumbled out of my mouth in a sloppy rush, and Jack chuckled. My head flopped to the side and I glared at him. At least, I was pretty sure I glared. It was really damn hard to keep my eyes open.

"Never said I was," Jack pointed out.

"Then quit calling me boy," I slurred.

"Quit acting like one," he shot back. I didn't need this shit from him. I had gone to Jordan's place hoping to forget about my inability to care for myself like a responsible adult. And what did I do? I wound up getting so hammered, I let myself be led out of the party by a dude who reminded me of my dad, all the way from his tailored suits to the disapproving tone in his voice.

Jack didn't say anything else, and as I drifted off to sleep, I offered up a silent prayer of thanks. If he didn't speak, it was easy to ignore him. But, the second he opened his mouth, it was like my brain couldn't *not* say something smart in return.

I didn't open my eyes when the car stopped. "Come on, sleepyhead. It's time to get you inside."

"Too far," I complained. "Just going to sleep here a little while longer."

"I knew there was a sweet, compliant little boy in there somewhere." I forced my body to remain still when he ran a hand down my arm. I didn't want to like him all up in my personal space.

"Fuck you," I retorted, but there was no heat in my words. As long as I didn't open my eyes, it was easy to pretend he was taking care of me because he wanted to, not out of some twisted sense of obligation to his brother. "Still not your boy."

"I'm well aware of that, Slade. And anytime I forget it, I'm sure you won't hesitate to remind me."

Jack's fingers grazed along my hip when he reached across the console to unbuckle my seatbelt. I swatted his hand away. I didn't need help.

But, then, I relaxed. I didn't want to fight him—not

tonight. Just for a little while, I could pretend he was here because there was nowhere else he'd rather be.

I waited patiently with my hands folded in my lap, while Jack came around to my side of the car. A blast of cold air hit me before he rested his arms on the roof, leaning in, creating a human windbreak for me. I glanced up at him, offering him what I hoped was a shy smile. In my inebriated state, I probably looked like some sort of psychotic killer, but if I was sober, I wouldn't have even made an attempt.

"You okay, boy?"

I bristled, biting down on my tongue hard enough I tasted blood. I wasn't going to let the sarcastic warning about not being his boy pass my lips. This was a gift I could give myself. Tomorrow, the world would come crashing down around me again and I would be alone, but I wanted this one night of someone giving a damn about what happened to me, even if it was all a farce.

"I'm fine," I told him. "I'm sorry for my behavior earlier." I glanced up at him through glassy eyes. He chuckled, running the tip of one finger across my cheek.

I chased the touch when he pulled his hand away, whining at the deprivation of his body heat. "What brought this change, boy?"

"I realized I was an asshole to you. You don't deserve that when you're just trying to help me."

Jack held out his hand, and I slid my palm over his, allowing him to ease me out of the car. I wobbled, nearly falling off the curb, and Jack pulled me tight to his side.

"Come on, let's get you inside where it's warm." I rubbed my hands up and down my arms. My bare arms covered in goosebumps. My arms that had been covered by a hoodie earlier. Shit.

Jack stepped in front of me, resting his hands on my

shoulders. "What is it? You have nothing to worry about, Slade," he promised me.

I believed him. Maybe it was stupid of me, but ever since he had stepped up behind me outside Jordan's place, something deep inside of me knew this man would never hurt me. Maybe part of why I didn't want to like him was because he made me want.

Or maybe he would hurt me, but only if I asked nicely. Jack had this intensity in his dark, whiskey-colored eyes. If I believed in that sort of thing, I would swear he was some sort of sorcerer, casting a spell that compelled me to him. What I felt whenever I caught him looking at me was that intense.

"It's not that." Even in the bitterly cold night, I felt my cheeks flush. It wasn't going to take me long to prove to him how incapable I was. "I hate to tell you, but I think you brought me over here for nothing."

"Why is that?"

Jack didn't give me an inch of space. He stood close enough to me that the heat radiating off his body warmed me. It would be so easy for me to bury my head in his chest.

So much for hating everything he stood for. If I wasn't so wasted, there was no doubt I'd be sporting wood. And hell, even now, I was resisting the urge to drop to my knees and properly thank him for his generosity.

"I think I left my hoodie at Jordan's apartment."

Jack's brow furrowed, and he drew in a few slow, deep breaths. "You can get it back from him tomorrow."

"You don't understand. I have no way to get into my place."

Jack's right hand slid down my chest before he reached into his own pocket. My eyes grew wide when I saw my key ring dangling from his fingers.

"I knew it was time to get you out of there."

I closed my eyes, replaying the end of the night, trying to figure out how he'd gotten my keys. Oh yeah, I'd practically dared him to dig in my jeans for them

"Sorry, I guess I forgot."

After tucking the keys back into his pocket, he reached up and threaded his fingers through my hair. "You confuse me, Slade. You run so hot and cold, it's hard to keep up with you."

"You think that's bad, you should try living in my head," I blurted out. Instantly, I wished I could take back the words. I really needed to learn how to keep my mouth shut.

Jack cupped my cheek, tilting my head back so I had no choice but to look at him. "Don't ever hide from me, Slade. I know it's difficult for you, but there are people who would love nothing more than to help you."

I shook my head as my eyes drifted closed. God, how I wished that was true. But when you allowed other people to help you, they either expected something in return, or they would cut you off the second you didn't toe the line they had drawn.

"Look at me, Slade."

Even my case of whiskey dick was unable to ignore that command. My cock twitched in my pants, but I didn't grow hard. What I did do, however, was open my eyes to find him staring at me.

"Where did you go just then?" He turned to face me, erasing every inch of distance between our bodies.

I inhaled sharply, wishing I knew the name of the cologne he was wearing. I wanted to find it and spray it on my pillows at night so I could remember this one. Long after Jack dumped me into my apartment and took off, I wouldn't forget how he had watched over me when I was too far gone to take care of myself.

"I'm a huge pain in the ass," I admitted. Jack threw his head back and laughed. I smacked his chest, allowing my hands to linger over his heart. "I'm serious, Jack. And I know you were just trying to be nice by giving me a ride home. You don't have to pretend it's anything other than a random act of kindness."

"Let's get one thing straight, boy." His hand slid around to the back of my neck, the tips of his fingers digging into my flesh. How in the hell was he so warm when it was cold as balls tonight? "There are very few things I will do out of obligation. I'm not here because I pity you or because I thought you needed to be rescued. I am not standing out here, freezing my ass off, because I was doing a favor for my brother's boyfriend."

"Then why are you here?" I pressed my chest against his, craning back so I could still look at him. His eyes fluttered and then closed as he bent down.

"You're going to be the death of me," he muttered under his breath a split second before his lips pressed against mine. I whimpered, my lips parting, inviting him to take things further. Now, I regretted drinking so much for an entirely different reason. Jack struck me as the type of man who wouldn't allow anything to happen while I was inebriated. And once I sobered up, my brain would engage again, and I would run for the hills.

Jack pulled away, frowning. Well, that was one way to keep a guy's ego in check. I tried taking a step back, but Jack tightened his grip on the nape of my neck.

"Don't run from me, boy," he commanded. "And don't sit there assuming you know anything about my motivations or what I'm thinking."

"You have to admit, seeing the guy who just kissed you, frowning, isn't reassuring," I told him.

Jack scrubbed a hand over his face. "I'm not doing this with you tonight, Slade. Not when you're drunk."

No, no, no. He was not going to do this. Didn't he understand it had to be tonight? Didn't he realize that a drunk mind spoke the truth we were too scared to admit when we were sober? At least mine did.

This time when I took a step back, I twisted my body, so Jack had no choice but to release me. I held out a hand. "I can get it from here."

Jack didn't respond, other than to walk to the front door of my building. He grumbled something under his breath and shook his head before pushing open the door. "You should live in a safer building. They need to have a security door at the very least. This isn't a great neighborhood."

"Yeah, well, shit like that costs money. If they worried about security, then they'd jack up the rent, and that would make this building unaffordable for the type of people who are willing to live here."

"And what type of people is that?" Jack held open the door and ushered me inside. I didn't look back as I walked down the hall to my apartment. For the first time in a while, I was truly ashamed of where I lived.

With Jack, I couldn't bring myself to get defensive. He was intense, but there was a sincerity in his concern. He might not like my living arrangements, but I didn't get the impression he was judging me. I stopped in front of my door and waited until Jack turned the key. Before he could push the door open, I placed a hand over his.

No way in hell could I let him set foot in my apartment. As if it wasn't bad enough that he had seen the deteriorating building where I lived, if he went inside, I would lose any shot I might have with him, and this bubble I'd decided to live in for the night would burst.

"Let's go inside, Slade."

"If you don't mind..." It shouldn't be this hard for me to make Jack see I had no intention of inviting him in. It was completely reasonable to not want a practical stranger in a person's home, wasn't it?

It was, but I wasn't ready for this fantasy to end. If nothing else, seeing the way I lived would be an incentive for Jack to take whatever he wanted from me and never look back once he said goodbye. I slumped against the doorjamb, my hand still resting on the knob. "Look, I don't have a house like you probably do."

Jack looked around as if to say, *You think?*

I scowled at him. "I mean it, Jack. I already told you I'm a mess. I meant that, both figuratively and literally."

"You've had a lot going on from what I've heard." I frowned. He'd heard? Great. The last thing I wanted was everyone discussing my business. Because that's exactly what it was—my business. "Slade, we all go through tough times. When that happens, everything tends to fall apart to some extent."

Maybe for some people, but for me, it was a natural state of being. It had been expected that everything be in its place when I was growing up, so as soon as I moved out on my own, I rebelled. But then, being a slob turned into a bad habit, and the longer it went on, the more incapable I became to pick up.

He pressed his palm to my cheek again. I closed my eyes and leaned into the touch, as his thumb grazed over my cheekbone. "I think you and I got off on the wrong foot. I will admit I'm a bit...exacting, some would say, in how I prefer things. I am a big fan of order, because it helps me take care of everything that needs to be done on a daily basis. That doesn't mean I'm going to think any less of you for whatever you might be trying to hide on the other side of the door."

I knew how he meant it, but that phrase had always amused me. Rather than hearing it as a reassurance that nothing would change, I always assumed the implication that whoever said it already thought so little of me, their view couldn't possibly get any worse.

"You say that now, but I won't hold it against you if you decide it's dangerous to your health to stick around."

"I am not leaving you, Slade. Not until you're sober."

"I already told you, I don't need a knight in shining armor. I am more than capable of taking care of myself, thank you very much." Whatever attraction I felt for Jack disappeared in that moment. It was a slap in the face to be reminded of what had brought him here. It wasn't attraction, he just didn't want me choking on my own vomit to weigh on his conscience.

I shoved him out of the way and pushed my front door open. Before I could slam it closed, Jack braced himself, holding the door open. He let himself inside, his fancy shoes clicking on the chipped tile floor.

As he stalked forward, I backed myself against the wall. He didn't stop until he stood so close his toes touched mine. He braced himself with a hand on either side of my head against the wall.

"I don't know what in the hell that was, but do not expect another free pass from me," he growled. He bent down and hissed his next warning against my ear. "You've already gotten away with far more than any other boy could have hoped for. Don't test my limits."

I pushed against his chest. My attempts to free myself

proved futile. He stood his ground while I wavered in my drunken state.

"I am not your boy," I enunciated every word as clearly as I could, pissed off when I looked up to see amusement sparkling in Jack's eyes. "You did what you came here to do. You made sure I got home safe."

"Surely, you aren't that naïve," Jack scoffed. He pressed his lips to the side of my neck. "You drive me crazy. I'm not sure if I want to kiss you or throw you over my knee and spank your ass until it's so red and welted you can't sit for a week without thinking of me."

"Such a romantic," I responded.

"Never said I was a romantic." Jack took a step back, curling his fingers around my wrist. "Let's get you cleaned up for bed."

"Are you going to tuck me in, too, Daddy?" I teased, desperately trying to gain the upper hand. No matter how badly I *wanted* to be taken care of, there was still enough of my brain engaged that I couldn't let go. A warning echoed in my mind that one night with this man would leave me desperate for more.

Jack's nostrils flared, then the corner of his mouth tipped up in a smirk. "I just might, but only if you're a *very* good boy for me."

"I thought you said you weren't going to fuck me tonight." The cold night air had sobered me up a bit, enough that the pieces of the night that had become hazy were coming into focus again. And why in the hell was there a pit in my stomach at the thought of Jack not wanting me?

"I meant it when I said that. When I bend you over and abuse that pretty ass, it's going to be because you asked me for it."

"I could ask you for it now," I teased. And, fuck, why in the hell couldn't my brain decide what I wanted from him?

"Oh no, boy, that would be far too easy." He stumbled over an empty box as he led me through the dark apartment. It would be far less dangerous if we turned on some lights, but it was less embarrassing if he didn't see the chaos threatening to crash down around us like an avalanche. "When you decide you're ready, you're going to beg me to take you. You will bend over freely, offering me that beautiful ass. And, you'll do it sober."

I couldn't stop the snort of laughter. No way in hell was that going to happen.

"Something funny, boy?"

I waved a hand over my body. "This isn't an open-ended offer. Tomorrow morning, I'll be sober, and my only regret is going to be not forcing you to say goodbye and part ways at the curb."

"What makes you say that?"

I gaped at him. "Come on, Jack. Even you can't be that naïve," I parroted his word back to him. "Look at me, then look at you. We're from such different worlds, we're not even in the same galaxy."

"And you've decided this based on what, exactly?"

"Experience," I responded cryptically. I stormed into the bathroom, slamming the door behind me. I splashed some water on my face before brushing my teeth. I didn't let the water run. I was determined to hide in the bathroom until Jack got tired of waiting and left. No matter what my brain told me to do in its moments of weakness, this was for the best. Nothing good would happen if I let him in.

6

JACK

I had been accused of a lot of things in my life, and being a patient man was nowhere on that list. I had a certain way I expected things to go, and when life deviated from that plan, I was not amused. But tonight, I had no choice but to wait.

Not true. You could engage your brain and leave. He's home now. He'll be fine.

But I couldn't leave, because he *wasn't* okay. Even once he sobered up, Slade would be broken and lost. But he didn't have to be. Exploring anything with Slade was a recipe for disaster.

The boy was right. He and I were as different as jet fuel and marshmallows. I was lists and routines, where Slade was impulsivity and chaos.

I checked my watch. He'd been in there six minutes. It had been three since the last time I heard the water running. I could almost picture him on the other side of the door, waiting for me to give up.

Well, I had news for him. I hated backing down from a challenge even more than I hated being kept waiting. I closed my eyes and leaned my head against the wall. I counted off the passing seconds, and when the standoff reached a full ten minutes, enough was enough. I took one step across the hall and rapped my knuckles against the door.

"You're stalling, Slade," I said in my most forceful tone. No response. "I already promised you nothing was going to happen tonight. I know you just met me tonight, but my word is my bond. I would never do anything to ruin the relationship I have with my brother and his men. Hurting you would do exactly that."

Why in the hell was I pouring my heart out to a thin door? If I wanted to, I could easily bust it open with one quick hip check, but that wouldn't get me any closer to my goal.

Goals. My entire damn life was comprised of them. And, until tonight, gaining the trust of this skittish, damaged boy was nowhere on that list.

I checked my watch again. Twelve minutes.

I tried the doorknob, unsurprised to find it locked. "Come on, Slade. It's time for bed."

Nothing.

His silence worried me. He had seemed to sober up a bit while we were outside, but I'd been around enough drunk people to know that was only an illusion. Whether Slade realized it or not, he had been through an emotional roller coaster tonight that heightened his buzz. I doubted anyone else noticed the way his mood rose and fell. I wondered if anyone—even Jordan, who claimed to be his best friend—had figured out what had him so upset.

While tonight had been a celebration for my brother and the family he was creating, it was a night of mourning for Slade. I saw it when Jordan first embraced him. Jordan, the sweetheart that he was, had no idea that him falling in love was like a dagger to Slade's heart. I doubted that was a revelation Slade had any intention of sharing, and, as I said, I relied heavily on my integrity. I would never betray Slade's trust, not even with this.

Fifteen minutes.

The games stopped now.

"Slade. Either you open the door right now, or you're going to be replacing it tomorrow," I informed him. This time, there was shuffling from the other side of the door.

The handle jiggled but didn't turn.

"Let me in, Slade." I bumped my forehead against the door. I couldn't remember the last time I had practically begged a boy to open up to me. And, make no mistake, that was exactly what I was doing tonight. I wasn't only asking him to open the door. I was asking him to give me a chance to prove myself to him.

I wouldn't take it easy on him, because that was the last thing he needed. What he needed was structure—someone to correct his course when he began to drift. Hell, right now, he needed someone to drag him, kicking and screaming, back to any sort of a constructive path.

And what makes you think you have the time to devote to him?

The voice of reason could always be counted on to splash cold water on me anytime I strayed too far from my own path. No, I didn't have time for someone as needy as Slade, but I couldn't resist the temptation. Something told me he would be worth it. For him, I might be willing to face some of my own truths, starting with the one Doug and Eli had been trying to hammer into my head for years. I had built a great life for myself, but it was like a home built on spec, standing empty, waiting for someone to truly live there.

Maybe it was time to live.

"Slade, please open the door." I rested my hand on the doorknob. "Even if it's just to tell me to fuck off, let me see that you're okay."

"Why does it matter?" He sounded so shattered. It was as if he honestly didn't believe my concern was genuine. I wanted to find whoever had made him feel so poorly about himself and strangle them. There was a shine to him some-where, but someone along the way had made him feel useless. Worthless.

I wanted to take him to bed and whisper things I had no business promising. I wanted to brush the hair away from his forehead and tell him he didn't have to worry anymore, that I was here to help him. I wanted to make him believe that it would all get better. He might hate me along the way, but, in the end, he would thank me.

"Open the door," I insisted again. "I am not having this conversation until I can see you."

The door cracked open and evil Slade poked his head out. "You've seen me. Happy now?"

"Not even remotely." I traced a finger down the bridge of his nose. Slade shivered as I allowed my finger to drag a line over his Adam's apple, then to his chest. "But let's not talk any more tonight. You need to get some sleep."

"Yes, Daddy." I glared at him, my mouth drawn tightly into a frown.

"The next time you call me that, you had better be prepared for what I'll do to you," I warned. I pushed the door further open, sliding my hand into Slade's. "Which way to your room?"

Slade quirked an eyebrow. "You're kidding me, right?"

"You act as if I should know where everything is. Remember, this is the first time I've been here. Hell, until a few hours ago, I had only heard your name in passing."

"All bad things I'm sure," he muttered under his breath. I was positive I hadn't been meant to hear it, but I had. Part of me wanted to try and figure out why he assumed people were talking badly about him, and another part of me wanted to sit down with Doug and Eli to see what they thought of him. But I had never once asked for outside guidance before, and I wasn't going to start now.

I worked to school my features when Slade pushed open his bedroom door. There was barely any floor visible. I would've thought the closet and dresser drawers would be empty, given the number of shirts and pants strewn everywhere, but a quick glance when Slade turned on the small lamp next to the bed showed the dresser drawers bulging to the point one was missing the face.

"I warned you I was a mess. I didn't just mean my head."

"Well, they say knowing is half the battle," I responded, trying to keep my tone light. "And I'm sure you'll pick up before the next time I come over."

"What makes you think there's going to be a next time?" Either Slade was attempting to dismiss me, or he was hoping to seduce me as he stripped out of his thin t-shirt. Next, he shimmied his hips as he worked the tattered denim down his legs.

Neither motivation would work. I stalked across the room, kneeling down to untie his shoes. He gaped at me, his mouth opening and closing as if he had a question he couldn't put into words. I tapped his leg and Slade lifted his foot. "There's going to be a next time, Slade. I refuse to believe this is it for us."

Once I helped Slade finish taking off his jeans, I leaned

in and kissed the front of his thigh. He wasn't hard. If tonight wasn't the first night we'd met, and if I hadn't promised him I wouldn't take advantage of him, I would have cupped my hand over his cock and balls, testing to see if it was a lack of interest or the alcohol keeping his libido at bay. When I kissed Slade's other thigh, he sucked in a sharp hiss of breath. "You don't want this to be it for us either, do you?"

I tipped my head back, holding my breath while I waited for Slade's answer. No doubt about it, I was a man who went after whatever he wanted, but when it came to sexual arrangements or relationships, I would never pursue a man who didn't want to be chased. "Answer me, Slade."

I slid my hands around to the backs of his thighs, never blinking while I gave him time to think.

When Slade responded, his answer was so soft I barely heard him. "No."

"I need more to go on, boy." His single word answer left far too much open to interpretation.

Slade's Adam's apple bobbed when he swallowed hard. "I don't want this to be all there is..."

The unspoken "but" hung thick in the air between us.

I leaned against the edge of the mattress for support as I stood. The grinding of my knees reminded me of every year I had lived before Slade had been born. "Whatever you're thinking, you can tell me, Slade." I cupped the back of his head, leaning in to place a tender kiss to the center of his forehead. "There are no right or wrong answers here, as long as you're honest with me."

Rather than elaborate, Slade flopped onto the bed, rolling away from me. He gripped the pillow tightly, hugging it to his chest for comfort. "Why are you pushing for this? You could leave, and I'm sure there is still time for you to find someone to service you before the bars close."

I couldn't help but laugh. "In case you haven't noticed, I am a man, not a car."

He harrumphed in amusement. I wished his back wasn't to me so I could see if my joke had made him smile. I hoped so. While I had yet to be granted anything other than a sullen or pissed off expression, I knew he'd be beautiful when he smiled. "You could have anyone. You don't need a wreck like me."

"True as that may be, I haven't walked away, have I?" I sat as far to the edge of the bed as possible without falling to the floor. When I placed a hand on Slade's side, he scooted back toward me.

Progress.

"I'm here because there's something about you I find intriguing. And I think we could be good for one another," I admitted.

"What could I possibly have to offer someone like you," Slade scoffed. "You don't need me."

"Let me be the judge of that," I responded. "You look at me and you see the tailored suit and my fancy car, but do you really know anything about me?"

Slade shrugged.

"Answer me," I insisted, my voice gravelly and rough.

"Not really," he admitted. "But I've known enough guys like you to realize you won't stick around for long."

"Then I suppose I will have to prove you wrong." The two of us could go back and forth like this all night, but we wouldn't get anywhere. I bent down and kissed Slade's shoulder, followed by his neck, and finally his temple. "Get some sleep. We can revisit this once both of us are rested. But don't think I'm going to let you off the hook, Slade. I know where you live now, and if I have to, I'm not above enlisting help from Doug and Jordan."

"Pushy bastard," Slade muttered. Alcohol and exhaustion were already pulling him under. I pulled my cell phone out of my pocket and stretched out on the bed next to him. Eventually, I would have to go, but I had meant it when I promised Slade I wasn't leaving until I knew he was okay.

I wasn't only talking about tonight.

I SLIPPED FURTHER into creeper mode with every passing minute. I never slept well when I was away from home, and tonight I had the added complication of Slade. He was one huge puzzle in need of solving. Every time I closed my eyes to try and sleep, my mind started racing with problems and solutions.

What to do about this attraction. *If I knew what was good for me, I'd ignore the way he made me feel.*

How to make him understand his own worth. *Far more work than I had the time to invest, but I'd be damned if that deterred me.*

How to combine the two without him shoving me away.

He would be well within his rights, of course. I had pushed further than I intended tonight. I couldn't help it. This was a boy who practically screamed for someone to help him, even if the words coming out of his mouth insisted the exact opposite. And the thought of anyone else lifting him up until he could stand on his own two feet, annoyed the hell out of me.

Hoping to assuage the guilt of not going into work, when I'd promised myself I'd only stay at my brother's for an hour or so before heading in to check on things, I pulled my cell phone out and started working while Slade slept.

No one had texted me with any catastrophes they couldn't solve. That could have been because it was a quiet night, or it just might be a sign I hired competent staff to take charge in my absence. I didn't *need* to spend every waking hour behind my desk, worrying about everything falling apart if I wasn't in the building.

Still, I fired off a quick text to Sam to get an update on how the night had gone. Then, I wasted some time checking email and skimming over the most recent reviews left for the Lodge. All was well there, too.

No one's indispensable, Jack. Not even you. Maybe Doug and Eli were right. Hell, Eli had let himself fall into this same trap, and it almost cost him the sickening happiness he had now. Maybe I *could* invest some time into helping Slade believe people gave a damn about him.

With that revelation, I set the phone on Slade's night-stand...if you could call it that. I doubted I'd sleep, but I had a lot to do tomorrow, so I swiped the phone and set the alarm for five o'clock, changing it to vibrate only so I wouldn't wake Slade.

As much as I would love to cancel all of my appointments and spend the day getting to know Slade better, without the alcohol and belligerence, I had made a promise to Sam. The kid seemed shocked I would listen to his ideas, and I wasn't going to let him down just because I had a new project I wanted to work on.

He's a man, not a fucking problem for you to solve. If that's how you're going to approach this, walk away now.

That admonishment sounded a lot like Colin, the only boy I'd ever truly loved. As it turned out, he had some very strong feelings about how I approached life. As he finished packing his bags to leave me, he let everything he'd been holding in escape.

My solution had been to never allow myself to get too wrapped up in a boy I played with. I was more like the cool uncle than their Daddy. Doing so saved both of us from hurting in the end.

Until now. I wasn't sure how I'd react if Slade kicked me out in the morning, and I didn't trust myself to go slow with him. I *wanted. Needed.*

I laid next to Slade, still fully dressed and on top of the covers so there were layers of protection from temptation. When he thrashed around, mumbling incoherently, I placed a hand between his shoulder blades, and he stilled instantly. I didn't remove my hand, and he scooted to the center of the bed, reaching out to me in his sleep.

"You're okay, boy. I'm not going to leave you." Still sleeping, Slade let out a soft sigh. I rolled to my side, draping an arm over his chest and threading our fingers together.

By three o'clock, I was more annoyed than anything. I needed to sleep. Maybe I could call Sam, once it was a decent hour, and ask him if we could push back our meeting. Not cancel it, because that would crush him, but push it back far enough that I could wake Slade, make sure he ate some breakfast, then run home for a quick nap and a shower.

Slade nestled against me, oblivious to how his ass rubbing against my dick affected me. I squeezed his hand tighter and he stilled, then I bit down on my lip to have something to focus on other than my arousal. And, eventually, I drifted off to sleep.

My phone vibrated on the overturned milk crate next to Slade's bed. Slade grunted his disapproval before burrowing deeper under his blankets when I released him and swung my feet over the edge of the bed.

Even in sleep, worry and anxiety were etched into Slade's features. I smoothed the thumb over his brow before kissing him lightly. "Relax, boy. I've got you. I'm not going anywhere."

It wasn't until I was across the hall in the bathroom, that I realized the truth of the promise I had made him. I had no business being here, no business pursuing him, yet, something about him made it impossible to walk away.

Once I decided to go for something, I was all in. Not having a notepad, I went into the living room, intending to make some notes on my phone. I wouldn't have believed it was possible if he had told me, but this room was even worse than the bedroom. I carefully piled the laundry at one end of the couch, broke down a few boxes, and gathered dirty dishes and empty take-out containers on my way to the kitchen.

I shuddered when I turned on the light. If the state of Slade's apartment was anything to go by, he was worse off than I had imagined. He fully expected me to run when I saw the state of his apartment, but all it did was strengthen my resolve to help him. It would've been easy to clean up for him—a nice surprise when he woke up and had one less thing to worry about—but that would do him no good in the long run. I neatly stacked the dishes in the sink and wiped down the countertops, using a bottle of spray disinfectant I found under the sink.

There were just enough coffee grounds in the bottom of the can for me to brew a pot. Thank God for small miracles.

The state of the refrigerator was unsurprising. Other than condiments and a couple of bottles of water, it was completely bare. I opened the notes app on my phone and began making a list.

It took some sweet talking, but as soon as the market down the street opened, I called and arranged for a delivery. We were heading into the end of the week, when work would be busy enough it would be impossible for me to devote the attention I'd like to Slade, but I was going to do everything I could before then to make sure he was taken care of.

The more layers of Slade's life I pulled back, the more distraught I became. I'd called Sam to reschedule for mid-afternoon, unsurprised when he very quickly agreed. That was the type of employee he was. But there wouldn't be time for a nap, there was far too much to be done here.

I waited until nearly ten o'clock before waking Slade. I had no doubt—given the glimpse I'd seen of his mental state—that he would happily sleep the day away if no one expected otherwise. With a cup of coffee in one hand, and a plate with two pieces of toast in the other, I very carefully made my way through the bedroom. The last thing I needed was to trip, sending the coffee cascading out of the cup.

"Time to wake up, boy," I whispered. He tossed the pillow over his head and grumbled something. That was a better reaction than I'd been expecting. I'd prepared for him to wake up swinging, either having forgotten last night, or regretting his weakness. I rubbed his back gently, allowing my fingers to drift toward his waistband. "Come on, brat. You need to get up."

"No reason," Slade grumbled.

I yanked the pillow away from his head and tossed it onto the floor. "I beg to differ. Even if you don't have anything scheduled today, you can't stay in bed."

"Wanna make a bet?" He swatted my arm before taking back his pillow.

I sat on the edge of the bed, with my hands folded in my lap to keep myself from touching him. When I spoke, my voice was low and steady. "I don't know what you expect to accomplish by hiding, but you have a hell of a lot of work to do today, boy."

"Like what?" Despite his protests, Slade sat up, pulling the sheet over his legs. He glared at me; his lips drawn tight.

I paused, gearing myself up for a fight. Slade was more compliant than I had expected him to be, but I doubted that would last for long. I could only hope. The one thing I couldn't do was walk away without testing the waters to see how Slade would react.

"First of all, you are going to get up and take a shower, after you finish your breakfast," I informed him.

Slade stared at the toasted bread I handed him as if it confused him. "I had bread?"

"No, but lucky for you I am well versed in ordering groceries for delivery. When you work as many hours as I do, you quickly get over any sort of need to pick out your own produce or the perfect cut of meat."

Slade scoffed and rolled his eyes. "Yeah, well good thing that isn't a problem for some of us. I'm not exactly trying to make a statement with my bare cupboards."

Slade swallowed hard and the color drained from his face. "You know I'm not gonna be able to pay you back for whatever you bought, right? You shouldn't have done that without talking to me first. I would've told you that I'm on a very tight budget."

More like nonexistent from the looks of it, but I kept that to myself. The last thing I wanted to do was sound like I was better than Slade and insult him.

"If I was expecting you to pay for it, then I absolutely would've talked to you first." I motioned for him to eat. His stomach growled as he took the first bite. The way he savored something so simple, made me wonder how infrequently he usually ate. That would certainly explain the way last night's binge affected him.

"I'm not your charity case, Jack," Slade spat out. "I let you give me a ride home and take care of me last night because I was too drunk and out of it to stand up for myself."

"You *let* me," I scoffed. "Let's get one thing straight right now, boy. No one *lets* me do anything. If I want to give someone a ride home, I will. If I want to watch him sleep all night to make sure he's okay, I will."

"That's kinda creepy," Slade said. I couldn't dispute it, but I also wouldn't change a damn thing about last night, other than possibly not making promises about keeping things strictly platonic.

"I'm not going to argue with you about giving you a ride home, taking care of you, or buying your groceries," I told him. "I did all of those things without any reciprocity expected. It's called being a decent human being. I'm not going to apologize for any of that, but I will promise to consult with you before any further acts of kindness."

"Thank you." Slade let out a huff of disapproval, crossing his arms tightly over his chest. His bottom lip jutted out, making him seem adorably innocent. I might have told him so, but I could imagine how he would've responded to being called either of those terms. Slade's attitude and defiance were armor he wore to protect him from getting hurt.

"After you shower—because I'm certain you aren't feeling the best right now—you're going to spend the rest of the day cleaning up this apartment." He opened his mouth as if to argue with me. I narrowed my eyes and glared at him, before standing and squaring my shoulders. "I mean it, Slade. I have to work today, but I'm going to stop by later and I expect to see a marked improvement."

"Oh, so I have one night of weakness and suddenly, you decide it's your God-given right to boss me around?"

"No, I'm pretty sure you *want* to be told what to do, but you're either too scared, or stubborn, to admit it. Possibly even to yourself." I braced myself for a second before Slade's fists connected with my chest. He wasn't able to move me. I curled my fingers around his wrists, holding him close. "Look me in the eye and tell me I'm wrong, Slade."

"Is this some sort of game to you?" Slade's voice wavered. I had shoved him out of his comfort zone, leaving him off balance. Good. At least he wasn't trying to lie to both of us.

"Tell me, boy."

"Fuck you," Slade spat out. Still, he didn't try to escape. His nostrils flared, and he deflated a bit.

"Tell me," I repeated, firmer this time.

Slade rose to his knees, pressing his stomach against my chest. Looking directly into my eyes, he smirked. "Make me, *Daddy*."

The little shit absolutely remembered the events of last night, and now he was taunting me. Well, he was about to learn what happened to little boys who tested me.

The words hadn't even escaped my lips when I wished I could take them back. Jack's eyes grew steely and cold. He wrenched my arms around, so they were pinned behind my back.

"Do you think you're being funny right now, boy?" When my gaze fell to the floor, Jack captured both of my hands in one of his, using the other to tilt my head back so I had no choice but to look at him. "Answer me, boy."

"Well, since the music thing doesn't seem to be working so well, I figured I'd try my hand at comedy," I quipped. "I'm hoping to take my stand-up routine on the road soon."

It was apparent, I had absolutely zero self-preservation instinct. If I did, I wouldn't have allowed Jack to stay in my apartment when I was too drunk to fend him off if he tried taking advantage of me. I would have told him to get the hell out of my bedroom when he walked in with toast in hand, as if I was incapable of feeding myself. And I sure as hell wouldn't have taunted him.

I knew exactly what I was doing. He had warned me last night that if I kept calling him Daddy, I was going to pay the consequences. I had considered saying it again immediately, just to see if he would follow through but, deep down, I knew he wouldn't. He had promised me nothing would happen last night when I was drunk, and I didn't want to scare him off before getting him to help me. I'd heard some guys talk about how submitting let them stop worrying about all the bullshit in their minds. I wasn't sure that was possible, but I'd reached the point I had nothing to lose. And, fuck, the idea of letting go and letting someone else deal with all the adult bullshit—even for just a few minutes —seemed worth whatever pain or humiliation came with it.

Jack's grip tightened to the point of being almost painful.

"Don't get smart with me, boy," he warned. "You won't be able to sit for a week if you keep that shit up."

I hummed, licking my lips, trying to look as eager as possible. I arched my back, pressing my dick against Jack's stomach. The air was knocked out of my lungs when Jack released me, and I fell back onto the bed. I grunted in pain when my head bounced on the lumpy mattress.

"The first thing you're going to learn is I don't appreciate little boys who try topping from the bottom."

I cupped a hand over my junk, giving myself a quick squeeze. "Oh honey, there's absolutely nothing little about this boy," I quipped. "I am all man. Would you like to see?"

"You are a disrespectful little shit, that's what you are." Jack balanced on one leg, pulling up his sock before stepping into his shoe. He did the same with the other foot. The opportunity was slipping away for me.

No. Dammit. This is not how this morning was supposed to go. I had been awake for over an hour, curled up against the pillow Jack had used last night. I had everything planned out. I was going to get Jack to give me exactly what I needed in order to take off a bit of the edge that had been threatening to cut me for weeks now.

At the very least, I figured I could suck him off, swallow his load, and then jerk off later to the memory of how he felt, sounded, and tasted. I lunged off the bed, gripping his forearm tightly. "I'm sorry. Please, give me another chance."

"Why should I?" Jack spat out without looking at me. "It's obvious that you think this is a game."

"It's not," I replied somberly. "I know that."

Jack turned to face me. The arousal and irritation from earlier had been replaced by a dull sadness in his eyes. I slid my hands up his chest. It took great effort, but I finally whispered, "Please, Daddy. Give me a chance to prove this isn't a joke to me. I *want* this, but I'm scared, too. It's not easy for me to step back and trust someone else the way I'm sure you'd demand."

Jack quirked an eyebrow, then scrubbed a hand over his face, mumbling something I couldn't understand. When he finally allowed his hand to drop to my shoulder, his eyes were a bit clearer. "You want to prove it to me, boy?"

I nodded, then remembered Jack's earlier instruction about using my words. "Yes, Daddy. Please."

Jack lifted a hand to cup my cheek. "I will be back at five-thirty tonight. If you've done everything I've instructed you to, then we can talk. If not, then we go our separate ways."

I nodded, willing to agree to just about anything if he was going to give me what I needed. His fingers twisted in my hair, yanking tightly so that I looked at him. "I'm serious, Slade. There are no more second chances. If you want this, you're going to have to prove it to me."

"Okay, so what do I need to do?" Jack bowed and shook his head as he walked out of the room. I followed.

"I expect my boys to pay attention when I speak to them,

Slade," he explained as he walked toward the front door. He wouldn't look at me and that hurt. I massaged my chest, trying to figure out why in the hell this mattered so much to me. Yesterday at this time, Jack hadn't even been a blip on my radar, but now I was ready to fall to my knees, wrap my arms around his legs, and beg him to stay. The disappointment rolling off of him was nearly palpable, and I fucking hated that.

"I was... I mean, I will," I corrected. "Tell me what I need to do. I'll do anything."

Jack held out his hand.

"Give me your phone," he demanded. I scrunched up my nose and gaped at him. Seriously? This is what he wanted from me?

"Don't keep me waiting, boy," he warned.

Oh, for fuck's sake, was the remote possibility of getting off with a sexy older man really worth all of this?

Yes, it absolutely was.

I hitched a thumb over my shoulder. "It's in my bedroom. At least, I think it is."

Jack jerked his head toward the bathroom. "No, you left it on the sink last night."

I had? I never left my phone lying around, especially when I wasn't alone. "Okay, I'll... I'm gonna..." Before I could make even more of an ass of myself, I backed out of the room to retrieve my phone. I handed it to him, and he tapped the screen, quirking an eyebrow when he noticed it was password locked.

I opened my mouth to give him the code. My teeth clattered together when I forced myself to stop. I hadn't even known this dude twenty-four hours and I was considering giving him the password to my phone? I might as well hand over my banking info if I was going to do that. Then again, if

I did do that, he'd probably make a pity deposit into my account when he saw the dangerously low number.

I swiped the phone out of his hand and quickly entered the code, carefully turning the screen so he wouldn't be able to see.

"Thank you, boy." Jack leaned in, placing a chaste kiss on my cheek. My freaking cheek. The only person who kissed my cheek was Mama Marino when I went to the restaurant for dinner with Jordan. Apparently, anyone who knew her boys was part of her adopted family. That was fine by me, since I didn't speak with anyone I was related to by blood.

I fidgeted while Jack messed around with my phone. Shifting my weight from one foot to the other, hands hanging at my sides, then crossing my arms tightly over my chest, before placing them behind my back, all as I tried to decipher what Jack expected of me. He was still an arrogant asshole, but I wasn't sure there would ever be another opportunity like this for me to get something I thought I might, possibly, maybe want. With this level of uncertainty, I sure as hell wasn't about to walk into a kink club and proclaim my submissive fantasies to the first guy who caught my eye.

Jack reached out, pressing a hand to my shoulder. "Settle, boy. You are restless enough, you're starting to make me nervous."

"I'm sorry." I spread my feet a bit wider, standing up straight, shoulders squared, back arched slightly. That was a good position, right? Jack chuckled and I deflated, then he stepped closer, sliding an arm around my back. He leaned in, brushing his lips gently across mine. "Relax, Slade. There's nothing to be nervous about, yet."

Yet? Well, that didn't sound ominous at all. Jack turned

his attention back to my phone, tapping out a quick message. His phone vibrated seconds later. He handed mine back to me as he pulled his out of his pocket. He started typing again, then it was my phone that chimed, alerting me that I had a new text message.

"You know, I've heard it's completely suitable to use verbal communication when you are standing in the same room as the person you are talking to," I quipped.

"And I was under the impression it was customary for one person to listen when the other person speaks, but you seem to be having issues remembering the simple tasks I gave you." He nodded toward the phone in my hand. "I figured it was for the best if I sent very clear instructions by text so there was no room for error."

Jack tucked his phone away and started walking toward the front door. "If you have any questions about anything, don't hesitate to ask. I won't be angry with you if you need clarification."

Curiosity got the better of me, and I pulled up the message from Jack. Instantly, my blood pressure spiked, and I felt my face grow red. "What in the hell is this?"

Jack let out an impatient sigh. "I already explained that to you, and I'm not going to do it again."

"But I thought you were going to discipline me," I protested. "You told me."

Jack closed the distance between us in three short steps. His toes covered mine, and I felt the hard leather soles pressing down on the tops of my toes. It wasn't painful. In a totally twisted way, it was... Comforting? "I have no doubt there will be plenty of opportunities for me to punish you, boy. But not everything is a sexy game."

"I already told you I was taking this seriously," I argued.

"I don't think this is a game. I know you see me as some sort of incompetent fuck up, but I'm not."

Jack tugged on my hair again, forcing me to look at him. It had always annoyed me when other people did that. I didn't appreciate being treated like an abused animal, getting led around by my hair. But with Jack, it felt different. I swallowed hard, blinking rapidly a few times. "Prove it."

Jack released me and walked out the front door, leaving me too stunned to respond.

I wasn't sure how long I stood there, gaping at where Jack had stood before my phone chimed again.

Words mean nothing without actions. Do you want this? You know what you need to do.

I was just about to throw my phone across the room in frustration, when another alert came through.

And for the record, the rewards for good boys are even better than the punishments you think you need.

Fuck him. Pompous asshole thinking he could tell me what to do. I stormed into the living room, swiped the remote off the floor, and started flipping through channels. Might as well enjoy the cable while it lasted.

Most days, I was perfectly content turning into a zombie as I stared at the TV without really processing what was happening on the screen. Today, I couldn't quit squirming around. I sat up, scrubbing my hands over my face.

"Asshole can't even let me wallow properly," I muttered to myself. I scooted closer to the pile of laundry at the end of the couch and began folding as I watched a documentary on the evolution of music over the decades. Once that pile was taken care of, I paused the show and retrieved another basket out of my bedroom. A quick sniff assured me I wasn't about to fold a basket of stale, nasty clothes. The show ended and another began, this one about the meteoric rise and tragic fall of a legend. If someone who saw that sort of success could fail, what did that mean for a no-name kid from a small town?

I thought about the second to last chore on Jack's list.

Call Eli. Swallow your damn pride and ask him for a job. You have people who want to help you. Don't turn your back on them.

Arrogant prick didn't know a damn thing about me. Or maybe he did, because, yeah, it *was* pride that kept me from seeing if there were any openings at Club 83. I wanted so desperately to be able to say I made it on my own that I refused to take the easy way out.

Besides, what skills did I have to offer Eli? I'd never had a real job. When I was still in school, my dad insisted I focus on my studies so that I could get into a good college.

The joke was on him, because I managed to screw myself hard enough during my senior year that no one wanted me. At the time, I figured it would be easier for him to accept that music was my life if it was my only option.

And that joke was on me. I knew I was talented. No one ever accused me of being insecure about my songwriting skills or my vocal chops. The problem was that the odds of making a living were slim enough without being part of a group who didn't take music as seriously as I did.

To them, it was nothing to walk away when they found what they really wanted in life. Not one of them had asked me how I felt about the band breaking up. None of them had called to check on me. This was why I didn't trust people. If my bandmates—people I swore were my chosen family—could turn their backs on me so easily, why would I believe everyone else wouldn't?

My phone chimed.

Have you blocked my number?

I cocked my head to the side, rereading Jack's message a

few times, trying to figure out what in the hell he was talking about. Had my shady ass phone eaten messages from him?

I couldn't help but laugh a little when I figured out what he meant.

You are still a jerk but, no, I haven't blocked you.

And have you thought about what I said this morning?

Rather than type out a reply, I sent him a picture of the piles of neatly folded laundry covering my couch.

Good boy, he responded.

I'm not a dog, Jack.

No, but I could totally see you as a puppy, he teased.

I groaned. Okay, so there was something disturbingly arousing about guys getting to run around and pretend they were pups, but it wasn't something that I wanted to participate in.

No thanks.

Oh, come on. You are exactly like a puppy. To you, any attention is good attention. You tend to act before your brain engages, and I'd be willing to bet you are full of excess energy you need to run off.

I couldn't deny any of that, but there was the whole tail and hood thing that was just bizarre to me. Then there was the whole collar and leash thing, which should be more offputting than it was.

Still not interested.

Duly noted.

Is that a problem for you?

Not in the least.

I released a breath when I read his answer. I still hated him for thinking a honey-do list was amusing, but I wanted to stick this out and see what sort of reward he had in mind.

I have a meeting soon. Do you have any questions for me?

Meetings. The tailored business suits. His fancy car.

Yeah, I had questions.

What do you do for a living?

That's a question better answered tonight. Any questions about the list?

No, I am fully aware of what a chore list is. Next time, maybe you can make me a chart and stick it up on the fridge. Give me stickers for doing a good job?

If that's something you feel you need, it is definitely something we can discuss later.

Another text quickly followed. *Talk soon, brat. I will be out of pocket for about an hour.*

I wasn't sure how to respond, so I didn't. I read over Jack's list, pleased with myself when I realized I could already cross off one item. All of the clean laundry was folded, and he could kiss my ass if he thought I was going out on a cold, rainy day to schlep my dirty clothes to the laundromat. We had a washer and dryer in the basement of the building, but I swore that every time I washed my clothes there, they came out smelling worse than when they went in.

I stood at the edge of the room after putting away my clothes, trying to figure out what to do next. Bile rose in my stomach. I might live in this dump, but somewhere along the way I had become blind to the mess. I was ashamed anyone had seen it in this state.

Where some people could grab a used shopping bag or a single kitchen garbage bag for a massive cleaning session, I dropped the full box of garbage bags on my coffee table. This was going to be a huge undertaking.

I was halfway through cleaning the living room when I heard the door open. It was Jordan with my hoodie draped over his arm. I jumped up, swiping the sweatshirt out of his hand.

"You didn't need to bring this over," I told him. He laughed as I shrugged into it, burying my hands in the pockets.

"It's okay, I wanted to check on you anyway. This just gave me a good excuse."

"Why in the hell does everyone think I need babysitters? I swear, it's like no one thinks I can take care of myself."

Jordan's eyes grew wide and he dramatically looked around the room. "I hate to tell you this, buddy, but you sorta do need a keeper."

He stepped past me and into the kitchen, letting out a low whistle. "Damn, dude. I wasn't aware you had counter-tops in here."

"You're fucking hilarious," I tossed back.

His eyes roamed over to a mountain of garbage bags and broken-down boxes stacked against the wall. "Is everything okay? You didn't get kicked out, did you?"

"Why in the fuck would you say that?" I stomped over to the fridge. Now that my hangover had subsided, my stomach was begging for more food than the toast I'd eaten earlier.

"It was the most logical reason for you to be cleaning. Look, I know you don't want to hear it, but I talked to Eli, and we want to help you."

"Better get at the back of the line." I gathered my hair, securing it with an elastic I found in the pocket of my hoodie. "Pretty soon, there is going to be a Help-Slade-Unfuck-His-Life community outreach project. Maybe you can sign up."

"Why do you have to be such an asshole?" Jordan asked as he poured a cup of coffee. His eyes grew even wider when he opened the cupboard where I kept the can of coffee grounds.

"Did you get a job and not tell me?"

"Yeah, that's why I'm spending the day cleaning my shit-hole," I retorted.

Please don't let him ask. Please don't let him ask. Please don't let him ask. I didn't want to lie to Jordan about how my cupboards were suddenly full, but I also wasn't ready to tell him about last night.

"I'd ask if you robbed the grocery store, but even I can't imagine you being stupid enough to run down the street with a grocery cart full of food you didn't pay for." Once Jordan had another pot of coffee brewing, he hopped up on the counter. "Seriously, man, I haven't seen this much food in your place since you moved in. What gives?"

My cheeks burned with embarrassment. I didn't want to tell him, but I couldn't keep secrets. Not from Jordan. "Jack took it upon himself to do some shopping while I was sleeping off last night's binge. Happy now?"

I slammed the fridge closed. God, could this be day any more embarrassing?

Apparently, it could.

"Jack? You mean, as in Doug's brother, Jack?"

"Unless there's another pompous asshole named Jack who seems to have a bit of a savior complex?" I quipped.

"Nah man, he's not like that. He's actually a down-to-earth guy."

I let out a snort of laughter. "Are you fucking kidding me? Who in the hell goes to a casual party at his brother's house wearing a three-piece suit? Someone who wants to flaunt their wealth, that's who."

"Not with him," Jordan insisted, and I rolled my eyes. "I get where you're coming from. I thought the same at first, but Jack is a really good guy. But I'm confused. If you think so highly of him, why did he buy you groceries? A better question... How in the hell did he know that you live like Mother Hubbard?"

"He gave me a ride home last night. You know that."

"Yeah, and it's one hell of a jump from being a good guy and giving someone a ride home, to whipping out his credit card to buy groceries."

"You don't even know the half of it," I muttered.

"Wait a minute." Jordan bit down on his lips to hide a smile. "Is he the reason you're cleaning? I hate to tell you, but if he gave you a ride home and was in your place last night, I'd say the ship has sailed on you trying to make a good first impression."

"It's not like that," I insisted.

Please don't make me explain. I dipped my head so Jordan couldn't see whatever humiliation was on my face. I knew he and his men didn't have a conventional relationship, but neither of us were the type to share those details. A man had to keep some things to himself. I wasn't prepared to admit that what had started as me lashing out at Jack for ordering me around had quickly morphed into fantasy, then a fucked-up goal I was determined to achieve.

"For what it's worth, Jack really is a good guy," Jordan reassured me. He hopped off the counter and pulled me in for a tight hug. "If you like him, go for it. I think he is exactly the type of man you need in your life."

"I don't *need* any man in my life. Remember?" I jabbed a finger against my own chest. "Anti. Relationship. I don't do hearts and flowers and candy, and all that other bullshit."

"You keep saying that, but it doesn't seem to be working out for you," Jordan pointed out. He tightened his embrace.

"Maybe it's time for you to figure out if there's something that would work better. Just think about it, okay?"

"Okay," I promised him. Little did he know, I had been doing nothing but thinking about Jack since the moment I woke up this morning, the scent of his cologne still lingering in the sheets. What terrified me the most was, for once, I didn't want to run away from the attraction. I wanted to run directly into his arms, slide down his body, and beg him to give me a chance.

S am gaped at me when I approached him at the main bar of The Lodge.

"That's a good look for you, boss," he remarked. There was something about the way he scanned my body that made me feel self-conscious. I glanced down with my brow furrowed. Granted, it was unusual for me to come to work dressed in casual attire, but I was heading straight from here to Slade's place, and he had made it apparent he wasn't a fan of my bespoke wardrobe. "If I didn't know better, I would think you'd been abducted by aliens."

"Come on now, Sam. Surely it isn't that strange for me to dress down. Believe it or not, I don't wear suits seven days a week." Now I wondered how others saw me. Did everyone think like Slade, assuming I was a pretentious asshole who dressed to flaunt his wealth?

"I know you don't, but I've never seen you dressed down when you come in here," he pointed out. "And the entire time I've worked here, I can't think of a single time when you called to say you were coming in later than you'd planned on. The only real options are a mid-life crisis or alien abduction."

"I apologize for rescheduling, Sam. Something came up last night that needed my immediate attention," I explained.

My phone buzzed but I ignored it. I had notified Slade that I would be unavailable for part of the afternoon. Whatever it was, I would wait until I wasn't in the middle of a conversation with Sam to attend to it. It would be far too easy for me to shift my entire focus to helping Slade get back on his feet, but that would do neither of us any good. Still, the sooner we got this meeting started, the sooner it would be over, and I could head over to see how Slade was doing with his chores.

I wasn't sure if I hoped he'd completed his chores so I could reward him, or that he'd fallen short so I could punish him. Slade made it obvious he *wanted* to be disciplined, but I was much more a fan of rewarding positive behavior. Preventative discipline was something we could address in the future if things progressed.

I hadn't realized how worried I'd been about how Slade would react until he'd sent me the first picture of his laundry piles. He'd have been well within his rights to ignore me and pretend he wasn't home. I probably would have if the roles were reversed. I'd crossed lines this morning, and even if they weren't sexual, I should have respected him more and asked for his input without charging in to take control.

I owed Slade an apology. It seemed I was doing a lot of that today.

"You okay, boss?" I blinked a few times, realizing that I had zoned out, thinking about Slade and how lucky I was that he hadn't laughed in my face.

"Yes. I'm fine. Why don't we head back to my office so we

can take a look at the proposal you put together?" The staff would start wandering in soon, and I didn't want them eavesdropping or interrupting us.

"That sounds... Uh, yeah. Okay." Sam leaned against the bar, closing his eyes, and taking a few breaths. I watched for a full minute while he muttered something under his breath that sounded like a pep talk. When he opened his eyes and looked up, I noticed his cheeks were flushed, and he quickly averted his gaze to the bar.

"Everything okay, Sam?" I stifled my laughter, not wanting him to feel any more insecure than he already did. He had nothing to fear; he was a brilliant kid with a bright future. I could only hope he meant it when he said he wanted to stick around The Lodge. Having someone like him as my right hand, would allow me the time to devote to...other pursuits.

"Yeah, sorry about that," he responded quickly. "Just a bit nervous, I guess. I really didn't think anything would come of me telling you about that project."

He grabbed himself a bottled water, holding it up. "You want one, too?"

"That would be great." My phone buzzed again. I decided it would be better to check in with Slade now, rather than give him an opportunity to think I was playing mind games with him. Something about his defensive walls told me that was what he expected. I didn't do head games. Psychological domination was a hard limit for me. "Why don't you meet me in my office? I need to make a quick call. I'm sorry."

"Don't worry about it, boss," Sam flashed me a brilliant smile. "I'm just grateful, and a little bit stunned, that we're having this conversation at all. Don't mind me, I can wait as long as you need. Would it be better for you if we did this another day?"

"Absolutely not," I insisted. "I haven't gotten as far as I have by blowing off meetings that I've set up. I'm not about to start now."

I wasn't sure if the speech was meant for his ears or mine. It may have been a reminder to myself that I wasn't going to get lost in the lusty fog of my attraction to Slade. "Just give me a couple of minutes, and I'll meet you there."

"Sure thing." Sam bounded down the hall.

There was nothing alarming about Slade's first message.

You better have one hell of a reward for me tonight, Daddy.

I smiled at the screen like an idiot. It was too soon for there to be any significant meaning behind him calling me Daddy, but I loved seeing it, nonetheless. He was such a cheeky little brat when he wasn't stressing about where his life was headed.

The second message wasn't nearly as optimistic.

I lied. I am never going to get some of this shit done. It's too much. I can't believe I let it get this bad.

My phone buzzed with, yet, another message.

Maybe you shouldn't come over tonight. If you give me another day or two, I might be able to get everything done.

And another.

I swear, I'm trying.

That was enough. I hit the call button, counting the number of rings and gearing myself up to hear Slade's outgoing voicemail message.

"Oh. Hey," he answered. "I didn't mean to bother you. I know you said you had meetings this afternoon. I do this sometimes. Just ask Jordan. I swear he ends up putting me on mute, so he doesn't have to hear his phone going off constantly."

"Boy," I said firmly, interrupting his insecure mono-
logue. "Take a breath, would you?"

"Sorry," Slade apologized.

"Don't apologize." I focused on the tone of my voice,
trying to keep it light and reassuring. "Breathe with me,
Slade."

I guided him through a couple of quick breathing exercises. After almost a minute, he exhaled audibly. "Wow.
Thought shit like that was a load of crap but it really
worked."

"Are you okay now?"

"Yeah, much better. Thanks."

"Glad to hear it. Now, I think it's time for you to take a
break."

"But I haven't gotten everything on your list done yet,"
he protested. "I want to show you that I am taking you
seriously."

This was a boy who was completely starved for affection and affirmation. There were red flags flying all over the
place. I shouldn't be this invested in his well-being when
we had only met a day ago. He shouldn't be freaking out
about how I would react. And the way his mood flipped,
worried me. There was more going on in Slade's head than
I could possibly help him with, and I wasn't sure he was in
the right mental space for getting involved with someone
like me.

"I want you to listen to me, Slade," I told him. I settled
onto one of the couches in the common area, kicking my
feet up on the ottoman. "I don't expect perfection from you.
I know I gave you more tasks today than you would be able
to complete."

"So, you're admitting you set me up for failure? If you
weren't interested, you could have just said so. You didn't

need to go on a power trip first." Trying to keep up with Slade's mood swings was going to give me whiplash.

"I promise you, Slade, that isn't what I was doing." I pinched the bridge of my nose and closed my eyes. I was out of practice when it came to dealing with needy boys. "Was I confident you would complete the list? No. But I had faith that you would do the best you could, and that is all I can ask of you. That's all I would ever ask of you."

"Wow. Okay. But what are you going to do if I don't get everything done? Now that you've told me you already knew I wouldn't be able to get through everything today, what if I say screw it and don't do anything else until you get here?" The emotional pendulum was coming back to center. I bit back my amusement.

"Well, I suppose there's nothing stopping you from slacking off the rest of the day. But even if I didn't know, you would. And I don't think you are going to disobey me like that blatantly, are you, *boy*?" I placed a heavy dose of emphasis on the last word, reminding him of what he'd asked of me, even if he hadn't fully realized what that would entail.

"No." Slade let out a disgruntled huff. "I still don't understand why I'm listening to you in the first place."

"Yes, you do."

"No, I really don't," Slade argued. "I could've told you to fuck off when you texted me that list."

"You're right," I agreed. "You absolutely could have. But you didn't. And do you want to know why that is?"

"Oh yes, please enlighten me." It was a good thing we were having this conversation over the phone, because I wasn't sure I would've been able to hide my amusement with Slade if he was standing in front of me. He was still a brat. But now that I was beginning to understand him a little bit more, I didn't think he was going out of his way to be disrespectful. This was yet another coping mechanism of his.

I leaned forward, resting my elbows on my knees. "I think you want exactly what you know I can give you. You don't want to have to make decisions or deal with the boring day-to-day tasks. It's much easier for you to accomplish things when you convince yourself you're doing it because someone else asked you to. And, deep down, I think the idea of being taken care of appeals to you."

"Maybe," Slade agreed reluctantly. "But it's probably stupid for me to say that to you, huh?"

"Why would you think that?" I wanted to hear why Slade thought he was being careless.

"Because I don't know you. What if you are some possessive asshole? What if you're doing all of this as a way to manipulate me? What if it turns out you really are a sadistic fuck who gets off on brainwashing the guys you're with?"

"You seem to have thought about this quite a bit," I remarked.

"Probably more than I should," he admitted. "Can't help it. I spend enough time alone in my apartment that I have plenty of time to come up with all these worst-case scenarios. Probably doesn't help that I am addicted to true crime shows when I'm not watching documentaries."

"Speaking of..." I paused, trying to figure out how to phrase my next question. Things seemed to be going well with Slade for the moment, and I didn't want to push too far, too fast. "Have you considered the last item on your list?"

"I don't think it's a good idea."

"Why not? You needed a job and Eli needs help. He's looking for both, bartenders and line cooks, so you could take your pick."

"Except there's one major problem with your magic solution. I don't know how to cook and the only thing I know about bartending is you have to put up with a whole lot of drunk assholes. Do you really think I'd be able to keep my mouth shut so I didn't get fired?"

"You can do it," I reassured him, even though he made a good point. Maybe the kitchen would be a safer place for him.

"You say it like it's easy."

"It really is Slade. And from where I'm standing, it doesn't seem like you can afford to be terribly picky right now." I cringed as soon as the words passed my lips.

Way to sound like the pretentious jerk he keeps accusing you of being.

The only thing that made me feel worse than imagining Slade telling me to get the fuck out of his life on the high horse I rode in on, was the crushed, defeated tone of his voice when he responded. "Maybe you're right. I'll talk to him."

"Thank you, Slade. Now, I am going to change things up a bit. I want you to forget about the list. I want you to call Eli and set up a time when the two of you can talk, then I want you to take a nap. Unless you've been lying to me, you've been a very good boy today. Tonight, we are going to talk a bit, and then I am going to give you your reward to show you how proud of you I am."

"No, you don't have to do that," Slade protested. "I want to see if I can get through most of the list today. I didn't understand the point of this exercise when I started, but I think I get it now. And I don't feel as defeated as I was before."

"That's wonderful, boy." Sam appeared across the room. I held up a finger, letting him know I'd be right there. He nodded and disappeared. I stood and began crossing the room. "You need this break. You're going to crash otherwise."

I should have anticipated this. I had seen glimpses of the boy who craved nothing more than to please me this morning, and I had taken full advantage of that. Now, it was time for me to pull back a bit and consider what was best for him, both immediately and in the long run.

"Call Eli, and then nap." I kept my voice firm, hoping he understood this wasn't up for debate. "I want you to set the alarm for four-thirty so you can get dinner into the oven. Is the living room clean enough that we can eat there tonight?"

"Yes. That was the first room I got done. The kitchen is almost done, too."

"Very good, Slade. It sounds like you've made more than enough progress for one day," I reassured him. I honestly hadn't expected to ever set foot inside Slade's apartment again. The fact that he had not only taken me seriously, but gotten so much work done, spoke volumes as to his work ethic. Now, if only I could make him see that today's lesson could be carried over into other aspects of his life.

"I'm going to let you go so I can get this meeting over with. Do as I said. I will text you when I'm on my way to your apartment."

"Are you sure you want to come over here tonight? Maybe we would be better off if you picked me up and we went out to eat," Slade suggested. "I can't afford much but if you'd be more comfortable..."

I hadn't done a good job hiding my displeasure with where Slade lived, and I got the impression he was offering for my benefit more than his own. That simply would not do.

"Boy, I want you to listen to me." I was beginning to feel like a broken record, but it was obvious I would be doing a lot of repeating myself. And I would do so gladly, as much as it took to make Slade understand he had nothing to be ashamed of unless he simply gave up. The fact I wasn't growing impatient with him, spoke volumes about the chemistry I wanted to explore. "The two of us are going to talk tonight, and there may be things you don't want random strangers to overhear. No matter what, I want you to be comfortable enough to say whatever's on your mind, even if you think I won't like it."

"But you hate my apartment," he pointed out. "I wasn't so drunk last night I imagined the way you looked when you saw where I live."

"No, I hate that your building doesn't have adequate security. It saddens me to see the disorder in a place that should be your sanctuary, because I'm pretty sure it didn't get that way because you're a slob."

"No, I'm not," he confirmed. Then he corrected himself. "At least, I wasn't, but then everything started falling apart and I couldn't bring myself to care anymore."

"That happens to more people than you realize, Slade. But we're going to get you on the right path, okay?"

"Why are you doing all of this for me?"

"Because my gut tells me you're worth it."

"Your gut lies," Slade muttered.

"Let me be the judge of that," I scolded him.

Sam popped his head around the corner again. The man's patience was never-ending.

"I really do need to get going," I told Slade. "I'll see you after a bit, okay?"

"Yeah, sure." I wished I had the time to convince him I wasn't trying to take him on as a charity case, but that would take days if not weeks. Instead, I said one final goodbye and hung up.

With that out of the way, I focused my attention on Sam. Instead of sitting behind my desk, I ushered him toward the small sitting area. Today, I didn't want him feeling as if I was the boss and he was my subordinate. From what I had seen of the proposal he'd done for his class, Sam had one hell of a mind for business.

I listened as he explained the general project outline, asking him questions in all the appropriate places, trying to get a feel for how much thought he had put into his suggestions.

"Anyone can open a BDSM club," he stated at one point, and I cocked my head to the side a bit. "I mean, no offense or anything, but it's not exactly a unique idea anymore. Perhaps it would've been, years ago when you opened this place..."

"Hey now, let's not make it sound like I am ancient or anything," I teased. Sam's entire face flushed red.

"That's not what I'm... I didn't mean..." He combed his fingers through his hair, rocking slightly, and muttering under his breath.

I held up my hands to stop him. I needed to remember who I was dealing with and that Sam tended to take everything literally at times. "Relax, Sam. I was just teasing you."

"Oh." He stared at me a moment; his brow furrowed in confusion. "Sorry, I'm not used to this side of you. You're always such a..."

I waited a beat, then two, as I gave him time to save himself. He slumped back in his seat. "An uptight prick?"

"No, that's not what I was going to say it all. You're just usually so serious all the time."

"So I've heard. I appreciate your candor, and I'm sorry if

I've given you the idea that I am unapproachable. It wasn't my intention at all."

"No, it's not really that. I have a hard time talking to most people," he admitted, then sank deeper into the cushions. When he pinched and tugged on his lip, I was tempted to reach out and stop him.

I pulled two of the presentation slides Sam had printed off and set them on the table between us. While all of his ideas were feasible, these were the two that caught my eye. "Tell me more. How would you make this happen in the space that we currently have?"

"When I was working on the project, I was working with all hypotheticals," Sam explained. "It may not even be possible without upsetting some of our existing clientele."

"That's not what I asked, Sam. How would you take these two concepts and bring them to life?" I leaned against the back of the couch, resting one ankle on the opposite knee. I steepled my fingers in front of my mouth, eager to see if his ideas matched my own. I would have ultimate say of course, since The Lodge was the only one of my businesses that I was hands-on for the day-to-day operation, but maybe Sam was right. Maybe it was time for me to bring in some new blood with ideas to innovate and reinvigorate, so we could increase the profit margin.

"Right now, you have three different public or semi-public areas," Sam explained. I cleared my throat to get his attention off his lap and on to me. "Sorry. I'm trying to work through everything in my head."

"I don't want you trying to figure out what you think I want to hear," I clarified. "Right now, all I care about is what you envisioned when you were working on this project."

"We don't need three open areas like we have now. Sure, there are some nights when all of them are you in use, but the space could be better served by taking the two smaller rooms and creating spaces where people from certain communities felt like they're not only welcome, but catered to." He glanced up at me, and I nodded.

"It's not part of the original project because I was worried about what people would say if I had to make a presentation, but I have some drawings and lists. If you'd like to see."

I held out my hand, trying to tamp down my impatience. This was his only misstep so far, and it was one I could forgive. Just asking Sam to sit down with me was forcing him outside of his comfort zone. He dug through his messenger bag and handed over another folder filled with papers.

He might have thought they were rudimentary, but I thought they were brilliant.

"I like these," I told him. "What would you say if I put you in charge of trying to get one of the two off the ground?"

Sam perked up, sitting straighter, and his shoulders squared for the first time since I had walked into the office.

"Which one are you most interested in?" The boy was practically bouncing in his seat. I had never seen him play at The Lodge, but I got the impression it wasn't a foreign concept to him when he had first applied for a management position.

Sam gnawed on his lip as he looked over both concept drawings. He glanced up at me, then back down at the paper, then back to me.

"Would it be okay if I take a couple of days to give you an answer? I will admit, I wasn't prepared for you to agree to anything, much less ask me to make a decision this big."

Thinking was the last thing I wanted Sam to do. I could see the color draining from his face the longer he considered which direction we should go. The more time I gave him, the more uncertain he would become.

"Let's meet again on Monday, next week," I suggested. "I'm hoping to take that night off, but I will have to come in and do some paperwork. We could talk then, and that will give me time to talk to my brother-in-law and get some contractor recommendations."

I wouldn't have to talk to Eli to get the list. I knew every contractor who had worked on the renovation of the dilapidated building in the district that eventually became Club 83. No one knew I had been the one who footed the bill to help my brother's partner achieve his dream. I was still a stakeholder in the club but, other than that, I was completely hands-off. Eli and I both thought it would be simpler that way so no one could come back later and say there was a conflict of interest or anything like that.

"This is a pretty big deal," Sam said. "Are you sure you don't want to be in charge of it?"

I shook my head. It was time for me to take a step back. For too many years now, I demanded complete focus for myself, and it'd come close to costing me everything. Sure, I had a well-padded bank account, but I was starting to realize monetary success was one of the least important things in life. "You are going to do this, Sam. And if the first concept is a hit—and I have complete faith it will be—then you are going to implement the other one as well. You're a bright young man, and I'm hopeful about your future here as long as you want to stay."

"Thank you, Jack. You don't know how much it means that you have this level of faith in me."

I was pretty certain I did. I stood, and Sam did the same. I shook his hand before gathering the papers. "Do you mind if I take these home with me?"

"Go ahead. I had copies made for you."

Of course, he did. Sam was nothing if not organized. He checked the time. "I'd better get out there. We're going to be opening soon, and I want to make sure everything is ready."

"Take a breath, Sam. Everything's going to be fine." I watched him leave and then flopped back on the couch. I scrubbed a hand over my face, wondering what the hell I was getting myself into.

I couldn't let a fleeting interaction with a broken boy change the entire course of my life.

Maybe this was the start of a midlife crisis. Only time would tell.

9

SLADE

Putting out place settings and finding a jar candle was probably overkill, but after busting my ass all day, trying to make sure Jack couldn't find any reason to be upset with me, I wanted everything tonight to go perfect. And wasn't that a load of fucked up shit, seeing as I had never—not once in my life—given a damn about trying to woo somebody.

Hookups were easy. Approach somebody at the bar, maybe even sit on my ass until someone swiped on my profile, get each other hard, get off, and get gone. And, yet, here I was trying to make a good impression on Jack. It was the least I could do after the lousy first impression I made last night. The only way that could've gone any worse would've been if I had puked all over the leather interior of his car, or on his expensive shoes.

My apartment smelled like a mix of lemon cleaner and some sort of frozen pasta Jack had picked out. The combination shouldn't make me smile, but it did. It smelled like hope that I could eventually pull my head out of my ass.

There was absolutely nothing Jack could fault me for.

After he texted to let me know he was about fifteen minutes away, I ran into the bathroom to check my appearance again. My hair was neatly pulled back into a low ponytail and the button-down shirt I wore over a simple black t-shirt looked brand new, because it was. I'd been panicking over what to wear when I remembered the purple and black checked-pattern shirt I'd tossed in the back of the closet as soon as I got home from Christmas with my family last year. The dark wash jeans did nothing for my assets, but they were the only pair I owned that weren't shredded, faded, or stained.

I glanced down at my feet, trying to figure out if I should put on socks and shoes.

Screw that. This was my house and I was going to be comfortable. I was already going way outside of my comfort zone. My stomach did a flip when there was a knock at my door.

He came back.

Of course, he came back, he said he would. The only thing that was up for debate was whether he would stay once he decided if I had made enough progress.

I felt damn good as I checked out the state of the apartment again. Although, I had been annoyed by Jack's demands earlier, now I was grateful to him for pushing me. It was amazing how much better I felt mentally, now that I wasn't being weighed down by my own mess.

Not only that, but I had gone above and beyond, getting everything on Jack's list done. I stood tall, with a broad smile on my face as I swung the door open. Jack would be—

Okay, so I hadn't expected a pissed off scowl when I answered the door. "What's wrong?"

Jack let out a frustrated sigh. He lifted a hand toward my face, dropping it to his side when he'd only been inches away from touching me. "Did you take a nap today?"

"I didn't need one. Once I got going, I sort of let the momentum carry me through everything on your list, and even a few other tasks," I explained.

"But I told you to take a break and get some rest." Jack shrugged out of his jacket, handing it to me. I hung it on one of the hooks behind the door. I couldn't remember the last time I'd been able to get to them without tripping over crap.

"I know, but I was afraid that if I stopped, I would lose the motivation to keep going," I admitted. "I thought you'd be happy."

Ugh, I hated the whiny, dejected tone in my voice.

"Make no mistake, Slade, I'm proud as hell of what you've accomplished. But if you want to make a good impression, you need to prove that you can *listen* when I tell you to do something. If I can't trust you to take a break so you don't kill yourself trying to get your apartment clean all in one day, how am I supposed to trust you to use a safe word if I push you too far in the bedroom?"

I hadn't thought about it that way. I'd been so gung-ho about trying to get through Jack's stupid little list, that I hadn't considered there might be an underlying lesson involved.

I hung my head as I shuffled toward the kitchen. "I'm sorry. I'll do better. I promise."

Jack squeezed my shoulder and spun me around. "Look at me, boy."

I couldn't. I didn't want to see the disappointment on his face. Just one time, it would be nice to do something right.

Jack squeezed my chin, forcing my gaze to meet his. "This is all new to you. I understand that. But we're going to get one thing straight right now."

The commanding tone in Jack's voice would've me hard if I wasn't so upset with myself. "Okay?"

"I knew who you were when I brought you home last night. I knew you were going to be a handful. You are going to challenge me, just as much as I'm going to push you, but that's part of the draw for me." He gave me a slow up and down appraisal. "I'm sure there are men out there who want nothing more than to be served, but I'm not one of them. When you fall in line, I want it to be because I've *earned* your submission, not because you think it's something you should hand over to make me happy."

"I thought you said you expect me to obey you." I massaged my temples, trying to fight off the headache I felt coming on. This shit was confusing as fuck, definitely nothing like the porn I may or may not have bookmarked on my computer.

"I absolutely do," Jack confirmed. "But I didn't give you that to-do list to see how compliant you would be. I fully expected the pushback you gave this morning." Jack's hand slid around to the back of my neck. I tilted my head to the side, resting my cheek against his palm. "I don't deal well with yes-men. That goes for, both, my personal and professional lives. I want to spend time with people who aren't afraid to speak their own minds. And, honestly, getting to punish you when you step out of line is a massive turn on. You wouldn't want to take that away from me, would you?"

I let out a weak chuckle. "No, I guess not."

"And, if you're honest with yourself, you want someone who will keep you in check, don't you?"

"I really don't know," I admitted. "I feel like an incompetent failure if I say yes. It's like I'm admitting I can't handle life on my own and I need someone to take care of me."

"There's nothing wrong with that if you're with the right person, Slade," he assured me.

I quirked an eyebrow. "And you think you're that person for me?"

Finally, I got to see a glimpse of Jack's captivating smile. I wanted to stand on my tiptoes and kiss both of his dimples before begging him to finally kiss me properly. All day, I'd been driven by thoughts of how Jack would taste, and how it would feel as he twisted my hair around his hands, completely consuming me, controlling me, owning me.

And now, I was getting hard.

"There's the cheeky little brat I figured you to be." Jack slid his hand down my arm, lacing our fingers together before guiding me into the living room. He looked around, nodding and humming his approval. "You did well, boy."

Jack sat down on the couch, his brow furrowing when he noticed the cheap vinyl placemats and silverware on the table. When I sat down, he stared at the space between us, then jerked his head, inviting me closer. I did, turning so I could drape my arm over the back of the couch and face him. He mirrored my position, our arms brushing, teasing me. I visibly shivered and Jack smiled.

"You feel it too. There's something here. Maybe it's the start of a relationship, or it could be something as simple as a sexual attraction that will fade in time. But, if you're up for it, I would like to see what happens. Am I the man you need to get your life in order? Only time will tell, but I think I am."

"I don't typically do relationships," I told him. It was important to me that I make that abundantly clear from the very start. Even if I did, I couldn't imagine I would ever rush into anything committed. There were far too many examples of people in my family who'd done exactly that, then spent the rest of their lives miserable because they were playing a game of emotional chicken. I came from stubborn stock—as my grandmother used to say—and no one was willing to be the first to concede failure. Except me. I was nothing but one failure after the next.

"I can respect that," Jack said with a nod. "Does that mean this could be nothing more than a casual affair, or would you be willing to explore all options?"

This whole conversation was surreal. Taken out of context, it would be easy to assume Jack was in the middle of a business meeting, rather than negotiating whether to bend me over, spank me, then fuck me until I begged him to let me come.

"I probably won't be any good at it."

"You don't have to be, as long as you try," Jack reassured me. "Let me ask another way... Do you *want* whatever we do to stay casual, or will you let go of whatever insecurities are holding you back?"

I sucked my bottom lip between my teeth. When I reached up to tug at my hair, I cursed myself for having it tied back. I couldn't pull out the tie without Jack seeing through my attempt to hide. He'd *just* asked me to do the exact opposite.

"I want to try," I admitted.

"And you promise you won't do or say whatever you think will make me happy?" Jack pressed. He trailed his fingers along the side of my arm. I squirmed, resisting the urge to laugh. I couldn't help that I was ticklish, but in the middle of, what felt like, a very serious conversation wasn't the time for laughter.

"I promise." I slumped against the arm of the couch, feeling as if a weight had been lifted from my shoulders. Jack probably didn't even realize the relief he'd given me. I would still obsess over whether or not I was making a huge mistake, but the idea that I didn't have to sort shit out on my own was definitely appealing.

Now what do I do?

Neither of us said anything else. The silence quickly grew awkward, and I began fidgeting in my seat. Jack placed a hand on my knee, and I stilled immediately.

"Did you start dinner when I told you to?"

"I did."

"Then let's eat." He stood, clapping his hands together once.

I gaped at him. "That's it?"

"That's what?" Jack crossed his arms over his broad chest. The motion drew my attention to the fact that he wasn't dressed the way he had been last night. He looked like pretentious perfection in his suit but dressed down he was sexy as fuck. His jeans hugged his body just enough that I could see the outline of his cock. The fact he wasn't even hard unnerved me. He was going to split me wide open.

"I thought for sure you'd want to have this long, drawn-out conversation about expectations and how I'm supposed to behave if I want you to believe that I'm doing my best," I admitted. And was it a little fucked up that I was upset he *hadn't* wanted to bore me to death? Probably.

"There will be plenty of time for all of that," he assured me. I groaned. Me and my big mouth. "But dinner is ready, and I don't know about you, but I would prefer to eat before it gets cold."

Okay. I guess that made sense.

"Glad you think so," Jack replied. The corner of his mouth turned up and he winked at me. Shit. I hadn't realized I'd said that out loud. "Give me enough time and I'll show you that I'm full of all sorts of good ideas."

"Do any of them *not* involve household chores?"

Jack pulled me up from the couch and our bodies crashed together. He slipped his arms around my back, cupping my ass.

"Just because you don't understand the meaning behind something, doesn't mean there isn't a reason for everything I do." Jack bent down, kissing the side of my neck. I tipped my head to the side, allowing him to continue, muttering under my breath when he stopped.

It hadn't been quite enough.

Jack squeezed my ass. Hard. "Would you care to repeat that, boy?"

"No." I dipped my chin, sticking my bottom lip out in, what I hoped was, a cute pout. Jack wasn't having any of it.

"No, what?" While he waited for me to answer, Jack yanked me into the kitchen where I had two plates stacked next to the stove. "Answer me, boy."

"I would if I had any clue what you expected from me."

"Fair enough." The conversation died again as Jack scooped huge portions of the meaty pasta onto both plates. No way in hell would I be able to finish mine without getting sick. "That's part of what I would like for us to talk about over dinner. It's not acceptable for me to scold you for disobeying rules that you may or may not know exist."

"Gee, you think?" Realizing what I'd said, I clapped a hand over my mouth. The filter between my brain and mouth could engage any time now.

But Jack didn't react the way I'd expected him to. Instead of scolding me for being disrespectful, he laughed. Again. Just like his speaking voice, his laughter was low and rich, sending vibrations through my entire body. I silently promised myself to do whatever I could to hear that more often.

"We are definitely going to have fun, Slade. Let's eat. You did a great job cleaning up the living room. I hadn't realized you had a romantic side." I followed Jack back into the living room, using my position to carefully inspect every curve of his ass. It wasn't tight enough to bounce a quarter off or anything, but it was still gorgeous. Everything about Jack was just a bit off from what I usually went for.

I couldn't help but let out a snort of laughter. "Pretty sure that's the first time anyone has accused me of being romantic."

I took a seat on the floor, leaving the place setting in front of the couch open for Jack.

"It's a nice touch," Jack reassured me, then stared at me for a moment. His brows furrowed, and his gentle smile flattened before turning into a frown. "Take out the hair tie."

"Oooookay." The word was drawn out as I slowly reached back to free my hair.

Jack shook his head; his lips still pursed tightly. "Take off the shirt."

I perked up a bit, smiling. Finally, we were getting to the good stuff. I didn't bother questioning him turning back on his insistence that we eat before dinner got cold. I quickly unfastened the buttons at my wrists and the top two nearest my neck, then yanked the shirt over my head, tossing it somewhere behind me.

"Boy." I swallowed hard at the warning tone in his voice. *What the hell had I done wrong now?*

"You spent all that time cleaning earlier and now you're going to throw your clothes around?" Jack sighed heavily and clenched his jaw. He leaned back, folding his arms over his chest again, not saying a word as he waited for my reaction. "Pick it up, fold it, and place it over there." He nodded toward the far end of the couch.

I sneered at Jack, just barely biting back a sarcastic retort. When I pushed myself up on the edge of the coffee table, it began to tip. Only Jack's quick reflexes saved our dinner from dumping all over the floor and me.

"Have a little bit of self-control," Jack scolded me.

"How exactly am I supposed to do that? This is how you get up off the floor." I cocked my head to the side and smirked. Jack sucked in a sharp breath, holding it, then releasing it slowly.

"You can do it without breaking the table, boy."

I fell back onto my ass, glaring at him. The staring contest continued until I finally rolled onto my knees and pushed myself up and backward.

I flashed Jack a sassy smirk. "Happy now?"

"That was much better, boy." He jerked his head toward the discarded shirt. "Now pick up after yourself."

I yanked the shirt hard enough that the edge of the fabric dragged through my plate.

"Attention, boy," Jack snapped.

"You're the one who wanted me to act natural," I quipped.

"True enough. But remember, little boys who throw attitude around get punished."

I debated crumpling the shirt into a ball and tossing it where Jack had instructed, just to see how he would punish me, but I didn't want to push my luck and have him decide I was too much work. Instead, I carefully folded the shirt with the now stained sleeve tucked in the middle, so I didn't get spaghetti sauce all over the couch. Not that it would ruin the furniture or anything, but knowing my luck, Jack would end up sitting in it later and he'd be upset with me.

Damn, this was way more thinking and effort than I had ever put into trying to get laid.

Maybe that's because you aren't just trying to get laid with this one. Damn that voice in the back my head.

Jack nodded, offering me a smile when I had followed his instructions. He took in my appearance again. I shifted my weight from one foot to the other, trying, but failing, to stand still. I couldn't decipher what he was thinking, and I hated it. The longer he didn't say anything, the easier it was to convince myself I still fell short of some bar I couldn't see.

"Come here, boy." Jack pointed to the floor in front of him. As I stepped closer, Jack stood. He reached up, combing his fingers through my hair. "That's much better, don't you agree?"

I shrugged, not knowing what he expected of me.

Jack tipped my chin back until I was looking at him. "You weren't comfortable before, were you?"

"I'm not comfortable with any of this," I admitted. "I feel sort of like I've been kidnapped and dropped into someone else's life, without any instructions on what I'm supposed to do or how I'm supposed to act."

"And how does that make you feel?" He gently squeezed the back of my neck. "There is no wrong answer here, Slade. What's going through your head right now?"

"I don't want to screw this up," I confessed. "Fuck knows why, since I've spent years running away from anything that resembled a relationship, but there's just something about you..."

I didn't know how to finish that statement. There was something about him that made me want to strip off all my clothes and bend over for him like a needy little slut. There was something about him that made me wait with bated breath for his next instruction. There was something about him that made me want to be a better person so he would tell me I had done a good job.

Jack pulled me closer, pressing my head against his shoulder.

"I know this is weird for you. And I know things are moving at warp speed. I hope you know this isn't a ploy for me to get inside your body."

I couldn't help but laugh. Jack had a way of making everything sound so damn formal. Part of me wanted to drive him crazy and make him lose a little bit of his polish.

"That's what has me so confused. If it was just about sex, things would be easier. And just so you are fully aware, I am always ready and willing whenever you decide you would like to be *inside my body*." I couldn't help but tease him for how stilted and formal his comment had been. Jack reached down, swatting me lightly on the ass. I leaned back with my arm still wrapped around Jack's torso. "What was that for?"

"Are you mocking me?" Jack lifted an eyebrow.

"Maybe a little," I admitted. "But you have to admit, the way you said it was weird."

"And what would you rather I have said? That I want nothing more than to drill your ass until your hole is wrecked and you can't sit properly for a week?"

Oh. Fuck. Yes. That was definitely more my speed. I tried taking a step back to put a little space between us so Jack wouldn't feel my erection pressing against his leg. Every twitch of my cock was a silent plea for him to do exactly that.

Jack glanced down before tightening his grip at my neck and around my back. His hand slid lower, forcing my groin against his leg. He moved, pressing his thigh against my erection. I couldn't help but hump his leg like a horny dog.

"We are getting off-topic, boy." His fingers dug into my hips, forcing me to stop moving.

"Sorry. I tend to ramble when I'd rather not talk about

serious shit," I apologized. "And you should probably know, that happens a lot. I am not exactly a talking type of person."

"With as smart as your mouth is, that doesn't surprise me at all." Jack chuckled. "You probably got used to your mouth getting you in trouble, but that's not going to happen here. I will always want to hear what you have to say."

"But you are still going to punish me, aren't you?" He'd practically promised he would. This was probably the first time in my life I *wanted* to get in trouble, because I felt confident that he would make me love the results.

Jack stuffed a hand into the back pocket of my jeans, gripping my ass tightly. "You'd better believe it, boy. But you're going to learn punishments aren't always what you think they'll be. If you *want* me to redden this pretty ass, it's not much of a deterrent. We may have to make spankings a reward for when you make me proud." Jack released me, then nodded to my place on the floor as he sat. "It's amazing to see how much more settled you are now than you were a few minutes ago. Why did you dress up if it made you so uncomfortable?"

"Because I didn't want to look like a slob," I explained. "This might be my apartment, and it might be a dump, but I was raised to look presentable when you know you're going to have company."

"Then maybe we need to make a new rule for you." Jack scrubbed a hand over his stubbled cheek. "I don't ever want you pretending to be someone you're not for my sake, Slade. I didn't come back tonight because you were a perfect boy who checked off a series of boxes. I came back because I was intrigued by the way you wear your emotions on your sleeve even when you think you're doing a good job of hiding from the world."

"And, because I'm broken and you think you can fix me," I pointed out.

"I wouldn't say you're broken, Slade." He picked up his fork and motioned for me to do the same. I could practically see him thinking as he enjoyed the first few bites of dinner. "This is very good. Thank you."

"I should be thanking you," I countered. "You're the one who bought it. All I did was put it in the oven."

"Boy, learn to take a compliment when it's offered." I dipped my head and reached up, pinching my bottom lip. With my gaze fixed on the floor, I didn't see his movement until it was too late. I jumped back when Jack swatted my hand away from my face.

"Don't do that," he scolded.

"Why does it matter if I fuck around with my lip? I used to have a piercing there and sometimes I still reach up to fidget with it. It's easier to think when I have something to do with my hands."

Why was I telling him all this?

"Why did you take it out?"

"Huh?" I picked up my fork and scooped a bite into my mouth. Eating was a much safer activity. If my mouth was full of food, I wouldn't spill my entire pathetic life story to him.

"The piercing," he clarified. "Why did you take it out? I bet you were hot with it."

I scrunched my nose up. Hearing Jack use such plebian words, was as hot as it was strange. He struck me as a man who had a large vocabulary and liked to show it off.

"Something funny, boy?"

"Not at all," I lied before taking another bite. Chewing gave me time to decide how much to reveal. Might as well lay it all out so Jack would understand I was a mess. "And, I took the piercing out before a family birthday party earlier this year and lost it."

"You lost it?" Jack sighed and shook his head.

"Don't act like that's so hard to imagine," I scoffed. "You saw what my place looked like earlier today. It didn't get that way overnight. Yes, I lost it. I set it down somewhere and couldn't find it when I got home. I would have gone to buy a new ring, but then shit started going south with the band, money got tight..." I waved my hand in the air. He could figure out the rest of the story on his own.

"Would you ever put it back in?" Jack narrowed his eyes. When he ran his tongue through the seam of his lips, I momentarily forgot he'd asked me a question. I was more interested in what had him looking ready to lunge over the table and devour me for dessert.

"I might. It all depends on where I get a job. A lot of places aren't thrilled about employees with facial piercings." Just one more thing to add to the list of reasons I dreaded job hunting. I wasn't the most conventional guy, and I didn't want to cut my hair, toss out my eyeliner, or never feel the sweet agony of a piece of metal piercing my flesh just so I could pay the bills.

"Eli doesn't have a problem with piercings or tattoos," Jack pointed out. "Did you call him today?"

"No, but I did talk to Jordan a little bit. He said Eli had some appointments, but I should stop down there tomorrow afternoon." And wasn't that a wonderful conversation. To his credit, Jordan didn't give me hell for being stubborn for so long. He knew I had to come around in my own time. Or, in this case, with the proper motivation.

"That's good enough." I sat up straighter, my lips involuntarily turning into a grin. I was practically preening. "I know it wasn't easy for you to admit to Jordan that you needed his help. I am proud of you for doing it anyway."

"Thank you," I mumbled, quickly shoving another bite of food in my mouth. The conversation faded off again, but it felt more natural this time.

Once both of our plates were clean, I neatly stacked them in the center of the table. I wanted to be closer to Jack, so instead of standing, I half crawled, half scooted around the table. Jack groaned. When I looked up at him, he was trying to adjust himself.

"Don't get used to me crawling around on all fours," I warned him. "I already told you, I'm not a puppy."

"And I think you shouldn't totally count it out until you try it," he replied. "But, you're right, I don't think you would be a good puppy. You'd get into far too much trouble. That lifestyle isn't one that's ever appealed to me anyway."

I could have easily joined Jack on the couch, but I was comfortable on the floor. I leaned against the couch, my shoulder brushing Jack's leg. He reached down and started combing my hair with his fingers again. My eyes drifted shut and I let out a hum of contentment. "What are you into then? Because something tells me store brand vanilla sex isn't your favorite."

Jack barked out a laugh. "Store brand?"

I shrugged. It was the best I could come up with in the moment.

"You're right. I am far from vanilla. Sometimes, I wish I could go out and have sex just for the sake of getting off. It would definitely make life easier."

"So why don't you? Even if you're typically into whips and bondage, that doesn't mean you can't have a raunchy one-night stand." I knew that very well. I'd built a good life on jumping from one bed into the next. Sometimes more than one in a night, but that wasn't something I wore as a badge of pride. Those were some of my lowest moments, encounters I hope Jack never found out about.

"If all I want is to get off, I have my own hands, as well as a sizable collection of toys."

"We're coming back to that," I quickly interrupted. Jack smiled, giving my hair a tug. "I mean, if everything goes well and you don't run out of here before the night's over."

"I'm not the one we need to worry about running, Slade." He bent down, kissing the top of my head. "My brother and I are similar in a lot of ways. Both of us like to take care of our partners."

He almost said something else, then stopped himself. I was about to assure him that I knew all about Jordan calling Doug, Daddy, but he continued before I could say anything.

"For me, I also like a challenge. I don't want a sweet, obedient boy who never steps out of line."

"Well, seeing as you're here with me, that's a damn good thing," I replied.

Jack twisted his hand in my hair. "Are you going to let me finish?"

"I'm sorry." But I wasn't. Not really. Pushing Jack's buttons was fun. "I'm assuming that means you're a Daddy? You are, aren't you? That's why you reacted the way you did last night when I was an asshole."

"Not an asshole," Jack corrected me. "You were a brat in the middle of a tantrum. But, yes, if I had to label myself, I am definitely a Daddy."

"Have you had boys in the past?" My stomach churned at the thought of him bossing anyone but me around. It was completely unrealistic to want him to have been saving himself for me, but part of me felt like he was the reason I hadn't even attempted a relationship in the past. I wanted him to be the one who shaped and molded me.

"Only a couple." Jack's expression fell. His eyes turned glassy, and he wouldn't look at me. I twisted around, lifting myself until I was kneeling before him.

"It didn't turn out well?" Jack shook his head, still staring at nothing in particular. I reached up, smoothing the creases in his forehead. He let out a soft huff and the corner of his mouth turned up in a grin. "You probably didn't do anything wrong."

Jack shook his head again, this time letting out a pained groan. "Oh, sweet boy. You have no clue. I'm far from perfect. I wasn't who they needed me to be and didn't see it until it was too late."

"Then maybe you weren't supposed to be together. I know that's shit to hear, but maybe you were doing everything right but for the wrong person."

"You sound like someone with experience," Jack remarked.

"Not firsthand, but I've seen enough decent people get themselves into shady situations to know it's not always easy to put all the blame on one person."

Jack took my face in both of his hands, bending down. Seconds before our lips brushed, he said, "Thank you, boy. Sometimes I forget that."

Then, he sealed his lips over mine. I placed my hands on his knees for support, scooting as close as possible, wishing I could crawl into his lap. For all his bravado, it turned out Jack wasn't a cocky, pretentious, know it all. He had plenty of his own insecurities he needed to face. Maybe it was possible the two of us were supposed to help one another.

"It's not the most comfortable, but we could move this into the bedroom," I suggested as my dick grew painfully hard. I didn't even care if I got off, as long as I could wipe the sadness and regret from Jack's mind.

"We could," Jack agreed. "But I thought you wanted to talk."

"Talking is *highly* overrated," I replied. "It's not so much that I wanted to talk, as I figured you'd be all demanding about things happening in a certain order."

"You're not wrong." Jack gave me a gentle push and I backed up. He noticed the plates stacked on the table at the same time I did. I knew what he was about to say and groaned. He laughed, pressing his lips to my cheek. "Come on, boy. We can talk while we clean up, then you won't have to worry about it later."

Jack was a smart man.

10

JACK

Slade had no idea how he affected me. I had always lived by a very clear set of rules. One of the reasons I enjoyed the kink community so much as a whole, was how clear cut everything was. But now, with Slade, I found myself ready to throw out all of the rules that had always focused me. I led him into the kitchen and started filling the sink with hot soapy water.

"You don't have to do that," Slade protested. "I'm pretty good at washing the dishes after all the practice I had earlier today."

He tried stealing the washcloth, but I held it over my head, out of his reach. He cooked, so I was going to clean. Living alone, I rarely came home to a hot meal ready to eat, unless I dug out the appliances my family insisted on giving me as a way to encourage me to cook for myself. They mostly collected dust because I didn't see the point in cooking a big meal for one, and all the recipes I found created more leftovers than I could eat before they went bad. Slade had actually done me a favor by heating up dinner before I got here.

"So I noticed," I responded, looking around the kitchen and nodding in approval. "You've done enough for one day, boy. Why don't you sit down, and I'll take care of clean up? There isn't that much, so it won't take very long."

Slade worried at his lip. I watched him for a few seconds, trying to picture him with a lip ring. While I typically wasn't a fan of facial piercings, I hadn't been trying to flatter him when I said he would've looked good with one. It would have rounded out the edgy rocker vibe he had going on. Without it, there was a sense of innocence about him. I didn't tell him that because, from the little I'd gotten to know him so far, I doubted he would appreciate the compliment. I was pulling him into uncharted waters, and I couldn't wait to corrupt him in only the best possible ways.

When Slade stayed rooted to the floor, I turned off the water, approached him, then hoisted him onto the counter. Slade spread his legs and I stepped into the gap, running my hands up and down his thighs. "I'm not trying to trick you. Relax."

"I didn't think..." His gaze lowered to the floor, revealing the lie he'd been about to tell. We'd have to work on his trust issues. Of course, a good starting point would be me not testing him.

"It's okay, Slade," I reassured him. "We're still getting to know one another. You may not believe me, but I like dividing labor. You cooked, so now I'm going to clean up before we get on with the rest of the night."

"Okay. That makes sense." He smiled shyly. "Man, you probably think I'm a total basket case."

"No, I think you're a beautiful young man who's avoided relationships. You wouldn't know how to act if this was just two men trying to see if there was something more than sexual chemistry between them," I explained, and Slade nodded. I rewarded him with a tender kiss. He hummed softly against my lips, and I massaged his neck. "Add in the...other stuff, and it's no surprise you're feeling out of sorts. So, tell me, boy, is this what you thought would happen tonight?"

"Not by a long shot," Slade confessed.

"And is it better or worse than you imagined?" I slid my hands down his back until they came to rest on Slade's hips. My dick had been hard since I forced him to take off that ridiculous button-down shirt and stand before me. My instincts screamed at me to throw him over my shoulder and take him to the bedroom, but he had been right to push for us to talk first.

Slade considered his answer before speaking. "Both?"

"Explain that," I replied, taking a step back. He reached out for me, and I quickly backed up to the sink. He was too much temptation. I needed to stay in control. While I waited for him to elaborate, I started scrubbing the dishes.

"I don't do any of this. I don't sit down and have cozy dinners with guys. Hell, I can't tell you the last time I got this far, without both of us being naked and the room reeking of sex." His voice shrunk, until the last of his words were delivered as little more than a whisper. "I probably shouldn't have told you that."

"I am not going to judge you, Slade." It was killing me to not turn around, but I got the impression it was easier for Slade if I wasn't looking at him as he spoke. "So, is that the better or worse part?"

"Both." This time, the word wasn't spoken as a question.

"How so?" Man, what should have been a simple conversation was like pulling teeth.

"I kind of like it. But not knowing what's going to happen next sucks."

"I can understand that. What do you *want* to happen next?"

"Jesus, Jack, what's with all the questions? See, this is why relationships are stupid. I don't know how to put any of the shit into words, and my head just keeps spinning." When I glanced over my shoulder, Slade had his hands twisted in his hair, tugging hard at the scalp. It had never been my intention to upset him. It hadn't even occurred to me that trying to have a casual conversation would be enough to set him off that way.

I swiped a towel off the counter and dried my hands. Rather than taking him in my arms the way I wanted, I leaned against the counter next to the sink. "Talking isn't a bad thing, Slade. It's a way for me to know what's going on in your head, rather than trying to guess. I know this is new for you, but if we're going to do anything beyond having dinner together, you are going to have to learn that I am a stickler for communication."

"I just don't understand why any of this matters. If I said that I didn't like having dinner together and wished you would've come in and talked to me, it wouldn't change anything. It's in the past. You can't change the past." Slade pinched the bridge of his nose and slumped forward enough that I darted across the room to catch him if he fell. His body sagged against mine.

I kissed the side of his head and rubbed his back. "You are right about that, boy. And both of us have pasts that we can't change. All we can do is take every moment as it comes."

"So, this is another life lesson with Jack moment?" I couldn't help but chuckle at Slade's snark. "No offense, man, but I'm not really interested in you trying to be some sort of self-help guru for me."

"That's good then, because that's not what I am trying to do." I released Slade and took a step back. "I didn't mean to upset you. I truly want to know what you're thinking. Both of us need to know what we're getting into, and we need to be on the same page."

"If I told you I just wanted a quick fuck and then never to see you again, you'd be okay with that?" He eyed me warily, and I wondered if he'd believe any answer I gave him.

"Okay? I wouldn't say that, but I would respect your decision. I'm not going to force you to do anything you don't want to do. That goes for inside the bedroom and out."

"And yet you made me clean my entire apartment," Slade pointed out. "I didn't *want* to clean today, but you told me I had to if I wanted you to come back tonight."

"I seem to remember I told you to take a break," I corrected him. "You are the one who decided to go above and beyond." I paused, scrubbing at my chin. "That reminds me, I owe you a punishment for that?"

"A punishment for finishing the list you gave me? That's sort of fucked up, dude."

"Dude? Let's get one thing clear right now, *boy.* I'm not your dude, your buddy, your bro, or any other stupid nickname guys your age use for their friends. You may call me Jack, Sir, Daddy, or even Asshole, but I am *not* a dude." I leaned in, biting Slade's earlobe. He hissed and his protests fell flat as his hips arched off the counter. I clamped my teeth down harder to see how he would react. He squirmed, reaching down to cup his erection. I curled my fingers around his wrist, yanking his hand away from his body. "Focus, boy. We are going to finish talking and then, if we are both in agreement and you behave yourself, I promise I will take you to bed and give you exactly what you need."

"I'd be able to think a lot better if you quit teasing me." Slade slid his hands over my chest. "Maybe you could give me a little taste of what sort of reward you have in mind. That might help me focus."

I removed Slade's hands from my body, twisting them around until they were pinned behind his back. "Nice try, boy. I'm getting way too many mixed signals from you to do anything just yet."

"I want you to fuck me," Slade said bluntly. "Is that a clear enough message for you?"

"But is that the *only* thing you want from me?" I had no clue what I would do if he said yes. I had meant it when I told him I wasn't a fan of casual sex. Sure, it was a way to achieve orgasm, but it was rarely satisfying for me. I needed the freedom to tease my boy. I wanted him to relinquish control to me—hand his body over to me like a gift.

"I don't even know how to answer that," Slade admitted. "Do I want you to fuck me and then take off? No. But I don't want the mess that comes along with more."

"More doesn't always have to be problematic," I told him. "That's why I insist on constant communication. If something changes for you, I want to know. If you need more than what I'm giving you, you need to tell me. If I'm moving too fast and things are too intense, I want you to feel confident telling me that, too."

"I'm probably never going to give you a straight answer. Too much shit up here." Slade knocked on the side of his head. "I don't think it's possible for me to have a healthy relationship, because I'm always thinking about everyone in my family and how fucked up they are. The worst part about that is you actually have me wanting to try."

"And why is that a bad thing?"

"Because I've gotten this far in life, swearing I don't *want* a relationship. That I don't *need* a partner to feel whole and content," he admitted. This time, I didn't stop him when he worried his lip. It was an unconscious comfort for him, and he needed that. For now. "But today, I started thinking about how it would feel if you weren't coming back just to check up on me."

"That's not why I said I'd be back tonight," I clarified. Handing him a task list was a way to see if he was interested in pursuing the type of relationship I needed, because I was too much of a coward to simply ask him. The way my ex left had done a real number on my confidence, and that was a bitter pill to swallow.

I cupped Slade's face in my hands. His breathing grew rapid and shallow. He whimpered when I remained still, my face a mere inch away from his. As much as I wanted to taste him again, I waited. And waited until, finally, the anticipation became unbearable. As soon as my lips closed over his, I pressed my tongue into his mouth. I twisted his hair in my fists, holding him captive as I drank my fill. "I'm here because I wanted to do that the first time I saw you, but I wanted to make sure you remembered how good it was."

"Pretty sure of yourself, aren't you?" Slade quipped, still gasping to catch his breath.

Hell yes, I was confident. As cliché as it sounded, the attraction had been palpable. If the party had been for anyone else, I would have ditched and taken him with me. "Was I wrong?"

"No." The corner of his mouth turned up, and his eyes sparkled with amusement. "I'd bet there are other things that would be even better."

"Not until we're done talking."

Slade glared at me. "What do you want to talk about now? Aren't you talked out yet?"

"What's the worst that could happen if we see where this could lead?" I ignored his pouting and huffing. If he admitted to his fear, maybe it wouldn't seem so consuming.

"Eventually, you're going to realize I'm too much work," he insisted. "Or, you're going to realize how much better you could do than a loser with no job, no band, and no fucking idea how he's going to pay the bills once his savings are gone. I *want* more than just sex from you, but I can't stop thinking about what's going to happen when it all falls apart."

"So, stop dwelling on what *could* happen, Slade." It was that simple. I watched him as I stepped back into the space between his legs, waiting for any sign of hesitation. When he gave me none, I took a deep breath, held it, then let it out slowly. If I was asking Slade to jump in with both feet, I had to be willing to do the same.

Slade shivered when my breath ghosted over his skin. I whispered, "You aren't the only one who's afraid, boy. But let me take care of you. Let me help you."

I nearly stumbled backward when Slade pressed his body against mine.

"I'll try," he promised me. He kissed his way up the length of my neck, wrapping his arms tightly around my shoulders. "Don't give up on me, even if I tell you to go away. It's the fear talking."

"I can't promise I won't slow down to check in with you, Slade. I don't ever want to make you feel like you can't speak up."

"Because of what happened before?"

I nodded, unable to speak around the lump in my throat.

"I want to do right by you," I said when I finally found my voice.

"You already have." Slade held my face in his hands,

running his thumbs over the stubble on my cheeks. "Are you ready to take me to bed now, *Daddy*?"

I should insist that we finish talking, but Slade was right; talking was overrated. He had promised me he would be honest if things got too intense, or if I was doing something he didn't want. For now, that had to be enough. And the way he looked at me when he called me Daddy? I was a goner.

I slid my hands under Slade's ass. When I didn't put him on the floor, he wrapped his legs around my waist, clinging to me as I carried him through the small apartment. Soon, I would ask him to my place. Not because I was turned off by where he lived, but because I wanted to do things to him that were clumsy and uncomfortable in his full-size bed.

"I like hearing you call me Daddy," I admitted as we crossed the threshold into the bedroom.

"Well, good, because I like calling you that," he confessed, burying his face in the crook of my neck. "I thought it was cheesy when I heard big burly guys being called Daddy in porn, but part of me wished I had that. But I'd convince myself it was dangerous and that no one would want to take care of me. Then you came along..."

More like, then he stumbled down the stairs at Doug's and I knew I'd do anything I could to keep him safe. But I didn't say that for fear of scaring him off. I carefully set Slade down on the edge of the mattress. When I turned on the light, I was stunned by the transformation in his bedroom. There was a chance everything was now shoved behind the closed closet door, but I wasn't going to question it.

"You did so well today, boy." I pressed my lips to his as I reached down and flicked open the button on his jeans. Slade moaned as my fingers grazed against the head of his cock. I took the opportunity to slide my tongue into his mouth as I coaxed him to lie down on the bed. He lifted his hips and I stripped him from the waist down.

My God, Slade was beautiful. *Too damn skinny*, I thought as I dragged my thumbs over the ridges of his hipbones. He writhed beneath me, squirming, trying to position himself so my hand would brush against his straining erection. "I'll get there, but not yet. Easy, boy. Let me inspect you first."

"I'm not a toy, fresh off the assembly line," Slade scoffed. I glared at him. "Please, Daddy, I need to come."

"And you will," I promised him. I placed wet, open-mouth kisses along his collarbones before shifting lower. Slade cried out when I flicked my tongue over his nipple. "Have you ever had these pierced?"

Slade's head thrashed back-and-forth on the mattress. I wasn't sure if that was his response to my question or if he was lost in the sensations. I moved to the other nipple, giving it the same attention as I pinched the left one.

"Tell me, Slade," I insisted when he clenched his eyes shut, and his lips pursed tightly. "You are so sensitive here. I bet you would love having barbells through both of your nipples. When you don't do exactly as I tell you, I could give them a quick tug. And when we're not together, you'd feel your shirt brush against them, reminding you who you belong to."

"Oh fuck, yes. Please." Slade opened his eyes, although it seemed to be quite a chore for him to look at me. "Please, Daddy. I'll do anything. Want to be yours."

He didn't mean that. Couldn't mean it, when it hadn't even been a full day since he was telling me what an arrogant prick I was. His assessment wasn't wrong, but it also wasn't one that bolstered my confidence that he meant anything he said in the heat of the moment.

"That's a dangerous offer, boy," I warned him. I reached

down, squeezing his balls tight enough he yelped. "Anything would include letting me take you to one of my friends and having him pierce you down here. Would you be up for that?"

Slade let out a squeak that didn't sound excited about the prospect.

"That's what I thought." Before Slade could freak out too much, I slid an arm between his back and the mattress, lifting him up so I could kiss him again. "Don't worry, baby. That's not something I would ever do to you." I gave his shaft a soft, teasing stroke. "The closest I would get would be shaving you. I like my boys totally clean."

My ex had balked at that request. He said it made him feel dirty, like I was only with him because he reminded me of a young teenager. It had nothing to do with that, and when he made the accusation, it had led to a frosty week in our home.

"Would you let me shave you, Slade? That way, when I want to slide a silicone ring over your shaft and your balls, we don't have to worry about you getting hurt." I circled the base of his dick with my thumb and forefinger, tightening my grip to simulate how the ring would keep him from coming.

"Can I think about that one?" Slade allowed his head to fall back and licked his lips. I was proud of him for saying he wanted to consider what I had suggested, rather than agreeing because he thought it would get him what he wanted. "No offense, but that's a lot of trust to put in anyone. You're talking about taking a razor to me in a rather tender area."

"I am," I confirmed, and Slade's face paled. "But you're right. That's something we can talk about down the road."

I laid down beside Slade and continued stroking him.

"You are such a good boy," I praised him. "I can tell you're freaked out, but you aren't pushing me away."

"Only an idiot would say no to getting off with someone as hot as you," Slade scoffed. "But I may change my mind if you don't hurry up."

I pulled my hand away, resting it on his chest. "Is that a fact? Sooner or later, you need to realize I don't put up with idle threats. Maybe I shouldn't let you come at all tonight."

"You wouldn't." Slade gaped at me.

I let out a low, rumbling laugh. "Oh, I totally would. If you want to test me, by all means, keep going."

Slade shook his head, pursing his lips.

I bent down and kissed the tip of his nose. "Smart boy."

"Are you going to undress? I'm starting to feel a bit self-conscious," Slade admitted, then fumbled for the button on my jeans.

I captured Slade's hand in mine. "Did you want something?"

Slade whimpered.

"Are you in charge here?" I pinched his nipple, twisting this time to get his attention. Slade's back arched off the bed.

"No, Daddy." I rewarded his quick response with an equally brief kiss.

"You know what to do if you want something, boy." I traced slow circles around his abused flesh, bending down to kiss it all better.

"Please, Daddy," Slade pleaded. "I showed you mine, now it's only fair if you show me yours."

"Life isn't always fair, Slade." I felt his body tense beside mine, and waited for a sarcastic retort, but it never came. And I felt like shit for pulling him out of his lust induced stupor. "Lucky for you, I'm feeling generous tonight."

I rolled onto my back, pulling Slade with me. "You may undress me, boy."

Slade planted his hands on the mattress on either side of my head. He bent down, cautiously kissing the corner of my mouth. "Thank you, Daddy."

I brushed the hair away from his face. "So sweet and polite for me."

"Weird, isn't it," Slade remarked. I wanted to force him to take the final steps out of his head, but that wouldn't happen tonight. Tonight was all about gaining my boy's trust. Slade kissed his way down the center of my chest. His hands ghosted over my sides, making me squirm. "Are you ticklish, Daddy?"

I reached around and swatted Slade's ass. The crack of flesh against flesh echoed in the room. "There is still time for me to take away your playground."

"My playground, huh?" Slade chuckled. "You know, I probably would've been a hell of a lot more interested in playing outside if there was equipment like this at the park when I was younger."

Slade cupped a hand over my groin. My dick twitched and I felt a damp spot forming at the front of my briefs.

"Take it out," I instructed him. Slade moved at lightning speed, as if he was worried I would take back the permission I had just granted. I lifted my ass off the mattress, allowing him to pull the jeans and underwear over my hips.

"Kiss it," I told him. "Just the tip. And no tongue."

Slade gaped at me, obviously unaccustomed to someone else telling him how to suck cock. I squeezed his ass. "Don't worry, baby. We'll get there, but I'm not as young as you. If you go too fast, or if you don't listen to me when I tell you to slow down, you aren't going to feel my dick filling your tight hole tonight. You don't want that, do you?"

Slade shook his head hard enough, his hair whipped around, slapping him in the face.

I chuckled. It'd been years since I enjoyed myself this much during foreplay. It was impossible for Slade to hide his enthusiasm, even if we did need to work a bit on his restraint. It felt damn good to be wanted. And, unlike the boys at The Lodge, Slade wanted me for what I had to offer him, not as a reason to brag to his friends that he had serviced the owner of the club.

It was an unfortunate drawback in my line of work. While there were some boys who were truly interested in letting me take care of them, even more saw me as a conquest. It was a part of my decision to remain celibate that I rarely discussed with anyone.

Once I felt a bit more in control, and less likely to explode the second Slade wrapped his lips around the head of my dick, I nodded for him to continue. I gathered his hair in my hand, holding it out of the way so I could watch as he took me into his mouth for the first time.

When his mouth closed around me, I bit down on my bottom lip to keep from crying out. His eyes never strayed from mine as he took my entire length.

"Good boy," I praised him. "So fucking hot and eager."

Slade hummed as he slowly released me. Before I could tell him what to do, he set his own pace, never applying too much pressure, his tongue swirling around my shaft as much as possible.

"One of these days, I'm going to keep you on your knees all day," I told him. Slade moaned his enthusiasm for that idea.

"We'll have to do it on a day when I'm not working so we aren't rushed," I continued. "I'll let you pick a few movies for the two of us to watch together, but you won't be allowed on the couch next to me unless I say. You'll sit at my feet, your head resting on my knee, your hand on my dick. Whenever the mood strikes, I'll pull you by your hair, reminding you where you belong. Because, sweet Jesus, you have a mouth that was made for sucking."

Slade tried to smile, gagging when I thrust deeper into his mouth. I pressed a hand to his shoulder. "You okay, boy?"

Slade nodded. I closed my eyes, savoring every wet slide of Slade's tongue over my erection.

Someday I would let Slade feast on my cock, but today wasn't that day. His tongue and mouth were wicked pleasures and, as much as I prided myself on my self-control, he was going to make me lose it.

"Move," I demanded, shoving Slade away from my dick.

He hurriedly scooted across the bed, nearly falling off the other side as he rummaged around on the floor. He held it over his head, whooping in victory. I reached for my jeans, pulling a single condom out of my wallet.

"A man your age should know better than to keep condoms in his wallet," Slade scolded me. "Do I need to check the expiration date? It hasn't been that long since you've had sex, has it?"

I swatted Slade's ass before pinning him to the bed. His hips arched off the mattress in search of friction. I dug the tips of my fingers into his flesh as I pressed him back down. "After that jab, I'm not sure you deserve anything else tonight."

Slade blinked slowly a few times, his mouth hanging open. "You can't be serious."

"Care to bet on that?" I stroked his cock slowly, stopping every time he bucked into my hand. He'd whimper and still, and I would start over again. "What did I tell you about being a brat?"

"Nothing, specifically," he pointed out. "You said that if I kept teasing you, you would punish me by not letting me come tonight, but I wasn't teasing you."

"No?" I pushed Slade's hair away from his face. Maybe I shouldn't have told him to take out the hair tie earlier. As beautiful as he was with his hair falling around his shoulders, it got in the way.

"Nope." Slade's lips popped at the end of the word. "When I was teasing you, I was making you horny for me. This time, I was simply making sure we weren't about to have a breakage incident that would ruin the night faster than my grandma walking into the room."

"Do you have a lot of experience with that?"

"Just once," he replied somberly. There was a story there and he was falling prey to the memories. I kissed his cheekbone, fluttering my eyelashes over his skin, grounding him to *this* moment. It worked and he smiled up at me. "But I don't want to talk about that right now."

He held the condom up between two fingers. "So, we are good here?"

"Yes, brat. I will have you know, the rest of the box that came from is sitting in one of my desk drawers. I can show you the receipt if you like. It's probably down in my car." My face shouldn't have flushed with embarrassment over the box I'd hastily shoved in the back of my desk.

My entire business was built on sex and kink, so it shouldn't matter that *I* was getting laid for a change. But it did, because I held myself to a much higher standard than anyone else, and I didn't do anything as reckless as obsess over someone I'd only just met. I wasn't the man who invited himself over to someone's house and fucked him so soon.

"You went out and bought these just for tonight?" Slade's

eyes widened slightly as if he couldn't believe I'd gone out of my way for him. He cupped my face in his hand, dragging his thumb over my lips. "Is it weird to say that's sweet?"

"I did." I kissed my way along the side of Slade's face, then up the other, before relenting and sealing my mouth over his. He didn't push for more this time, just simply allowed me to control the moment. "And no, it's not weird. You deserve someone who's willing to prove that you're special, even if that's by grabbing condoms to be sure nothing could interrupt the night."

I'd tipped my hand too far. Every word was true, but Slade wasn't ready to hear any of it. I needed to remind myself there were no guarantees we'd last beyond the next orgasm. "Now, I thought you said you were done talking."

"No more talking is good," Slade confirmed.

"Then roll over and show me that tight little hole," I demanded. In his excitement, Slade kicked me in the stomach. I bit down on my lips to keep from lashing out and telling him to be careful. And I supposed it was endearing, in a way, to see how reckless he became when he was aroused.

While Slade got himself comfortable, I flicked open the cap and drizzled some lube onto my fingers. Spreading him open with my left hand, I dragged the slick fingers through his crease.

Slade whimpered. "Don't need any prep. Please, Daddy, fuck me."

"I am not going to hurt you, Slade. And you'd better believe I'm going to make you wait. It'll be better that way."

"Like hell it will," Slade protested. "I've been thinking about you filling me all day. Just do it already."

"Like this?" I pressed my middle finger against his hole, pressing inside slowly. So hot. So tight. And, the deeper I pushed, the more Slade's muscles clenched around my digit. I caressed his back, planting soft kisses along his spine. "Relax for me, boy. Once I am inside of you, I'm not going to be able to hold back."

"Don't want you to," he blurted out. "Want you to fuck me hard. Just like you said you would. Don't need sweet and tender."

The sharp slap to his hip was anything but tender. Slade cried out but rocked his hips as if he was seeking out another blow. "You like that? You want Daddy to spank you?"

"Yes, please." Slade's head dropped to the pillow. I struck him three more times, massaging his hole in between each sharp slap.

"Don't hide from me, boy. I want to hear you—your pain." I slapped him again. "Your pleasure." I buried my finger deep inside his body. "Everything." I draped my body over his, biting his shoulder. "Give it to me, Slade. Don't hold back."

"Fuck me, Daddy, and I promise I'll give you everything."

How I wished that were true. Sure, Slade would open up for me, as long as we were both naked and the endorphins addled his brain, but I wasn't stupid. Once the aftershocks of our orgasms faded, I knew Slade would shut down on me. This was intense, even for me, and it was only natural that he would be terrified of the connection I knew damn well he felt. I sat back on my heels watching his hole tighten as I rolled the condom down my shaft. I covered his back with my body, lacing our fingers together. "You ready, boy?"

"I've been ready since the first time you touched me on the stairs last night," Slade admitted. When he buried his face against the pillow, groaning something about being stupid for saying that out loud, I yanked his hair, forcing his head back.

"You're not stupid," I insisted. "It's never a bad thing to say what's on your mind."

"I thought we were done with life lessons for the night." I swatted Slade again, this time light enough that it did little more than frustrate him. "Please, Daddy. Fuck me."

My hands shook as I took hold of my dick, lining it up at his entrance. This was more than I had prepared myself for. It was a point of no return. That thought gave me pause. Slade wasn't the only one who needed to be certain of what he was giving up.

"What's wrong?" Slade squeezed my hand that was still entwined with his. "If you're not into this—"

"That's not it at all," I scoffed. I kissed Slade's cheek. "I just needed a second to get my bearings. As you pointed out, it's been a while since I've done this."

"Just like riding a bicycle," Slade reassured me. He wiggled his hips. "Or in this case, just like riding a boy, hopefully fast and hard. But don't worry, Daddy, I won't let you crash and burn at the end."

God, how I wanted that to be true. There was nothing to be done, no reassurances that could give either of us confidence that we wouldn't have a catastrophic ending. The only thing I could do was center myself in the here and now.

I closed my eyes tightly as I entered Slade's body. He made such dirty, delicious sounds as I continued pressing inside until I was fully seated with my pelvis against his ass. Both of us stilled, allowing our bodies time to get used to the sensation of a new lover.

Slade moved first. In the future, I wouldn't let him get away with topping from the bottom, but tonight I think I needed him to prove to me that he knew and accepted what he was getting into. I curled my fingers into his hips, bracing myself as I withdrew.

"You ready, boy?"

"I'm not going to answer your stupid questions. If you can't feel how much I need you, we have bigger problems." I growled before biting down on the back of his neck. "I'm just saying."

"Well, we will see what you have to say about this," I replied, then started fucking him at a brutal pace. The entire bed slammed against the wall. Slade had to brace himself to keep his head from crashing into the headboard at an awkward angle. And, still, I didn't slow down.

Every one of the strangled cries that escaped Slade's lips fueled my need for him. I wanted to break him. I wanted him to be a crumbled mess I could put back together by the time I was done.

I felt my orgasm racing down my spine quicker than I would've liked. I clumsily reached for the lube, coating my palm before reaching around to stroke Slade's cock. I wanted him to come first. Wanted to feel his hole strangling me, milking every drop of cum from my body.

"Eventually, I'm going to do this without the condom," I told him, and he shivered in response. "You want that, boy? You want to feel Daddy's cum leaking out of your hole?"

"Please, Daddy, give it to me," he pleaded. "Mark me. Make me yours."

"Oh, sweetheart, you already are," I promised him. "And if I have anything to say about it, I'm never letting you go."

I wrapped my arms tightly around Slade's stomach as he came. I pulled both of us upright, his chest pressed against my back, as I drilled him even harder.

"You are such a beautiful boy," I praised him. "You have no clue how much of a gift you are." Slade shook his head, and I kissed the side of his neck. "Don't argue with me, boy. Life will be a whole lot easier once you realize Daddy knows best."

Slade reached back, holding my ass as I continued drilling him. "Give it to me, Daddy. Fill me."

I closed my eyes tightly, imagining what it would feel like to fill him—another thing to put on our list for someday. I collapsed on top of Slade as I shot my load into the condom. Every muscle in my body seized and spasmed. I had nothing left. I didn't even want to get up long enough to dispose of the condom and get us cleaned up for bed.

Luckily, my boy didn't seem to have the same problem. He swatted at my hip. "You have to get up, Daddy. You're crushing me."

"Are you saying I'm fat," I scoffed as I rolled to the side. Slade whimpered as I withdrew my dick from his hole. I felt the same way.

Slade flipped onto his side, draping an arm over my chest. He ran his fingers through my damp chest hair. "I like the fact that you aren't ripped. Nobody likes cuddling with a boulder."

"So, are you telling me that cuddling isn't something you reserve for when you're too drunk to hold back?" I teased.

In answer, Slade burrowed himself closer to my side. He buried his face in my armpit, inhaling deeply, then he hummed the same way he had last night as he drifted off to sleep. "I'm not usually this clingy," he told me. "Then again, I am not typically a lot of things I am when it comes to you."

"Same, boy. I think it's time for both of us to rewrite what we thought we knew about relationships and ourselves."

"That sounds like a good plan to me." When I tried lifting Slade's arm so I could get up and relieve myself, Slade tightened his grip on me.

"Relax, boy. I'm not going anywhere. I'll be right back."

"You'd better be," Slade warned me. "I don't feel like getting arrested for indecent exposure if I have to chase you down the street while I'm naked."

"We definitely wouldn't want that to happen, would we?" As I disappeared across the hall, I considered everything that had changed in twenty-four short hours. Slade wasn't the only one stepping outside of his comfort zone. I could only hope I had half the courage he did.

11

I couldn't remember the last time I had gotten a full night's sleep without the help of a good buzz. I felt, both, refreshed and like I could drift back off for a few more hours. The latter was all because of the heat radiating off the body draped over mine. Who needed to adjust the thermostat when I had Jack in bed with me?

Jack.

I opened my eyes as I slowly rolled onto my other side, so I was facing him. Last night hadn't been a dream. I had bent over and begged him to fuck me. I shifted on the bed. From the way my ass felt, he had given me exactly what I asked for and more.

It was awesome waking up and still feeling the effects of the night before. Too many guys saw my slender body and delicate features and assumed I was fragile. I couldn't even remember how long it had been since someone had manhandled me the way Jack had as he plowed into my ass.

Getting used to the way he made me feel was dangerous. I was in serious trouble, because I wasn't flipping shit about him still being sound asleep in my bed this morning. It left me open to hoping for more nights like last night, followed by more mornings waking up in his arms. It was completely foreign to me.

That's because he's different, the voice in the back of my mind reminded me.

"You can't know that," I muttered out loud. Jack scrunched his nose, tightening his arm around my waist. A sense of peace washed over me as I slid lower in the bed. The shitshow that was my life would still be waiting for me later. For now, I was going to savor every second I had of feeling like there was someone out there who not only gave a damn about me, but cherished me.

Again, I was dreaming up scenarios that couldn't come to life. No way would he stick around. We were oil and vinegar, night and day—we might complement one another, but we were never made to coexist. Eventually, he would quit slumming it and head back to his fancy house in his fancy car, and he would change back into his fancy suit and head off to his fancy job. Meanwhile, I would sulk around the house, complaining about how miserable my life was but too paralyzed to do anything about it.

Okay, so maybe sleep wasn't going to happen.

"Go back to sleep, boy," Jack mumbled, tightening his grip on me.

"Too keyed up to sleep," I admitted. Still, I scooted back so I pressed against Jack's morning wood.

He pressed a hand firmly against my stomach. "Keep that up, boy, and I can't be held responsible for what I do to you."

"Maybe I want you to do something," I teased, giving my ass a wiggle. Jack groaned, and I laughed. Not the half-hearted chuckle I let out when it was expected of me, but a sound of honest enjoyment. No matter what happened once reality set in, I would always be grateful to Jack for giving me a brief respite from my shitty life.

"You're not too sore?" Jack shoved a hand between our bodies. I winced when he pressed a finger against my hole, grateful that I was facing away from him. If he saw my discomfort, I knew he would refuse to fool around, and I didn't want him to put on the kid gloves now. Without knowing if this had been a one-time deal, I wanted to get my fill before we got out of bed.

"I'm good," I lied.

Jack's palm cracked against my hip, causing me to jump. "Don't lie to me, boy. If you hurt, you tell me."

"I'm fine," I insisted. "A little sore, sure, but I like it that way. Besides, you're the one who warned me he was going to make sure I didn't forget what we did last night."

"As true as that may be, I never want to hurt you." A lump formed in my throat at the tenderness in Jack's voice. My eyes drifted shut when he reached up and began threading his fingers through my hair. "You like that?"

"Mm-hmm," I hummed. "Feels good. Going to put me to sleep if you keep doing that."

"Good. I don't have to be up early today, and I can't think of a better way to spend the morning than in bed with you." As I drifted to sleep, it was almost possible for me to imagine this as my new normal.

A while later, I awoke again with Jack's body still plastered against mine. I lifted his arm, easing my way off the mattress. Nature called and, no matter how sexy he was, I couldn't wait any longer.

I leaned against the wall as I took my morning piss. Once I was done and had washed my hands, I stared in the mirror, scrubbing a hand over my face, still trying to wrap my head around how much everything had changed in the past few days. I waited for dread to settle in my gut, reminding me that this wasn't a life I could have. It never came.

In its place, there was hope. Jack didn't run off as soon as we were done fucking last night, so maybe he was telling me the truth when he whispered in my ear that he thought I was a good boy, that I was sexy, and that he planned to keep me, as long as I wanted to be with him.

When you do something often enough, you tend to become immune to certain emotions. In my case, I shuffled out of the bedroom every morning and was immediately consumed by dread over the state of my apartment. It had become my normal, and I don't think I fully realized how horrible I had gotten used to feeling on a daily basis until, suddenly, I exited the bathroom and caught a glimpse of the living room on my way to the kitchen.

There was a sense of peace that washed over me. It was like I had been suffocating in my own despair, and now I could breathe. Sure, I still had to worry about finding a job so I could keep paying the rent and, maybe, someday, move into a place I could, if not be proud of, then at least not be ashamed of. I'd never believed people when they said they felt lighter when they weren't stressed out, but that's the only way to describe the way I practically floated through the apartment knowing Jack was still sleeping in my bed.

I found myself humming as I pulled the canister of coffee out of the cupboard and started brewing a pot so I could surprise him with breakfast in bed. I paused, trying to place the melody. It wasn't familiar and, yet, I couldn't stop myself. I barely caught the container before it crashed to the ground. Coffee could wait.

It wasn't until I raced into the living room and began scribbling down notes, that I realized what was happening. I was writing again. Maybe it was a fluke, but I wasn't about to let this chance get away from me. I felt around under the couch, rejoicing when I found a rubber band. I quickly threw my hair into a messy bun, then hunched over the table, tapping out a rhythm then doubling back to work out each line of notes. The song was slower and less angry than anything I had written in over a year, but something in my gut told me this was what I was supposed to be doing.

"It's never easy to let go of something you want. And even though it's not exactly my type of music, I can admit that you have a hell of a lot of talent. Have you ever thought about going solo?" When Eli had made the suggestion, it was all I could do to not laugh in his face. Me? A solo act? Not a chance in hell. I needed a band behind me, supporting me, or at least I thought I did.

There was no point in getting ahead of myself. I had the start of one ballad that may or may not suck. Even if it was good, I wasn't sure there was a market for it. My shoulders slumped as the voice of self-doubt shouted over the melody.

Who in the hell was I fooling? Just because I'd managed to pull my shit together for a single day, didn't mean I was ready to grab life by the balls and make it my bitch.

"I was wondering where you'd run off to." I jumped at the sound of Jack's voice behind me, the pen in my hand scratching across the paper. When I attempted to stash the notebook under the couch, Jack captured my wrist. "What's that?"

"It's just something I was working on this morning," I told him.

"Can I see?" I glanced over my shoulder at Jack as he sat on the couch behind me, straddling my body. I shook my head, and he let out a disappointed sigh.

"It's nothing personal," I quickly told him. "I don't

usually show my projects to anyone. Not even my band-mates get to see anything until it's polished. I mean, my former bandmates."

Saying those words out loud felt like a punch to the gut. I was finally accepting that being a part of the band was my past, not my future. Whatever I did from here out, I'd have to do it on my own.

Jack tugged the hair tie out of my hair and began finger combing it. I leaned my head back, allowing my eyes to drift shut.

"If you keep that up, I'm going to think you're only with me because you're fixated on playing with my hair," I teased him.

Jack leaned down, nibbling on my earlobe then the side of my neck. "Boy, if you really think that, then you haven't been paying attention at all."

He slid a hand down my chest, tugging up the hem of the t-shirt I had thrown on because I was cold. I arched my back as his hand drifted higher, his fingertips teasing over my nipple. He twisted hard, sucking on my neck until I was certain there would be a mark later.

Now that I had allowed self-doubt into my head, I found myself struggling to silence it. "It makes about as much sense as anything else."

My head jostled as Jack wrapped my hair around his hand before tugging backward so I was forced to look at him. "None of that. I was standing over there, watching you scribble in your notebook for almost five minutes. It felt like a gift, getting to see a glimpse of you in the zone, so passionate about something that you were oblivious to everything around you. You were like a totally different boy than the one I met at the party."

"Not really," I argued. "Still the same wreck trying to find any way to avoid reality."

The lie felt bitter as it passed my lips. Why in the hell couldn't I be normal? I wanted to go back in time to when I woke up and everything felt good for a change. What the hell was wrong with me that I constantly had to find a way to sabotage myself?

"Do we need to go back to the bedroom for a lesson in what happens when you lie to me?" My dick reacted to the growly, demanding tone of Jack's voice.

I pressed my lips shut to keep from begging him. Something told me I wouldn't like whatever punishment he had in mind.

Instead, I slumped back against the couch, resting my head on Jack's thigh. He continued running a hand over my hair. "You can't expect everything to change like a light switch turning on, Slade. There is nothing wrong with you."

For a moment, I thought I had spoken the words aloud. Jack leaned forward, pressing a kiss to the side of my head. "Last night was intense. You're still trying to come back to center."

"Center?"

"Think of your emotions as a pendulum," Jack explained. He continued massaging my scalp, and I closed my eyes, focusing on the low timbre of his voice. "You were at one extreme before. You felt lost and hopeless. But then, last night, I took you out of that. You were able to forget everything, even if only for a little while. You soared, letting excitement drown everything else."

"You sure think highly of yourself," I scoffed.

He spoke the truth, but I couldn't hand over the power to Jack. If he knew how much of an effect he had on me, I would be vulnerable and even more desperate when he eventually left. Because, as amazing as last night had been, and as badly as I wanted to believe everything he had whispered about keeping me, there was still that nagging voice in the back of my head, telling me this would never last. Once Jack and I said goodbye, he would see how much of a drain I was on his life.

Jack tightened his fist in the back of my hair again. "This is your last warning, boy. Don't lie to me again."

"I didn't lie to you," I argued.

"So, you're just being a cheeky little shit this morning?"

"Maybe." Was that a lie? Would he see it that way? "Okay, so maybe I am struggling a little bit to believe this is all real. You keep talking about more than just whatever happened last night, but I don't do relationships."

"Just because you haven't in the past, doesn't mean you're destined for a lonely life," Jack argued. The knot in my gut loosened. The way Jack talked made me want more out of life.

I twisted around so I could kneel at Jack's feet, facing him. "Yes, last night was fucking mind-blowing. I still don't understand why I liked a lot of it is much as I did, and that's scary. I let you tell me what to do and didn't tell you to get lost. You might not realize it, but that's *huge* for me."

"You don't have to have all the answers right away, Slade. When was the last time you simply allowed yourself to feel without second-guessing everything?" Jack's hands wandered across my body. It wasn't sexual, but every caress was more intimate than anything I'd ever experienced.

"Never," I admitted.

"Then maybe it's time for you to start."

"How?" The question came out as a whiny plea.

Jack hitched his hands under my armpits and tugged me onto his lap. It felt awkward at the same time it felt perfect.

His arms were wrapped tightly around my waist, and I rested my head on top of his. I could feel every gentle exhale of breath, and I wanted to stay just like this.

"I know it's a lot to ask this quickly, but do you think you can trust me?"

"I want to." And, fuck, if that didn't scare me to death. There were very few people in the world I trusted. After the bullshit with the band, the only person I trusted implicitly was Jordan, and yet, I wanted nothing more than to place Jack on that list.

"Have I done anything so far to violate your trust?"

I shook my head, afraid to speak, because I wasn't sure what I would say.

"Let me help you, Slade," Jack pleaded. The vulnerability in his request startled me. "I'm not promising you forever, but I'm asking you to take one day at a time with me. Believe it or not, this is new ground for both of us."

"But you've been in relationships like this before?" He told me he had, but I hadn't asked for any details.

"I have, but I've never met someone like you, Slade. And it's been a hell of a long time since anyone has had this sort of pull on me."

I sat up a little straighter, proud that I had an effect on him too.

"We're going to get everything sorted out for you, that much I can promise." He pressed his lips to my hair again, this time staying there. Silence washed over the room. I focused on his breathing now, smiling when he sucked in a sharp breath as I ran a hand over his chest.

"What's in this for you?" Just because I wanted to trust him, didn't mean I did. Men like Jack didn't do shit like this for someone without expecting something in return. I still didn't know what he did for a living, but everything about him screamed shrewd businessman. And the price tag on his car said he was damn good at what he did.

Jack's chest rumbled with laughter. His hand slid lower, his fingers dipping beneath the waistband of my sweatpants. "I'm assuming you mean other than access to this beautiful ass?"

"Yeah," I agreed. "Besides that. I am not a fan of feeling like a kept boy. This isn't Pretty Woman, and I'm not going to let you throw money at my problems to make them go away."

"And that, right there, is why I'm willing to help you, Slade. I look at you and I see a boy who has lost confidence in himself. I hope that someday you'll trust me enough to explain how you wound up where you are, but for now, it's enough to know that you want to be better. You're not happy with the status quo. And, for the sake of honesty, it gets me hard seeing the way you light up when you follow my instructions. If you're game, I'd like to continue seeing you."

"You mean like dating?" I scrunched my nose up.

"Exactly like that," he confirmed.

Dating complicated things. And I wasn't sure where Jack thought he could take me that we wouldn't be a spectacle. Even if I had the money to go out and buy a new wardrobe, Jack and I were still like night and day. He was polished and refined, while I would always be rough around the edges. I wasn't going to change myself that much just to be the perfect boy for him.

"I've never dated before," I admitted. "I'm not sure…"

I'm not sure I'd be any good at being a boyfriend. I'm not sure I could keep it together and not embarrass you. I know I'm not good enough for you.

"You're dwelling again," he scolded me. He wasn't wrong. "And I can practically hear all the crap your brain is trying to tell you." He pressed his palms to my cheeks, pulling me down for a hard, fast kiss. "Your insecurity lies to you. There are so many places I would love to take you, Slade. And don't sell yourself short; when I show you off, I guarantee everyone's going to realize that I am the lucky one."

"We'll see about that."

Jack's stomach growled.

"Oh shit, I was going to surprise you this morning, then I got distracted. Dammit. Why does this always happen?" I squirmed, trying to get up. "I do this all the damn time. Stupid."

"Slow down, boy," Jack urged me. Instead of letting me up, he held me tighter. "There's some fruit and yogurt in the fridge that will make a good, quick breakfast. I'd come in to remind you to eat. You need to take better care of yourself, starting with eating breakfast every morning."

"If I wait, I don't spend the entire day starving," I admitted.

"That shit stops right now. If you need food, you tell me."

"I already told you, I'm not taking your charity," I spat out.

"Fine, we will keep track and you can pay me back once you get a job," he conceded. I eyed him warily, finding it hard to believe he'd caved so quickly.

"And you'll take the money when I try to pay you back?"

"I will," Jack promised. "This isn't about you being a shiny toy for me to play with, Slade. And even though I would love nothing more than to spoil you rotten, because I get the impression you haven't had nearly enough of that in your life, I respect that it's important for you to be self-suffi-cient. It's an admirable trait and one I can fully support."

I hopped up from Jack's lap, turned around and held out a hand for him. "Fine, I'll let you help me, but only if you let me pay you back every penny. We can put the receipts in an envelope."

"Whatever you say, sweetheart." He ruffled the top of my head, and I scowled at him. The fucker had the audacity to laugh before motioning for me to move. Jack followed me into the kitchen and began dishing up the fruit and yogurt while I brewed the pot of coffee I had abandoned earlier.

We sat in companionable silence as we ate. I still had plenty of unanswered questions, but I didn't know where to start. And, for once, I didn't feel like I needed to speak just to fill the silence.

"What do you have planned for today?" Jack asked after he was finished eating.

"I need to talk to Eli," I replied. "I'm not sure he'll have anything I can do, but Jordan isn't going to let up until I ask Eli for a job."

"Give yourself some credit, Slade. You can do just about anything you put your mind to." He gathered the dishes, then stopped me with a single raised eyebrow when I stood. "Sit. I've got this."

I flipped around in my chair, resting my arms across the back as Jack washed our bowls and silverware. I probably should've fought with him, telling him he was a guest and didn't have to clean up, but this felt weirdly right. I let out a huff of amusement. Weirdly right, pretty much summed up how everything with Jack felt.

"The way I see it, you're holding yourself back," Jack explained, glancing over his shoulder to make sure I was paying attention to him. "You've got it in your head that you're going to fail because the last thing you tried didn't work out. It's easier to give up than risk failing again. But Slade, that's no way to live in the long run."

"More life lessons with Jack?" I teased.

Jack shrugged. "It's not intentional, I swear. But dammit, Slade, you're a good man. Eli sees that, and he'll be happy to help."

"You're wrong," I argued. "Eli doesn't know me well enough to have an honest opinion, but I'm pretty sure he's not my biggest fan. He might laugh in my face and tell me to get lost."

"He won't," Jack said with certainty. "If he does, you let me know and I'll call him."

"You're not my knight in shining armor," I reminded him. "Let me do this on my own, please."

Jack held up his hands in surrender. "Fine, but don't forget that you don't have to do everything on your own. And I'm a pushy enough bastard that I'll step in if I think you need help but you're being too stubborn to admit it."

I didn't want to get into this with him. I didn't want to explain that on my own was the way I did everything. So, I did what I do best. I changed the subject. "What about you? Do you have any meetings today?"

"No, but I will have to go in tonight. Business picks up toward the end of the week, and it would be nice to get things set so I can try to sneak over here to see you at least once this weekend."

"You don't have to do that," I told him. "I'm a big boy. I'll be fine on my own. And really, I'm not as fragile as you seem to think I am."

Jack stalked across the room until he was hovering over me. "It's not about thinking you're incapable. If anyone here needs a reminder of just how capable you are, *it's you*. I want to make time to visit you, because your mouth and your ass are addictive as hell. It's all about not wanting to deprive myself, really."

"Oh, well as long as it's all about you," I teased. I'd fully expected Jack to wake up this morning and make his excuses, but here he was telling me he was going to rearrange his work schedule for me.

"It's a shame I don't work typical business hours, or I'd be tempted to whisk you away somewhere for the weekend."

Yes, a total shame. Although, I wasn't sure we were at the point of weekend getaways just yet. Then again, I'd *never* been at that point, so maybe it was a totally normal part of most relationships.

"You don't strike me as the type of guy who works nights and weekends. Don't you have people to work the shit hours for you?"

"I do, but I am a firm believer in being around during the height of business. It's easier to handle any...issues that arise." His scowl made me wonder just what he did because, again, the suit didn't seem to fit with any job that would have weekend emergencies.

"What do you do that there would be that many problems on the weekends?"

Jack sucked his bottom lip between his teeth. For a few drawn-out moments, I wondered if he was going to ignore the question. "Have you ever heard of The Lodge?"

I barked out a laugh. Of course, I'd heard of it. Everyone had heard of The Lodge. I nodded.

"Well, that's my place."

"Are you fucking kidding me?" I buried my hands in my face. I couldn't have been more off the mark if I tried. I wasn't sure why, but I had always imagined whoever owned that place, walking around in leather pants with a round, fuzzy belly and a harness over his burly chest. The place wasn't seedy, but I'd pictured the owner as borderline sleazy, given the fact he ran a sex club.

But Jack? Fuck me, now I wanted to know if the suit was

his casual attire because the leather pants didn't breathe. I licked my lips as I imagined pulling them down his legs, burying my face in his groin. The only thing that would possibly smell any better than Jack, was Jack's arousal combined with leather.

I squirmed in my seat, my dick tenting the front of my pants.

"I know you probably think it's all sex, all the time, but it's really not," Jack said, interrupting my fantasies of dropping to my knees for him at work. "Part of why we're as successful as we are is we've worked to become a safe haven for the kink community in the area. We are firm believers in keeping things safe and sane, which is why we have monthly education events."

I held up my hands to stop him. His voice grew loud and almost argumentative. Well, this was one thing he didn't have to fight with me on.

"Is that why you've stayed single for so long?" I stood, tired of craning my neck so I could look at him. "I'd think that you'd have boys falling all over you. You must have quite the following if I've never even been to The Lodge, and even I know it's the place to be."

"While it's reassuring to know you've heard good things about the club, that's exactly the problem," Jack explained as he led me back to the living room. He sat down on the couch, one leg hanging off and the other stretched across the cushions. He pulled me onto his lap, wrapping his arms around my waist. I settled with my back against his chest and my head on his shoulder. "There are plenty of perfectly suitable boys out there, but it's hard to distinguish those who have a genuine interest in me from those who want to sleep with the owner of The Lodge because they think it'll make them more intriguing. There's no shortage of shallow, self-serving people in this world, and I'd prefer not to get mixed up with them."

"Instead, you decided to pursue someone you didn't know it all?" I traced patterns in the hair on Jack's forearms. He gave a little shiver and I smiled. "Don't get me wrong; I'm glad you did. But what was it about me that made you think, 'Hey, if I'm not having any luck with guys at the club, maybe I'll hit on the train wreck at my brother's place'? You should probably know the only reason Jordan was even able to convince me to go to the party was because there was free food and booze. When you're as broke as I am, you never turn down those offers."

"You say that, but I think there's more to it." Jack pressed his lips against my hair. Now it was my turn to feel a chill rush through my body. I had never allowed myself to feel this intimate connection with anyone, and now I wondered why I had deprived myself for so long.

"So, tell me, oh wise one, if I didn't go for the food and alcohol, then what lured me away from home when I hate being around people I don't know?"

"You put on this front like you don't need anyone or anything," Jack explained. "But, secretly, I think that's a way to shield yourself from getting hurt. The way you opened up to me so quickly is proof that you're desperate to feel connected to somebody, even if the very thought scares you. You've kept yourself at a distance because you figure it's safer that way, but you're not happy."

Fuck, this man really had my number. If this was how he read potential members at The Lodge, it was no wonder they were known for being overly cautious and weeding out the troublemakers before they were allowed entrance. "Am I wrong about any of what I just said?"

"No, Daddy. You're not wrong." I realized too late that I

had slipped and called him Daddy. I waited for it to turn awkward, but it didn't. It also didn't feel creepy to think of him that way, even when we weren't in the bedroom. After all, the first thing he had done for me wasn't sexual at all.

And, damn, I wanted to make Jack proud as his boy. I would start by doing everything I could to have as much faith in myself as Jack already had in me.

12

SLADE

Jack finally left shortly after two in the afternoon. I would have felt bad keeping him from whatever he had going on in his own life, but it had been his decision to relax on the couch and watch a movie while we chatted, getting to know one another a bit better. This whole situation was backward as fuck, but I wasn't feeling as hopeless as I had been, so I was going to ride the wave as long as I could. I rummaged through the clothes I'd taken the time to neatly fold on Jack's insistence, trying to find something suitable for a job interview.

You're stalling, that's what you're doing, self-doubt scolded me.

I wound up pulling on the pair of pants I'd worn last night when I'd been trying to impress Jack. If I got a job at Club 83, I would likely have to add to my tab with Jack so I could get some clothes suitable for a real job. I showered as quickly as possible, knowing if I waited too long, Eli would have the opportunity to blow me off, saying he had to get the bar ready for tonight's rush.

No, he won't. It's like you didn't listen to a word he said when he cornered you the other night. Seriously, self-doubt could take a flying leap.

I didn't call Jordan to let him know I was stopping by. I didn't want him making a bigger deal of this than it was. Plain and simple, I was just a guy who needed a job, walking into a bar that needed employees. Nothing more, nothing less. I knew it was too late not to have him put in a good word for me. Hell, he'd probably done that the first time he realized I was struggling financially.

And you should be grateful you have friends willing to stick their necks out for you.

"Shut the fuck up," I muttered aloud as I locked my front door. Okay, so I probably looked a bit crazy to the old guy walking down the hall to his apartment. "Sorry, not you."

Old dude grunted, shook his head, and rolled his eyes as he passed me. That was probably the most interaction I'd had with any of my neighbors in months. This wasn't the type of place where you got to know one another and had impromptu dinner parties.

The bar was almost empty when I arrived. It was strange being here so early. I was used to music blaring from the high-end sound system Eli had installed when he opened the bar, and wall-to-wall people. It was a little eerie, honestly. The only noise was from Hank, the cook, prepping for the night, and a TV at the corner of the bar.

I sat down on one of the stools and started playing around on my phone. No one was behind the bar, and I figured Jordan was most likely in the stock room pulling bottles to make sure they didn't run out of anything during the rush. Knowing him, he was probably dreaming up whatever this weekend's wicked concoction would be. I envied my friend. He had both talent and the support of the entire staff. Even before he had gotten together with Eli and Doug, it was like this was Jordan's stage and everyone else who worked here played back up to him.

They'd do the same for you.

I knew that, if I was being honest. Apparently, two nights of sharing a bed with Jack had stripped me of the lies I used to shield myself from one day to the next. The tight-knit friendship of the employees at Club 83 was part of what held me back from applying sooner. Everyone knew everyone's business, and that didn't work well if you were trying to hide.

"Hey man, everything okay?" I glanced up and smiled when Jordan pushed through the swinging double doors.

"Eli around?" No sense procrastinating any longer. If Jordan and I got to talking, it would be far too easy for me to chat with him until customers started trickling in, then walk out without doing the one thing I came in to do.

"He's still upstairs," Jordan told me. The corner of his mouth turned up in a shy smirk. "You finally ready to suck it up and talk to him about a job?"

"Not like I have much choice," I scoffed. "I can probably make it another couple of months if I cut back on how much I'm eating, but after that, I'm screwed."

Jordan rolled his eyes. "You can be such a stubborn asshole sometimes, you know that? I think you should have gotten a job months ago, based on the way you're looking."

I smoothed a hand over my shirt. Sure, it hung looser than it used to, but it wasn't like I was all skin and bones.

"Screw you. You're just jealous because I'm still hotter than you," I teased.

"It's the hair," Jordan deadpanned. "No matter what, you'll always be hotter because you got that rocker vibe going on. Add in a bit of eyeliner, and there's just no way to compete."

Jordan set down the cases of beer he was carrying and slid onto the stool next to mine. "Seriously though, what made you change your mind? I've been telling you for how long to come down and talk to him?"

"Yeah, well maybe I'm sick of being miserable all the time. I know it's time to get a job, and at least Eli will probably be cool if I decide to do something with music again in the future."

"You totally should," Jordan remarked. "And Eli would definitely be cool with working around your schedule. Maybe this could be a good thing. You could talk to him about setting up on nights we don't have anybody else booked in. You get the exposure and he doesn't have an empty stage. I bet he wouldn't even charge you for it."

"Let's not get ahead of ourselves," I told him. "Right now, that's still a pretty big *if*. I think it's for the best if I treat music like it's part of my past until I'm back on even footing."

Holding onto pipe dreams was how I'd found myself in this position in the first place. Trying to find a job that wouldn't make it impossible to play had helped me dig the hole even deeper. Putting music on the back burner seemed like the only sensible choice for the time being.

Jordan tipped his head to the side and stared at me. I squirmed under his silent assessment. When he shrugged, I wondered if he found what he was looking for. Then he let out a grunt, shook his head, and turned away.

"Just spit it out." Jordan got like this sometimes. He wanted to be nosy, but when it came to me, he had always been careful about asking questions he might not want the answer to.

"I'm just wondering why the sudden change of heart," Jordan said after a long pause. "Does it have anything to do with the car that's been parked out in front of your building the past two nights?"

"Jesus, Jordan, have you been stalking me?" To his credit, Jordan never broke eye contact. However, I wasn't used to the pissed off glare he shot my way, and I held up my hands in surrender. "Hey, you have to admit, it's a valid question. How else would you know there's been a specific car outside my apartment?"

Jordan practically bounced on his seat. "Well, I didn't, but now I do. So, tell me all about it. He wound up coming back yesterday?"

"There's nothing to tell," I lied. Even if I was the type to kiss and tell, I wouldn't have made a big deal about it. Whatever was happening with Jack was still far too fragile for me to go blabbing about, especially knowing Jordan's complete inability to keep secrets from his partners.

"So, did the two of you know one another before he gave you a ride home from our place the other night?" Oh, Jordan was getting good at needling for information. He'd obviously spent far too much time with Eli.

"No." I figured it to be easier to give Jordan a little bit to go on and hope that Eli showed up before he could try to draw every raunchy detail out of me. There were still things I didn't fully understand myself, so I wasn't about to try to explain what was going on to Jordan. "He stuck around that night because he was afraid that I was going to choke on my own vomit and die. Can't blame a guy for not wanting that on his conscience."

Jordan just scrunched his nose in disgust. "That has got to be one of the grossest visuals ever."

"You're the one who asked." I stood on the bottom rung of the stool, reaching across the bar for a glass. Jordan looked like he was about to say something when I reached for the soda gun and poured myself a cup of water.

Jordan's brow furrowed and he tipped his head to the side again. "I don't know what Jack did to you, but he needs to keep it up."

"What makes you say that?"

"You're...different. You're not nearly as grumpy as you used to be, and you have more color today."

Funny how not starving yourself changed things. I kept that to myself as well, not wanting another lecture about my dietary habits or my reluctance to ask for help. I checked the time on my phone. "So, when do you expect Eli?"

Jordan checked the time and tapped away at his phone. "He's just about to head down now. You want me to hang with you a bit longer?"

"Nah, I'll be fine," I assured him. It wouldn't make a good impression on Eli if his partner/star employee was slacking off when he should be working. And it was far more important to me now, than it had ever been before, to make good impressions on people who might be able to help me. Even if I'd sworn I didn't want their help.

My stomach flipped when I heard the back-door slam shut. There were very few people allowed to use the alley entrance and, given the fact Jordan had said Eli would be here soon, there was little doubt whose heavy footfalls were stomping toward me. The friendly smile Eli gave me, as he extended a hand to shake, nearly knocked me off my stool. This wasn't the version of Eli I was used to. As a business owner, he was always friendly with his customers, but he had little time for those who posed a threat to his success. I had always imagined I was in the latter category, because Club 83 had been one of my favorite hunting grounds for the next hook up.

"Slade," he greeted me with a firm handshake. "It's good to see you. Jordan said you were hoping to talk to me?"

I dipped my chin and twirled my hair around my finger. As soon as I realized what I was doing, I dropped my hand back to my lap. My heart raced and my stomach churned. Despite everyone telling me all I had to do to get a job here was talk to Eli, I couldn't stop myself from thinking of all the different ways I could screw up this interview.

"Yeah, I was hoping... I mean... Shit..." I blew out a harsh breath and scrubbed a hand over my face. I was doing a stellar job of selling myself as a competent addition to his staff.

Eli pressed a hand to my shoulder. "Relax, boy."

Hearing the endearment from Eli didn't have the same effect it did when Jack called me boy. And, yet, it did settle me in a way I hadn't expected. Grounded me. Reminded me that Jack's approval was one of my motivations for dragging my ass down here today.

"Sorry, this isn't..." What'd I even want to say? Did I want to admit to him that burying my pride and begging him for a job was about as much fun as a root canal? That probably wouldn't serve me well. I closed my eyes and imagined Jack guiding me through a series of breathing exercises. When my heart rate slowed and my brain started firing properly again, I started over. "Sorry. I know I probably shouldn't be nervous, but I don't have a lot of experience trying to get a job. I don't have experience but, I promise, I can be a hard worker."

"There's nothing to worry about here," Eli assured me. "I understand that you've been plenty busy with music until recently. Would it help you to pretend I am the owner of a bar and you're trying to get me to hire you for a gig? You may not have much conventional work experience, but I know from some other owners in the area that you don't put up with any shit when you're negotiating show dates and fees. That's part of why I was hoping you'd come and see me."

I had to chuckle because, when he put it that way, I did feel more confident. And, really, this wasn't all that much different. Sure, I wouldn't be standing on stage, screaming out angry lyrics over the guitar and drum lines, but he *was* the bar owner. The only difference was the "gig", as he put it.

I sat up a bit straighter and turned to face Eli. He gave me a reassuring nod. "Thank you, Eli. I promise I'm not always this scatterbrained."

This time, it was Eli who laughed, and he squeezed my shoulder again. "Don't bullshit me, Slade. I've heard plenty about you and I've seen you around enough to know this is exactly who you usually are. But I'm still willing to take a chance on you."

"Why? It's not like I have any skills you need," I questioned.

Way to go, self-doubt lectured me. *Why don't you just start listing up all the reasons he'd be a fool to hire you?*

"You have one skill I most definitely need," Eli corrected me. "You're good with people."

"I'm really not," I disagreed.

Eli scowled at me. "Would you let me finish?"

My shoulders slumped forward. "Sorry," I muttered. "Go on. I won't interrupt again."

"Thank you." Eli rapped his knuckles on the top of the bar. "When you let go of the paranoia that everyone is judging you, you're actually quite a personable young man. I've watched you plenty. I've also seen how my customers interact with you. Not to sound like a sleazeball or anything, but in order to keep a place like this thriving, I need good looking boys in customers' eyes."

"So you're hiring me to be eye candy?" I might joke with Jordan about who was better looking, but that was yet another smokescreen. It was better than pointing out how my nose was too pointy and a bit crooked, my eyes were dull, and my hips too skinny—even before I'd cut back to eating once a day.

"I would like to offer you a position as a bar back." Eli relaxed, with an elbow resting on the bar. It didn't seem like he cared much, one way or the other, if I took the job. Then again, he probably didn't. This sounded like a made-up job because he couldn't admit he was hiring me to walk around looking pretty.

"I know next to nothing about the bar," I reminded him.

"I understand that," Eli said. "This would be a good way for you to learn, if you'd like. When the club is busy, you'll be responsible for keeping everything, from the beer coolers to the ice wells, fully stocked. Essentially, you will be doing all of the grunt work that keeps my bartenders from serving customers as quickly as possible. We have a lot of big events coming up, and I'd like to have you start as soon as possible so you can be up to speed before Pride weekend."

That was only a few weeks away. Even though Eli swore I didn't need to know much, I doubted I'd be efficient by then.

"You'll also be helping out on the floor," he continued as I opened my mouth to protest. I clamped my lips shut, because I'd promised I wouldn't interrupt him again and I was determined to follow through. "Wiping down tables, bringing empty glassware back to the dishwasher, helping Bear watch for any problems."

That didn't sound so bad. It would be boring as hell at

times, and I wasn't thrilled about being a glorified errand boy, but work was work.

"What you say, Slade?" Eli's question startled me. I needed to quit spacing out.

"Sounds great," I told him with as much fake enthusiasm as I could muster.

"If things work out, and you decide you'd like to learn about tending bar, I am sure we can get Jordan to teach you when there are lulls in business. That would mean you'd get tipped on your own, rather than whatever the bartenders throw your way."

Well, shit, now he had my attention. I hadn't realized tips would be part of this made-up barback gig. Sign me the hell up! If I paid attention and did a good job, I could pay Jack back and not have to borrow any more money from him.

"I can start whenever you'd like," I told him.

"I was hoping you'd say that." Eli chuckled, and I got the feeling I'd just walked into a trap. "If you're free tonight, we'll go back to my office and do some paperwork. Then, you can help Jordan finish setting up for the night. It's probably going to be too slow to need you up front, but there are some odd jobs that keep getting pushed aside lately. You game?"

"I'll do whatever you need," I said through gritted teeth. This had definitely been a trap, and I was a sucker. Still, it wasn't like I had many other prospects on the horizon.

As I followed Eli to his office, I pulled out my phone and sent Jack a quick text.

You'll be happy to know I'm officially employed.

His response came instantly.

I'm proud of you. I take it things went well with Eli? I shouldn't have to stay here too late tonight. You want me to pick you up at your place so we can celebrate?

Hell yes, I wanted to spend more time with him. Unfortunately, I'd agreed to work. I could ask Eli how long he wanted me to stay, but that probably wouldn't go over well on my first shift.

Can't. Eli's putting me right to work. Raincheck?

After I sent the message, I remembered Jack saying he'd be busy all weekend at his own club. This sucked.

*C*an't. Eli's putting me right to work. Raincheck?

Slade couldn't have known how his reply to my invitation to get together affected me. From the little I knew about him—and, logically, I knew we were still practically strangers—he wouldn't believe me if I told him that was the perfect response. He'd tapped the brakes while I was going full throttle. Until I could explain why I was so drawn to him, I needed to be careful to keep from overwhelming him.

I pocketed my phone and stood, needing to touch base with Sam before we opened for the night. I found him at the bar, hunched over a stack of papers. After grabbing each of us a bottle of water, I slid onto the stool next to his, watching him scribble notes, referring back to his original class project. "You know I don't expect perfection before Monday, right?"

He startled, as if he hadn't realized I was there, quickly shuffling the papers into a neat stack and turning them over. "Sorry, I know I should be finishing the inventory and processing a few membership applications, but I had an idea and wanted to get it written down before I forgot."

I placed a hand on Sam's shoulder, giving it a gentle squeeze. "Sam. Relax. I'm not upset. On the contrary, I love seeing you so passionate about this project. Now, show me what you've been working on."

We spent the next hour going over the progress he'd made so far. It was hard to believe he'd only told me about his ideas yesterday. It seemed as if an entire lifetime had passed in twenty-four hours. His plans were solid, and his proposed budget was realistic, yet conservative.

An alarm played on Sam's phone, and he started packing away his drawings and lists. It was odd not to be the one calling the shots for a change, but his determination to not let the new project distract him from his duties at The Lodge was admirable.

I envied Sam as I watched him stuff everything into his messenger bag, then bound off for his own small office down the hall from mine. How many years had it been since I felt that sort of excitement and anticipation about anything?

"Too damn many," I muttered to myself.

As if to emphasize the years I'd spent drifting through life on autopilot, my knees creaked in protest as I pushed off the stool. There had to be work I should be attending to in the office,

but there wasn't. There rarely was anymore. I spent my nights flipping from one program to the next in my computer, scanning the week's invoices, and just trying to appear busy in general to affirm my need to be in the building, ready for the next crisis.

"Fancy meeting you here." I barely had time to register the low rumbling voice before I felt a broad hand clamp down on my shoulder. "I was starting to think you were like the Wizard of Oz or some shit."

"I'm not that bad," I protested.

"Actually, you are," William argued. "It's been months since you sat in on any of the education events. The only time we catch a glimpse to know you're still alive is if you're sneaking to the bathroom. We barely see you anymore."

"I'm here every night," I told him.

"Of course, you are," William agreed. I stared at him as he walked around the end of the bar and poured himself a drink. What was he doing here this early? The doors weren't even open to the public yet. "You practically live here, Jack." He swiped my, now lukewarm, bottled water off the bar and replaced it with a cold one. "But you sit back in that cage of yours, safely away from anyone who may want to get close to you."

"Are you seriously criticizing me for setting boundaries?" I scoffed. "You know how fast shit can go wrong if you blur those lines."

The moment I saw William flinch, I regretted my words. The two of us both took our work seriously, but for years, William had much more dire consequences than I could have dreamed of if he'd pursued any sort of relationship. And yet, William found ways to get what he needed.

So do you, a little voice, that sounded suspiciously like Slade's, mocked me. *You just took your sweet time about it.*

"True enough, but you're never going to move on if you keep hiding from the rest of the world." William slid onto the seat I'd just vacated, pulling out another with his foot, urging me to sit.

"Who says I'm hiding?" I crossed my arms tightly over my chest and flashed him a smug grin. "For all you know, I might be spending all my time in the office because I have a pretty little boy on his knees under my desk, waiting to take care of me."

William let out a bark of laughter.

"What? It could happen."

"It could," William agreed. "But we both know that's not the case. You're not the type to keep secrets. When you have a new toy, you like to show him off—maybe even let your friends play with him, just so they know what you've got that they don't."

I sneered, a low growl escaping my lips. William wasn't lying, but there was something different about Slade. I didn't want to let him play with anyone else. As long as he was mine, I didn't have to worry about him realizing how much better off he would be with someone younger. Someone who wasn't a workaholic and could pay him the attention he deserved.

"Holy shit!" William's eyes grew wide. "There really is someone, isn't there?"

He stood, and I pulled him back to the stool before he could march into my office to see someone who wasn't there.

"I'm not sure I'd go that far," I argued. My stomach churned at the truth of those words. It was just a couple hours ago that I had been stunned over how much my life had changed in the past few days. No, I wasn't going to rush into things and declare myself off the market. Not that I had been on the market before meeting Slade, but whatever.

"Bullshit. You don't get growly and possessive. Ever. So, tell me about this boy you claim you don't have." William never knew when to leave well enough alone. He was like a damned hound dog, nosing around until he wore the other person down to the point that they shared far more than they were comfortable with. "You might be able to evade most people, but I'm not most people. I was starting to think you'd never get your ass back in the game after Colin."

"You and me both," I admitted. "And I'm not sure you can say I am back in the game, just because I had one really good encounter with a boy. Hell, all I meant to do was give him a ride home from my brother's. Then I started to see him and I don't think he's used to that, so I couldn't leave him. I wanted—"

"You tried to fix him, didn't you?" William massaged his temples and let out a loud sigh. "You can't do that, Jack. It never ends well for you. Haven't you learned anything?" He shook his head and took a drink of his water. "Well, the damage is done now. Did you, riding in on your white horse work?"

God, he sounded so much like Slade when the boy accused me of trying to be his knight in shining armor.

"For a day or two, yeah. But how do I know he's not going to get sick of me and block my number?" It might feel as if he'd always been part of my life, waiting in the wings for me to notice him, but I needed to remember this was all new. At some point, we'd both slow down, and I wasn't confident he'd still accept my guidance when he realized what he'd done.

"Seriously, Jack, insecurity is not a good look for you," William pointed out. "What's the real problem here?"

"I like him," I replied. William chuckled at the confusion in my tone as I admitted that I genuinely liked Slade. Not as a fun little toy to blow off some steam with, but as something more. He'd offered me tiny glimpses of what lay under the mask he wore to keep everyone at a distance, and I was determined to strip him until he was vulnerable and couldn't hide from me.

"You say that like it's a bad thing."

"It is. He needs someone, there's no doubt about that." God, if ever there was someone who needed a Daddy to keep him in check, it was Slade. I had The Lodge to worry about, and even if I had been considering turning more of the responsibilities over to Sam, I still needed to be here. At the end of the day, this was my business, and its success or failure rested on my shoulders. I had no place taking on a needy boy right now. "But I don't know that I'm the right man for the job."

"It's only as bad as you make it in your mind, Jack. If I know you, you've already written out a bullet point list of all the reasons you are the wrong Daddy for him."

I shrugged.

"That's a horrible way to live, Jack." William squeezed my shoulder until I looked up from the scuffed bar to meet his eyes. "For once, I dare you to do what feels good, instead of what you convince yourself is right. Rip up all the lists and spreadsheets. Stop thinking of your life as a set of goals to be met. Because, I've gotta tell you, if you get to the very end and look back, you are going to have a hell of a lot more regrets if you're sitting there alone than if you weren't here seven nights a week."

"You make it sound like I live here," I argued.

William's face twisted up in disbelief. "You said yourself that you're here every night. When was the last time you didn't at least stop by just to check on things?"

He had me there. The Lodge was centrally located to everything else in my life. I'd done that on purpose, because this club had always been the one project I took on for myself. It wasn't someone else's business to throw money and reap a percentage of the profits. The Lodge was my own brainchild, and I wouldn't step aside and let anyone else mismanage it.

But you have a strong staff now, the voice that sounded like Slade pointed out. *You don't have to micromanage everything anymore.*

William opened his mouth to say something, but cut himself off, grinding his teeth for a moment before his lip turned up in disgust. He jerked his head toward the lounge area. "Let's take this someplace else."

I checked over my shoulder and saw Cory, the lead bartender, making his way in from the break room. He was sporting a sheepish look, as if he was nervous about facing William.

What the hell was going on there? How did I not know why both of them looked upset about seeing the other?

"Easy. As much as you tell yourself you're here to keep an eye on things, you're really just hiding out," William responded.

Shit. Had I said that out loud?

As if sensing my embarrassment, William squeezed my shoulder. "This is exactly what I'm talking about, Jack. You can lie to yourself and say it's critical for you to be here every day of the week, but, the way I see it, you're not doing anybody any good if you are sitting behind that slab of mahogany, shuffling papers from one stack to another, trying to feel important."

As I lowered myself onto one of the plush, tufted leather couches in the corner of the room, I blinked a few times, seeing the club through fresh eyes. At one point, the room felt cold and somewhat uninviting. That was by design, because it was what the market research I had done before opening the first King club in Annandale told me people wanted.

But, somewhere along the way, things had subtly changed. Nothing major, but enough to make a huge difference. A pile of oversized throw pillows and a few velvety blankets, carefully draped over the back of some of the couches, transformed the space into something inviting. It felt like a contemporary living room on steroids. I liked it, and owed Sam kudos for the initiative he'd obviously shown. The fact he'd done all this without me knowing was like a bucket of cold water, waking me to the realization that William's criticism was both warranted and probably a long time coming.

"Fine, maybe you're right," I conceded. Somewhere along the way, I'd stopped spending every minute working and I'd buried myself in a facade. I bent at the waist, resting my elbows on my knees as I tangled my fingers through my hair. "But how am I supposed to relax if I have no clue what's going on? Sam is damn good at what he does, but he's about as anti-confrontational as they come."

"You're not wrong about that." William chuckled, scrubbing a hand over his stubbled cheek. "What if I offered to help you? I know this place as well as just about anyone, and you trust me. Give me the keys and let the troops know there's a new general in town when you're not here."

"Why would you do that? Every time I've tried putting you on the payroll, you act like I've offered you a poisoned apple."

"That's because the thought of working for you is about as appealing as a root canal," William quipped. "I'm not trying to needle my way into a job here, Jack. I am trying to help out a friend who took care of me when I was in a rough spot. The way I see it, this boy who's got you running scared isn't the only one who needs a set of rules. The problem is you need someone big and bad enough to put you in your place."

William flashed me a feral grin and cracked his knuckles. A lesser man might have been intimidated. Me? I was more annoyed than anything.

"If you think I am going to let you dictate how I should run my life, you've got another think coming. Not sure you've noticed, but I'm not so good at being the one taking the orders," I admitted. William laughed, and I felt my cheeks flush. There'd been one time when I had stepped in to help him with a class. To say things didn't go well was an understatement, and William still liked to give me a hard time about it every now and then.

"I'm pretty sure no drastic measures will be necessary this time. But, dammit, Jack, I've watched you circling the drain for far too long. If someone was keeping track, I'd be willing to bet the number of hours you spend in the building goes up every single week, while the number of minutes you spend out here actually socializing with anyone goes down." The way William maintained eye contact as he leaned in, had me fighting the urge to squirm. "You have to make a change, Jack, otherwise you're going to be miserable and alone."

"I'm not an anti-social hermit, just because I'm trying to maintain a professional distance from the customers that I rely on to keep the doors open," I argued. I'd long ago grown tired of having to turn down every sub who approached me, thinking their not-so-subtle advances would be the ones I couldn't resist.

"Bullshit, Jack," William spat out. "You and I both know why you withdrew into your office. I'm not gonna call you out on that because it sounds like—if you get your head out of your ass—things are starting to turn around. Now, you just need a little bit of help getting yourself on the right track. A wise man once told me that I'd be no good to my boy if I didn't take care of myself first."

"Sounds like a crock of shit if you ask me," I huffed. Man, having my own words thrown back at me sucked. Still, I knew my friend well enough to know that he wasn't going to let this drop. I slumped back on the couch and closed my eyes. "So, tell me, oh wise one, what are these rules you think I need in my life?"

"I'm glad you asked." William sat up straighter, scooting closer on the couch. "First, I want you to tell me which two days of the week I can come down here and not see your ugly mug. I don't want you sneaking in the back door. If I have to, I'll tell Sam to ignore you if you try calling him. You gave that boy a management position, now it's time for you to show him that you believe in his abilities to run this place in your absence."

"What if there's something that needs my immediate attention?" I argued.

"Nope, not going to get a loophole here, Jack. Keep pushing me, and I'll tell you to take a full week off just so you can detox."

My brow furrowed as I tilted my head to the side.

"You're an addict, Jack," William clarified. "Your drug of choice isn't alcohol, or anything illegal, but that doesn't make your vice any less harmful. And, lately, you're not even doing that very well."

"Gee, way to bolster a man's ego," I grumbled. "And I'm not a workaholic."

"Prove it," William dared me. "Call that boy of yours and take him somewhere special."

I barked out a laugh. No way in hell was that going to happen. If I couldn't stand the idea of having no contact with the club for a couple of days, there was no way I'd make it an entire week.

"Yeah, that's what I thought." William rested a hand on

my knee. "But don't worry, we will take baby steps until, eventually, you'll be able to take a much-needed vacation. Maybe once you prove to yourself this thing you're building with your boy isn't just a flash in the pan, you can take him up to the lake. You still have your house up there, don't you?"

Bile churned in my stomach. I did, but I wasn't sure why I held onto the place. After Colin left, I couldn't bear the thought of visiting the little lake house the two of us had bought as a getaway. It had been his suggestion, because he claimed I was addicted to work and needed a place where there was limited phone service and lousy internet, so I'd be forced to disconnect for a while. I had fought him, saying it wasn't necessary but, because I loved him, I had given in.

In the year after we bought the house, we'd only visited a few times and, in the aftermath, it felt like a tangible reminder that he had been pleading with me to pay attention to him. That I'd chosen this place over him. And, since then, I'd done everything in my power to convince myself I hadn't made the wrong decision.

"Don't do that shit," William scolded me. Bastard. He and Doug were the only ones who could see past my walls. He knew exactly what I'd been thinking. "You can't change how things went down with Colin. The only thing you can do now is decide if you're going to learn anything from losing him. Are you going to do things differently with this new boy, or are you going to dig in your heels, pointing at the past as evidence of why you don't deserve to be happy?"

"It's not that I think I don't deserve to be happy," I argued. "But with everything going on, it's not a good time."

"And that brings me to rule number two," William interrupted. "You, my friend, need to learn how to delegate more. Even on the nights when you are here, you have staff who can do a lot of the work. This place could run on autopilot if you'd just let it. You could be out here mingling. People miss you, Jack."

"I have been delegating," I countered. "Hell, I let Sam run with his ideas for turning some of the educational spaces into themed rooms. If that doesn't show I'm not a control freak, I don't know what does."

"Great, so you've got a start on that one." I paused, wondering what William thought when he looked across the building to the rooms that were currently closed off. Maybe I should have consulted with him before jumping in to change everything. While I didn't have to answer to him as the majority owner, it would have been courteous to at least talk to him first. Plus, he would be directly impacted if we had to change some of the programming he was in charge of. If he had any reservations, he didn't mention them. "Now you have no reason to hide away."

"You know damn well I do." I visibly shuddered at the thought of hanging out on a busy night. When I'd opened The Lodge, I hadn't realized the consequences of being out as a Daddy.

"So, bring your boy down here some night and a lot of your problems will go away," William suggested.

"How's that?"

"The boys want you because they all see how lonely you are." William flagged down Corey, holding up two fingers. It was a bit early in the day for a drink, but one wouldn't hurt. "Most of the boys who come here are dying to serve someone. They see your pain and they want to be the one to fix it."

"Bullshit." Corey approached, setting down two glasses of whiskey. It was undoubtedly from the private stash William didn't think I knew he kept hidden under the bar for after he'd finished playing for the night. I waited until Corey was safely back at his post before continuing. "They want me because I'm a status symbol to them."

"Think pretty highly of yourself, don't you?" William chuckled and shook his head.

"Are you going to tell me I'm wrong?" I crossed my arms over my chest, waiting for him to dispute me. The couple of times I did mess around with anyone I met here, they were more in love with the idea of me spoiling them rotten, or being able to tell their friends they were with me, than they were interested in what I was actually offering them.

William let out a loud sigh. "Whatever you say, man. Either way, they respect you enough that if you bring your boy down here, word is going to spread. And everyone knows you are a one boy Daddy. They may not like it, but they'll back off."

I had to admit, it wasn't a horrible plan. But, first, I needed to see where this thing between Slade and I was going. In order to do that, I needed to get my head out of my ass. And that meant finding time to talk to Slade this weekend. Waiting until Monday wasn't an option if I was going to prove he was a priority.

"About to unlock the doors, boss," Sam called out from the other side of the bar. "If you're going to make your getaway, now's the time. It's mixer night, and you know what that means."

I glanced over to William who was barely able to contain his amusement at my discomfort. Yeah, fine, he'd made his point. "Piss off. Just to prove you wrong, I might stay out and mingle tonight."

God help me.

"Yeah, I'll believe that when I see it," William replied.

"You've got to be one of the only kink club owners on the east coast who's repelled by the attention he receives."

"Again, piss off." I tipped back my whiskey, allowing the amber liquid to coat my tongue. I was going to need a little liquid courage, because no way in hell was I doing this stone sober.

14

SLADE

Being an adult was highly overrated. Three nights into having a "real" job and every muscle in my body ached. I had assumed working at Club 83 would be a cakewalk once Eli explained I would be a glorified gofer. After all, I had always done more than my share of loading and unloading equipment into the back of Jesse's van whenever we had gigs. That did jack shit to prepare me for hauling cases of beer from the storage room up to the bar at warp speed. Eli pulled me aside at one point to tell me it wasn't a race, but if this was the only job I could get, I was damn well going to prove I was the best bar back he had ever seen. Plus, Jordan and Max seemed to appreciate how quickly I retrieved whatever they hollered out they needed.

I glared at the sign taped to the front of the elevators in my building. It was too fucking late—or early—to deal with the stairs. What was four in the morning classified as anyway? Not nearly as much fun when you were getting off work as it'd be if you'd been out drinking, that's for damn sure. I had run my ass off for ten hours, and I was soaked in stale beer—thanks to a mishap on my way to the dish area.

All I wanted to do was stumble into my apartment and fall flat on my face. Was that too much to ask?

Apparently, it fucking was, because the cheap-ass owners of my shit hole building couldn't be bothered to fix shit when it broke.

With a resigned sigh, I trudged to the end of the hall, throwing open the door to the stairwell. On my trek up the stairs, I became painfully aware of muscles I wasn't even aware I had.

Did I mention I fucking hurt?

I let out a sigh of relief and tossed my head back when I reached my apartment. Less than a minute and I'd be able to get out of my damp, smelly shirt and the boots I needed to replace as soon as I got my first paycheck.

And just because the universe felt like kicking me squarely in the dick tonight, my key got jammed in the lock. I couldn't do a damn thing. A shower and my bed were just on the other side of the door, but I couldn't get there. I kicked the door hard enough to leave an imprint of my combat boot.

"Not like that's going to do a damn thing anyway," I muttered to myself. I took a step back twisting my fingers through my hair as I sucked in a few slow breaths. "Come on, man. Keep it together. It won't always be this bad."

I stepped forward, trying the lock again. Nothing. And now, the lock I'd reported no less than half a dozen times, was holding my keys hostage.

Fuck it. Maybe I didn't need a bed. If they couldn't maintain shit around here, I'd sleep in the hall. I fucking dared anyone to say a word. Hell, I hoped one of my busybody neighbors got the super down here, just so I could give the lazy fuck a piece of my mind. Yeah, that seemed like a damned good plan.

Mind made up, I slipped out of my hoodie before settling on the floor, knees pulled up to my chest. It was uncomfortable as hell, and I probably wouldn't be able to move tomorrow, but I was too damn tired to keep fighting with the door. And if I kicked in the door, which I probably could without too much effort, I'd have to worry about someone coming in snooping for shit to steal. The joke would be on them because, other than my TV and gaming system, I didn't have shit.

I yanked out the elastic holding back my hair, allowing it to fall around my face, shielding some of the sterile light from overhead. It wasn't long before I drifted off to sleep.

"WHAT ARE YOU DOING OUT HERE?" The deep, pissed voice sounded faintly familiar. I flipped to my other side, hoping he'd realize that was a stupid as hell question and leave me be.

I'd been wrong. Once I laid down and rolled my hoodie up like a pillow, sleeping in the hall wasn't all that uncomfortable. I swatted a hand in the air when I felt the toe of a shoe poking me in the ribs.

"Go away. Sleeping," I mumbled.

"I see that." The asshole who was trying to wake me actually fucking laughed. Ha-fucking-ha. Look at the little lost boy who can't even get into his apartment. Not in the mood for his judgment, I curled into a ball, silently pleading for him to give up and walk away.

"Slade." The voice was closer now. And with the way my name rolled past his lips, I knew instantly who'd caught me. I scrubbed a hand over my eyes, trying to wake up. "Come on, sweetheart. Wake up and tell me what happened."

When I opened my eyes, Jack hovered over me, his brow furrowed with either irritation or concern. I hoped for the latter, but given our few interactions, it was more likely the former.

"Couldn't get into the apartment. Stupid key got stuck in the stupid lock. I was too tired to fight with it," I explained. My brain was still foggy enough I struggled to form complete thoughts.

What god-awful time was it, anyway?

"Why didn't you call me?"

"Because it was four in the morning and I didn't think you'd want me bothering you with my problems?" My response came out as more of a question than an answer. It didn't make sense that he assumed I would wake him up in the middle the night for something like this.

"You figured wrong," Jack responded. He gently pushed me upright, and I watched as he slid down the wall next to me. When he draped an arm over my shoulder, I reflexively leaned into his side. His body was solid and warm. I didn't realize how cold I'd been until I felt the heat of his body searing mine.

"What are you doing here?"

"It's Monday," Jack responded as if that was any sort of explanation. I was still too damn exhausted for riddles. I lifted my head from his shoulder and scowled at him. "I told you the last time we saw one another that we would spend today together."

Was I supposed to admit I hadn't believed him? And when the few text messages I sent trying to strike up a conversation with him went unanswered, I had been even more certain his suggestion that we meet up after the weekend was simply a courtesy to keep me from realizing he was trying to ghost on me.

"I'm sure you have better things to do." I reached back and gathered my hair into a low ponytail. "Don't feel like you have to be here just because you made an off-handed comment about it."

"Wrong again, Princess," Jack responded. My eyes fluttered closed when he reached up to tuck a loose strand of hair behind my ear. I normally bristled when anyone called me that, but from Jack, it felt like a term of endearment. "One of these days, you are going to believe me when I tell you I don't do anything out of obligation. If I didn't want to be here, I wouldn't be. For that matter, if I hadn't been interested in seeing you again, I wouldn't have made plans."

"But why?" I wasn't even certain what I was asking him. So many things about this situation made zero sense. Why was he here? Why was he interested in me? What in the hell made me worth him showing up at ass o'clock on a Monday morning to hang out?

"Because there is something about you I can't ignore. All weekend, I wondered what you were doing and if you regretted last week." Jack grunted as he struggled to stand.

"Easy there, old man," I teased, hoping to ease the conversation away from all...this. He was the one who left my messages unanswered, not the other way around. If he was thinking about me, all he'd have had to do was pick up his damn phone. "Wouldn't want you out of commission."

Jack reached around, giving my ass a tight squeeze. "That's the last time you call me old," he warned me. "Next time, there will be consequences."

"Is that a promise?" I slid a hand up his chest to his shoulder, pressing my body against his, tilting my head back, silently begging him to kiss me.

Jack chuckled and shook his head. "As tempting as you

are, Princess, why don't we take this someplace a little more private?"

"You inviting me back to your place?" I glanced down at the keys still stuck in the lock of my door. "In case you forgot, I wasn't sleeping in the hall for shits and giggles."

Jack slipped around me, lifting up on the doorknob with one hand as he wiggled the key with the other.

"You're wasting your time," I informed him. He ignored me and gave the keys a tug. "I already tried that." Paying me no attention, he eased the key into the lock until it turned. At least, I thought I had tried everything. When the sound of the bolt sliding back echoed in the hall, I wasn't so sure. "How in the hell?"

Jack pressed his palm to my cheek, leaning in to kiss my forehead. "There's a lot you don't know about me, Slade. Just because I wear expensive suits and drive a fancy car doesn't mean I was born with a silver spoon in my mouth. He swung the door open wide, ushering me inside. "I lived in places even worse than this one until a few years after college."

I highly doubted that. I rolled my eyes as I passed him. Now he was just trying to make me feel better. Well, it wasn't going to work. All this morning had done was prove, yet again, how different we were.

"Think what you'd like, but I didn't get where I am by spending money like it's my last day on earth," he explained. "I knew from a young age that I wanted to make something of myself. To do that, I had to save every penny I could until there was enough to invest. Once I did that, I did it again and again."

I wandered into the kitchen, swiping the take-out containers on the counter into the trash can. Jack let out an audible sigh as he slipped past me. I couldn't look at him; I knew that noise. He left me on my own for one damn weekend and I'd started sliding back into bad habits. "Sorry. I..."

"Don't apologize to me, Slade. You're the only person you're letting down when you don't pick up after yourself," Jack told me as he reached for the can of coffee grounds as if he'd done it a million times before. "If we'd set rules before I left last week, then it might be a different story. The fact you feel guilty is quite telling though."

"How do you figure?" Since he'd taken over coffee duty, I was left feeling pretty damned useless in my own home. My brain was still foggy from too little sleep and too much work. Nothing he said seemed to make sense.

Jack finished setting up the coffee maker, not saying a word until it was brewing. He cupped my ass, lifting me onto the counter. When he stepped between my legs and tipped his head back to look at me, my breath caught. His lips were drawn into a tight line, but his gaze was soft. No one had ever looked at me like that, and I wasn't sure how it made me feel.

"I can't say for certain, but I have some ideas." I shivered when Jack ran his hands over my thighs. His thumbs stopped so damn close to my dick, I started to get hard. With anyone else, I would have tried goading him into getting off together, but I doubted Jack would give in as easily as the guys I'd fucked around with in the past.

"Like what," I asked. As I stared down at Jack, I was overcome with the urge to lean in and suck on his plump bottom lip. He kept exploring my body with his hands, his thumbs dragging over the now stiff fabric of my t-shirt. I might still be out of sorts and sleep-deprived, but, now that I was awake, I swore I could feel the stale beer dried on to my skin. I tried scooting away from him, but he dug his fingertips into my hips preventing my escape.

"Don't run, Slade," Jack pleaded. "I know this is all new for you, but I promise we will take things at whatever speed makes you comfortable."

"It's not that," I reassured him. "I'm just... All I wanted last night was to get into my apartment and take a shower. I may have had a little...incident with a bus tub and the swinging door. I probably smell disgusting."

When Jack buried his nose in the crook of my neck, taking a deep breath, I squirmed again, trying to get away. When he held me tighter, I swatted at his hand.

"Quit it," I scolded him. "I already know I reek like sweat and alcohol. I don't need to ruin the illusion by you knowing it, too."

"Princess, it's going to take a hell of a lot more than that to turn me off. No matter what you look like or how you smell, I'm still going to be completely caught up in you." He peppered a trail of kisses along the side of my neck.

"But why?" I repeated. Relationships were something I didn't have a lot of experience with, and, on paper, the very concept of Jack being this interested in me made zero sense.

Jack brushed his thumbs across my cheekbones. He leaned in, kissing the tip of my nose and then my forehead. He pulled out the elastic restraining my hair and began combing it with his fingers. "You are absolutely beautiful, for one thing." He slid his hands down my arms, tracing the tattoo on my forearm with a single fingernail. "You are a walking, talking contradiction. Pretty but masculine. Soft but strong. Guarded but needy. I want to break down the walls you constructed and show you just how amazing you are. I want to challenge you to be everything I'd be willing to bet someone in your past convinced you wasn't possible."

"You can't possibly know all of that this quickly," I scoffed. "You say this shit, but you don't really know me." It freaked me out that he was sitting here acting like I was an open book, just because he had seen me in a moment of weakness last week at the party. I liked to think I was better than that at hiding all the shit I didn't want anybody to know.

"Fair point," Jack conceded. "But that's what everyone faces when they begin pursuing someone. Unless you are entering into a relationship with someone you've been friends with for years, there are always secrets waiting to be revealed. All of the great romances in the world start with little more than a simple hello."

I stifled my laughter over the cheese factor of Jack's statement. He pursed his lips and narrowed his eyes, as if daring me to dispute him again.

"Fine." I let out a huff. "You win. But there have to be some rules here."

"I agree," Jack responded without hesitation. "I might be completely off base here, but I think that's why you were initially drawn to me. You are a free spirit, longing for someone strong enough to tether you to the ground. Everything you were ashamed of last week comes down to the fact you had no one holding you accountable. If you'll let me, I'd love nothing more than to be that man for you."

"Oh, you thought I meant rules for me?" I retorted. Again, I was trying to shift the focus off my own needs. The only thing worse, in my mind, than jumping into some sort of freaky power exchange relationship, was tipping my hand to show Jack how vulnerable I actually was. "No, I meant in general. For both of us. If we're doing this, I'm setting some rules of my own."

"Let's hear what you have in mind."

"Really?" I gaped at him when he turned away and started pouring two mugs of coffee. Then he opened the fridge, pulling out a package of pre-cut fruit. It didn't take a genius to figure out why his brow was creased and his lips were pursed when he turned back to me. I hadn't touched any of the food he'd bought. I scrubbed the back of my neck, my cheeks heating with embarrassment. "Sorry. It was a long-ass weekend, and I didn't have time to eat at home. By the time Eli let me out of there, I was dragging ass, so I just got something to go."

"While that may be convenient, it's neither the healthy option nor cost-effective," Jack scolded me, and I bristled. If these were the type of rules Jack planned on setting for me, I was going to have to rethink this entire arrangement. There was nothing sexy about him lecturing me as if he was my father. If I wanted that, I knew exactly where to go.

"True, but I'm pretty sure burning down my apartment because I am too tired to cook when I get home from work isn't the best idea either," I quipped.

Jack pulled another container out of the fridge, along with a carton of eggs, and started putting together breakfast.

Okay, now, this I could get used to. I didn't cook for myself because I was crap at it. But if Jack was volunteering for the job of being my personal chef, I could deal with some un-sexiness.

Unable to sit around and watch him do all the work, I hopped off the counter and started cracking eggs into a bowl. Even my limited cooking skills allowed me to do that much. I decided to see if we could get on with the boring stuff so that we might be able to lay down and take a nap after my belly was full.

"Tell me about these rules?"

"There will be time for that later, Princess."

"Are you gonna call me that forever?" I whined. As far as endearments went, it wasn't one I preferred.

"Would it bother you if I did?"

"That depends. I know I have long hair and fine features, but if it's some sort of backhanded jab because you think I am overly feminine, I am going to get pissed off in a hurry," I warned him.

Jack sat the knife down, and, before I had time to process what he was doing, he pinned me against the counter, his hips grinding against my ass. He forced a hand between my body and the lower cabinets, giving my dick a hard squeeze. I couldn't hold back the whimper when he bit the side of my neck. "I am completely aware of how much of a man you are, Slade."

"Then why call me your princess?" My voice was raspy and my breaths quick and shallow.

"Because it fits," Jack answered simply. "Is that okay with you?"

"I suppose."

"And you'll tell me if it's not at some point?"

"Yeah," I agreed breathlessly as Jack continued stroking me through my jeans. "I think I can do that." I allowed my head to fall back against Jack's shoulder. "Keep that up and you could get me to agree to just about anything."

Of everything I expected to happen next, Jack stepping away wasn't on the list. I was instantly chilled by the loss of his body against mine. I crossed my arms over my stomach, hugging myself tightly, trying to regain some of the warmth I'd felt. And I'd be lying if I said it was only physical temperature he made me feel.

"You're a damned distraction, you know that?" Jack picked up the knife and resumed swiftly chopping a green pepper. I didn't have the heart to tell him I couldn't stand most vegetables. Hell, knowing him, he'd take that as a challenge and load up whatever he was making with even more boring stuff.

"I like to think of that as part of my charm," I quipped. I chewed on my bottom lip, wondering how much I could get away with before I truly annoyed him. Since I was kind of digging having someone other than my own thoughts to keep me company, I decided against pushing my luck today. I picked up another egg and got back to work. "How many of these do you want me to crack?"

Jack craned his neck to peer into the bowl. "That should be plenty. Do you have a whisk?"

I let out an inelegant snort of laughter. "Oh, no. In case you haven't noticed, the kitchen isn't exactly a place I spend a lot of my time."

"We're going to have to see what we can do to change that," Jack remarked. "I need you to take care of yourself, Slade. I am a very needy, demanding man. You need to keep your energy up."

Well, now one part of me was up at least. I twisted slightly so my back was to Jack long enough for me to adjust myself. I pressed my palm against my erection, willing it to go down, since it was obvious Jack wasn't going to give me any relief.

"No," Jack scolded me. "None of that."

"Let me guess, another one of your rules?" Of course, it would be one of his rules. Hell, it was on the list of demands he made the morning after we met. I'd hated it then, and I had no doubt I was going to hate it even more now.

"That's right." Jack stepped up behind me again, brushing his knuckles against the front of my jeans as he nibbled on my neck. I brushed my hair out of the way and tipped my head, allowing him easy access. "I like to tease my boys. Sometimes, I might spend the entire day tormenting you without letting you come."

"Oh God," I groaned. My exhausted body went limp against his. "It's not fair for you to do this to me."

"Do you want me to stop?" He sucked on my neck hard enough there was a good chance I'd have a mark later. Good. I needed a reminder that this wasn't all a sexy dream if I woke up and he wasn't next to me.

"God, no," I sighed. "Don't ever stop."

"But I have to, sweetheart," Jack remarked. "You need something to eat and a few more hours of sleep. I don't have to be anywhere until tomorrow afternoon, so we have plenty of time."

"Don't need sleep," I protested. I turned in Jack's embrace, pressing my erection against his, as I cupped his ass. "The only thing I need is you."

"Then I suggest you behave, otherwise you're going to be a very frustrated boy by the time the sun goes down." Jack pressed his hand to my cheek, and I leaned into the contact. He bent down, brushing his lips against mine in a barely-there kiss. "If you behave, I promise I'll give you everything you want and more. But, until you show me that you're willing to take care of yourself, I'm going to make it my mission to force the issue."

"Such a buzzkill." There was no heat behind my words. I wasn't going to tell him, but it felt damn good to have someone care about me for a change. Sure, Jordan always worried about me, but even he hadn't seen how much I craved exactly what Jack had to offer. "So, tell me, Daddy, what are the rest of these rules you have for me?"

"It's quite simple, really," Jack explained as he whipped the eggs, then poured them into a pan I hadn't even realized he had heating on the stove. "For the time being, there will only be a few from my side."

While the eggs cooked, Jack leaned against the counter, stretching his legs out in front of him. I couldn't stop myself from staring at the bulge in his pants, my hole twitching as I remembered what it felt like to take him inside of me. Even holding back, that had qualified as some of the best sex of my life. I didn't want him to hold back next time. I wanted him to hurt me, leaving an imprint that would take a lifetime to fade.

"All I want is for you to promise you'll take better care of yourself," Jack explained. "That means no more take-out food. If you would like, I can help you put together some simple meals you can reheat when you get home at night."

I'd much rather live a different life, where I could come home to this sexy silver fox every night, and he would set me down at the table with a plate of food, watching me carefully until every bite was gone. The two of us could talk about our days as I ate, and then he would drag me into the bedroom to abuse me in whatever way he saw fit until both of us passed out.

"You also need to make sure you're getting enough sleep," he continued, oblivious to my erotic imagination. "I can't promise I'll have time for you every day, but whenever we're together, I want to know that you're well-rested and ready for whatever I want to give you."

"That sounds..." My voice cracked, and I had to clear my throat a few times. When that didn't work, I reached for my coffee mug, taking a long drink. "I..." Fuck. Why was it so hard to form a simple sentence? Words completely failed me. Instead, I nodded dumbly. "Yeah, I... That sounds good. Will you come and tuck me in at night when you aren't busy?"

"As often as I can," Jack promised solemnly.

Shit. I'd been joking, but he seemed deadly serious. I wasn't sure I had ever been tucked in, in my life. Even when I was little, my parents could hardly be bothered to get up from their places in the living room to say good night, much less read me a bedtime story and wish me sweet dreams.

"Fuck, why is that so hot?" It wasn't until I noticed Jack staring at me with sad eyes, that I realized I'd spoken the question out loud.

Jack turned off the burner and moved the eggs to the other side of the stove so they wouldn't burn. "I told you, Princess, whether or not you even realized it, you've been waiting for your prince to come and rescue you."

I opened my mouth to protest, but Jack silenced me with a fierce, demanding kiss. His tongue forced its way between my lips, exploring every inch of my mouth. By the time he was done, I couldn't even remember what we were talking about.

"I know you said you don't need saving, but you're wrong, sweetheart. I want to see you come to life in ways you never thought were possible. Even if this thing we're building doesn't last, I could die a happy man knowing I had some small part in you living a full life."

My nose itched and I felt my eyes beginning to water. No, I was not going to get emotional over this. I wasn't going to break down, just because a man cooked me breakfast and told me I was something special.

He was wrong. I was just Slade—the guy who fought growing up with everything he had. The man who hung onto his dreams until he risked losing everything when they didn't pan out.

Still oblivious to the turmoil in my mind, Jack started plating our food. He jerked his head to the side and led me into the living room. He settled onto the couch, and I sat on the floor next to him, leaning against his legs for support. I couldn't say why, other than it felt like this was where I was supposed to be. When I looked up and saw the reverent way Jack was looking at me, I knew I'd done something right.

15

JACK

Slade and I fell into bed after we finished eating. At one point, I worried I was going to have to spoon-feed him, or he was going to fall asleep and face plant into his plate. As soon as he finished the last bite, I propped him against the front of the couch long enough to wash our dishes. When I returned, his head was lolling to the side, and he could barely keep his eyes open. With little resistance, he allowed me to guide him into the bedroom.

When I stirred a few hours later, my boy was still sound asleep next to me. When I shifted to sit up so I could get some work done on my phone while he slept, he let out a frustrated grumble and burrowed deeper into my side. It was easy to imagine every morning spent exactly like this. But those fantasies were dangerous. Slade and I had yet to have a completely sober and well-rested conversation about what we were doing and what I expected of him. I was hoping that could come later today.

As I watched him sleep, I offered up a silent prayer that this wouldn't blow up in my face. I had let my guard down, and I was falling for him hard and fast. The kicker of it was, for the first time in my life, I wasn't sure I wanted to slow down or take a step back. With Slade, I wanted to race ahead at full speed, knowing damn well that the inevitable crash would kill me.

It was well after noon when Slade finally stirred. He scrubbed a hand over his face, blinking a few times. A smile like I had never seen from him, nearly split his face in half. God, he was gorgeous. I reached out and traced a finger down the center of his face. When Slade caught the tip between his teeth, sucking my finger deep into his mouth, I let out a low growl.

"Feeling feisty, sweetheart?" I gently lifted him up so I could roll onto my side.

"Have I been a good boy, Daddy?" Slade batted his long eyelashes dramatically, sucking his bottom lip between his teeth as he awaited my answer.

"You did take a nap without too much fuss," I pointed out. "Although, that may be more due to the fact that you were about ready to fall asleep while you were eating breakfast, than you were trying to behave." Slade scowled, shaking his head furiously.

"No, Daddy," he responded. I had to purse my lips to keep from laughing at the very serious look on his face. "I'm trying very hard to be a good boy. Do I get my reward now?"

I slid a hand along his side, loving the way he shivered at my touch, then dipped a hand under the waistband of his bright purple briefs. "What sort of reward were you hoping for?"

"Fuck me?" The uncertainty in his request had me hardening. My situation didn't go unnoticed, and Slade slid a hand over my dick. "I want to feel this inside of me again. You don't even have to get me ready. I like it rough."

"And what if I want to take my time with you?" I slid a

finger between his ass cheeks, pressing against his hole. "If you're going to be my new toy, shouldn't I play with every inch of you to see which is my favorite part?"

"Later, Daddy," Slade pleaded as he ground himself against my thigh, and I allowed just the tip of my finger past his entrance. I flipped Slade onto his stomach, yanking on his underwear. He lifted his hips, wiggling, as I stripped him naked.

"I want to take a good look," I told him. As I spread his cheeks wide, I allowed two fingers to slip inside. He winced in obvious discomfort. I gathered a pool of spit in my mouth and bent down, using my own fluids to provide some lubrication. Slade's body tensed when I pressed my fingers against his hole. He keened as I pushed inside without hesitation.

"Oh God, Daddy, please keep going. Give me more. Give me your dick." His rambling was adorable, and I was tempted to cave. Even Colin had never been this needy for my dick. He'd talked the talk, but I'd never felt like he was handing himself over to me completely. It was a role for him, where for Slade, it was who he was only beginning to realize he was at the core.

I pulled out and Slade whimpered at the loss. The bottle of slick wasn't where I'd found it last time, and I didn't have the patience to go on a scavenger hunt for it. "Where's your lube?"

"On the floor." He made a vague gesture toward the other side of the bed.

"Hold yourself open for me," I demanded. "I want to look at you."

"Do you have to?" he groaned, and I swatted his hip. "Sorry, Daddy. Whatever you want."

I bent down and bit his shoulder. "That's a good boy."

As quickly as possible, I grabbed the lube and coated my fingers as I climbed back onto the bed. "Do you have a condom?"

Slade let out a string of curses. Taking that as a no, I grabbed my jeans off the floor, hoping I'd remembered to put a new one in there after last time.

I let out a sigh of relief when I found what I needed. I sat back on the bed, studying the lithe body in front of me. He was gorgeous, and my body ached with the need to be inside him.

"Did you mean it when you said I didn't need to prep you, boy?" I asked as I tore open the packet. I'd prefer to make sure he was ready, but if the burn was something he needed, I'd give it to him. I was quickly realizing there wasn't much I *wouldn't* do for Slade.

"Just fuck me already," Slade begged.

To teach him a lesson, I delivered a series of fast, sharp blows to both sides of his ass. "How does a good boy ask, baby?"

"Please, Daddy," he begged, arching his back to stick his ass higher in the air. "I'll do whatever you want if you just get that dick inside of me."

"Show me how much you want me, Slade," I demanded. I knew he was uncomfortable with the request, but I was determined to help him through this. Slade reached around, clawing at the air as he tried to touch me. "Not like that, sweetheart. Show me that pretty little hole."

A flush crept over Slade's entire body. He buried his face in the pillow and groaned. He wasn't comfortable being on display, but I didn't care. It was time for him to realize every single inch of him was beautiful, including the parts that he was too embarrassed to show.

"I'll give you what you want as soon as you do the same."

I kneaded the flesh of his ass. It wouldn't have taken much for me to sit back on my heels, spread him wide, and stare at his hole until he squirmed. But I wouldn't, because I needed *him* to take the next step to prove he was on board with this.

"You're evil," he complained when I stood my ground. He dropped his shoulders to the bed and turned his face away from me as he reached back.

"Look at me, Slade." I ran a hand down the center of his back.

He shook his head, making his hair fan out, curtaining his entire face. That wouldn't do. I shifted to the edge of the bed, and carefully leaned over to grab a hair tie I had seen while I was grabbing the condom. I combed my fingers through his hair before, very carefully, pulling his locks back into a loose, low ponytail. My cock twitched, imagining all sorts of fun I could have with that. Eventually. But not right now.

"Let me see you, Slade."

"You've already seen too much," he protested. The words were so quiet, I wasn't sure I had been meant to hear them, but I had. I bent down, kissing the side of Slade's head. "You can trust me, baby. I won't do anything to hurt you."

It wasn't the first time I'd made that promise to him, and it wouldn't be the last. I'd repeat those words every single day if that's what it took to get Slade to trust me.

"Please," Slade begged.

I leaned in close to his ear so I could whisper, "You know what to do."

His hands visibly shook as he reached back again, this time spreading himself wide. I poured some more lube onto my fingers and dragged it through his cleft. His hole contracted as I got close. "This is such a hungry little hole.

You're going to make me come too fast if you keep that up."
He clenched, causing another tight contraction, and I was
left imagining what that squeeze would feel like around my
cock.

"Just means we can get into round two that much sooner," Slade quipped. I ran my finger around his hole, never
entering him. I'd given him a set of directions and, so far,
he'd only obeyed one.

"Come on, sweetheart," I urged him. My own tone was
growing impatient and needy. My balls ached with the need
to release inside of him, but I couldn't back down. I wouldn't
set the expectation in his mind that he could get away with
only obeying the commands he found pleasurable. "Look at
me, Slade. Let me see how much you like me toying with
you this way."

He slowly turned his head. His mouth hung open, and
he gasped for breath as I pressed a finger inside of him. He
offered me a crooked, sex-drunk smile, as I pushed deeper
inside of him, then his eyes drifted shut.

"Keep them open," I demanded. "Don't try to hide your
reactions from me."

"Can't help it," Slade admitted. "Feels too good."

"I'm sure it does. Are you going to hide from me
anymore?" Slade shook his head. "Say it, Slade."

My hands stilled as I waited for him to answer. Both of
us knew I wasn't only talking about him trying to turn away
from me while I fucked him. He was stripped bare at this
point, and it was time to start building him back up.

"I promise, Daddy." He reached out for me, and I
threaded our fingers together as I positioned myself on top
of him. He'd faced his fears, now it was time for his reward.

"Just like that, baby." I coated myself with a bit more
lube. He wasn't nearly as loose as I would have liked him to

be, but this was my way of showing him that I trusted him to know what he needed as well. He might learn to defer to me about a lot of things, but that didn't mean we weren't equals.

Slade cried out as the broad head of my cock stretched his hole. His entire body tensed.

"Breathe, baby. Breathe through the pain, and I'll make it good for you."

"Already is." Slade tugged on our still joined hands, pressing his lips to my knuckles." I can take all of you. I need to burn. Reminds me I'm alive."

My heart skipped a beat. From the very little I knew about Slade, I was sure he hadn't meant to say those words out loud. An ache formed in my chest as I wondered if there'd been a time when he had wished he wasn't alive. I hoped not, because I couldn't imagine a world without Slade in it.

I didn't pause as I shoved into Slade's body. He cried out, throwing his head back, muttering incoherently, then begging me to fuck him hard. I was already giving him more than I was comfortable with by fucking him without prepping him first, I wasn't about to rush things. Besides, I wasn't as young as he was. He might be ready for round two relatively quickly, but I knew that once I came, I was going to need the rest of the day to recover.

Slade never let go of my hand as we settled into a slow rhythm. Every time Slade tried to thrust back, I dug my fingers into his hip, holding him until he settled. Sweat dripped from my face to Slade's back. I rubbed the fluid into his skin, the first of many marks I would leave.

Slade's body vibrated with need beneath me. I shoved a hand between his body and the mattress, stroking him in time with my thrusts into his ass. "Such a good boy," I praised him. "Do you think you can hold out just a little longer?"

"Not... oh, shit... If you..." he stammered.

I buried my face in the crook of his neck to stifle my laughter. I loved the fact that I had rendered him completely incapable of coherent thought. I pounded into his ass harder—faster. My own release was so close. I jerked Slade faster, silently pleading with him to come. I had no doubt his muscles clenching around my shaft would get me the rest of the way there.

He cried out, throwing his head back as his ass strangled my orgasm out of me. Come coated my hand, slicking the way for me to keep fucking him with my fist as my body slammed against his ass. It only took a few more powerful thrusts before I screamed out, filling the condom with my seed. The aftershocks of Slade's orgasm milked the last of my release from me. I collapsed on top of him, worn out and unable to move.

Slade reached around, squeezing my ass, holding me tight against him. "Don't want to crush you, sweetheart."

"You won't," he assured me. "I am not as fragile as I look."

"Never said you were," I pointed out. "That doesn't change the fact that I've got at least sixty pounds on you."

"Stay there just a little bit longer," he pleaded. "Want to keep feeling you inside of me."

"One of these nights, I'm going to sneak into your apartment when I get done with work, and I'm going to take you while you sleep," I warned him. It was risky telling him about some of my darker, more twisted fantasies, but Slade deserved to know what he was getting into with me.

"Only if you promise you'll fall asleep with your dick still inside of me."

My eyes shot open. If I didn't know better, I'd think this was some elaborate hoax. No way in the world did someone this perfectly suited for me exist.

"You want to be my cock warmer, sweetheart?" I held my breath, worried I'd pushed him too far.

"Is that what it's called?" I wrapped my arms tightly around Slade's torso, dragging him with me as I rolled to my side. He held on tighter, as if he was as reluctant as I was to break the physical bond between us. "Is that something you like, Daddy?"

"It is," I admitted quietly. As we lay there together, coming down from the high of our orgasms, I kissed my way along Slade's shoulder. "You make me want things I've kept locked away for a long time, baby. I know this is all new and confusing for you, but you have to know it's just as out of character for me."

Slade shifted his upper body slightly, craning around to try to look at me. "How so?"

"There are so many things I've wanted to explore, but I had convinced myself I would never find anybody interested in the same things," I admitted.

"Like what?"

"This, for one thing." I gave a gentle thrust into Slade's ass. It was far more intimate than sexual. "I don't know that I've ever just laid with a man after we got off. Most of the time, my partners have wanted to get cleaned up as quickly as possible."

Slade let out an irritated huff.

"Something wrong, sweetheart?"

"Hasn't anyone ever told you it's bad form to talk about past lovers when your cock is still buried in somebody's ass," he scolded me.

"Right you are," I agreed. "But you asked, and it felt important that I be honest with you."

He gave my hand a squeeze. "Thank you for that, I guess."

I laced our fingers together and rested our joined hands on Slade's hip. "What's something else you want to try but you never have? If you're trying to show me all these new things, it's only fair that I try and be your first something."

It was on the tip of my tongue to tell Slade that he already was so many firsts for me, but I didn't want to ruin the moment.

"I'll have to think about that a little bit," I told him. "For now, this is plenty."

"And maybe the whole sneaking into my room to fuck me while I sleep," Slade added. "That sounds hot as hell."

"Yeah? You don't think it's weird?"

"No weirder than you sitting there, on your phone, watching me while I sleep," Slade quipped.

"If you'd prefer, I can stop that, too."

"No way," Slade protested quickly. "Otherwise, you'll get up and go out to the other room when you wake up before me. I don't like that idea at all. I sleep better when you're next to me, keeping me warm."

"Noted. Then I suppose you'll have to deal with me watching you sleep when we nap together and fucking you awake when we don't."

"Damn, such a hardship," Slade teased, draping an arm dramatically over his eyes. "However will I survive?"

As nice as it was lying next to Slade, still joined with my cock inside of his ass, the cum drying on his skin couldn't be comfortable. I wrapped a hand around the base of my cock as I pulled out of him. He whimpered, digging in his fingers, trying to force me to stay inside of him.

"I'll be right back, sweetheart. I'm going to show you so much attention, you'll soon be sick of me."

"Not fucking likely," he muttered as I walked out of the room. Those words were music to my ears. I wanted him to be as needy for me as I was for him.

16

I hated Jack for all the ideas he put into my head. Every night I went to bed hard, hoping that would be the night Jack snuck into my room like he promised, waking me with his fingers pressing inside of me, readying me for his cock. I even made sure to clean myself, no matter how tired I was, wanting to make sure the experience was as good for him as it was for me. And yet, here we were, almost a month in and he had yet to deliver on his kinky suggestion of getting started while I was still asleep.

It was, yet, another night I was sitting home alone. Jack was busy with the renovations at The Lodge, and, now that all of the work Eli had been putting off until he had time to tackle it was finished, I was bored out of my mind. Eli had never promised me full-time hours, and I considered myself damn lucky that he'd given me as much work as he had. Now, I was down to working three nights a week, which left at least one night alone every week while Jack was at the club.

I shuffled around the apartment, trying to find anything I could to clean. There wasn't anything out of place, because

I had made it a point to clean up every day. Just one more way I was changing to try and keep Jack happy. I didn't want him to have any reason to find me lacking. So much for never compromising my independence for the sake of a lay —no matter how hard he rocked my world.

I loaded up a first-person shooter game on my console, but my mind kept racing and I was unable to concentrate. After the fourth time my character was killed, I tossed the controller to the other end of the couch and eased my way onto the floor. I reached under the couch, quickly finding what I was looking for. I pulled out the notebook Jack had brought me about a week after we decided to see where things went. He'd been shockingly cool with me setting rules for him, too.

When pressed, I hadn't been able to think of many, other than no radio silence. I didn't cope well when I felt ignored. I'd added at least one day a week that was for us, because I'd wanted to see if he'd agree or not. He had and, since then, every Monday was spent together. We usually did boring stuff, like grocery shopping, but he always made it worth my while to not whine.

"You're an artist, sweetheart," Jack had pointed out, handing me a small gift bag. Inside, I found a bound note-book and a set of pencils.

"I think you may be confused about what type of art I create." These looked better suited for someone who couldn't help but sketch whatever inspired them the moment the mood struck. Calling it creating was almost as much of a stretch as claiming I was a songwriter. Mostly, I sat around my dark apartment, bleeding out onto the paper. I wasn't even sure most of my shit was all that good. Lord knew we never even got a tenth of the response when we played my original songs as we had covering other's hits.

"Don't sell yourself short. No, you don't draw, but that doesn't mean you aren't making art. I want you to start spending a few minutes a day writing something. Maybe the words turn into songs, maybe they don't, but you'll never know if you don't put the pencil to the page. And for your information, I chose pencils instead of pens because you're bound to make mistakes and need to go back to fix things."

Holy shit, he'd really thought about this. The lump in my throat made it hard to breathe. Jack guided me into the living room. He sat back at one end of the couch, grabbing the remote, but he didn't turn on the TV immediately. Instead, he watched me, waiting to see what I would do. I settled at his feet the way I almost always did. I stared at the bag, scared to take out the gift he brought me. Would he expect me to show him? Would he check up on me to make sure I was writing every day? That had never been the way my mind worked. It truly was an emotional outlet for me, nothing more.

At the time, I'd thought it would be impossible to write every day, but, again, I seemed weak to push back when Jack added a new rule to my list. Most days, I pulled out the notebook from where I kept it hidden and set a timer for myself.

I flipped through the pages, reading over lines that only I had seen. I worked through both lyrics and melodies, scribbling a few notes in the margins of the pages. So far, I hadn't worked up the courage to pull out my guitar. If I put the pieces together, I'd want to play for Jack, and I worried he'd pressure me to talk to Eli about playing at the club. But, damn, if I didn't want to play for him and face whatever challenge he threw down for me. Even if I never made music from a stage again, I longed to perform for an audience of one. I wanted to say to him through a song everything I couldn't bear to say directly to him.

But it was too soon, wasn't it? A month wasn't long at all, especially for someone who spent as much time as I had insisting that he would never get trapped in a relationship. I was just getting into the second verse of a new song when I heard my phone ringing from the bedroom.

Before Jack, I would have ignored the noise and continued working. Now, I hopped up, racing through the apartment. My heart faltered a little when I saw a ridiculous selfie of Jordan staring back at me.

I shouldn't feel that way about my best friend calling, and now my insecurity had been replaced by a heaping dose of guilt. I'd given Jordan a piece of my mind when he had ghosted me for the two men he now lived with in some sort of freaky triad relationship. I didn't get how you were supposed to make a relationship work with two people, much less more than that, but it worked for them so who was I to judge?

"Hey man, what's up," I answered.

"Eli gave me the night off," Jordan informed me. "He said I should call you and see if you wanted to hang out."

"Way to make a guy feel pathetic," I grumbled. I knew he hadn't meant anything by it, but the fact that one of his partners had to suggest we spend some time together was an indicator that we were drifting from one another. That sucked. I didn't want to think a day might come when Jordan and I were just coworkers. "You know, there once was a time when the two of us were inseparable, J. What happened?"

"We fell in love," he responded. With the wistful tone in his voice, it was hard to not imagine little hearts floating in the air over his head. He was lost for them, but me? Nope. Not going there.

"Speak for yourself," I retorted.

"You can try and deny it all you want, but you and I both know damn well you are gone for Jack." I wished Jack and Doug weren't brothers. I wanted to be able to talk to my best friend about my issues with the relationship we were building, but it didn't feel right to talk to Jordan when he was sleeping with the brother of the man that I was completely hopeless for.

And I was, wasn't I? As much as I swore it would never happen to me, I truly loved Jack. I hated when Jordan was right.

"Are you still with me, Slade?"

"Shit. I must've zoned out. What were you saying?"

"I was telling you to get dressed. I'll be there in twenty and we're heading down to The Ginger."

"Do we have to?" I hadn't been to The Dandy Ginger since the night of the band's last show. We'd always considered that to be our home base of sorts, and I worried going back there would put my head in a bad place.

"Come on, Slade. You can't avoid it forever. I know things have been tough since the band split up, but it's time for you to show everyone they're not going to keep you down."

"Have you been moonlighting as a motivational speaker," I teased. Jordan had always maintained a sunny outlook, with the notable exception of right after he and Tyson split up, but even that had turned out in his favor. During a very brief pity party, he had managed to snag himself two sexy daddies who would kill for him.

And thanks to them, you found one of your own, the voice in the back my head reminded me.

Fine, so maybe I should take Jordan's advice and get back on the horse, so to speak. I was also nervous about heading back there, because I had spent years relentlessly pursuing Rusty—the slightly overweight, sexy in an unconventional way, owner of the bar. I wasn't sure I trusted myself to tone down the flirtation now that I was in a relationship. And how would I respond if he asked me to fool around? He'd been the object of my obsession for so long, I worried I would cave.

Yeah, fat chance that would ever happen, the voice in my head scoffed. *If he had wanted you, he would've taken you up on one of the hundreds of times you propositioned him.*

My conscience wasn't wrong, but I wasn't sure I was strong enough to turn him down.

"You're starting to worry me," Jordan said, interrupting my freak out. "Twenty minutes, Slade. Don't try and weasel your way out of this. We're going to go out, I'm going to repay you for the last time when you got me utterly shit-faced, and you're going to tell me what's got you tied up in knots."

"Fine. But could we skip the getting shitfaced part?" Knowing my luck, the night Jack decided to sneak into my apartment, would be the night I was too wasted to get it up. No thank you. No night out with a buddy was worth missing out on that.

"We'll see. No promises. Twenty minutes." Without giving me a chance to say anything else, Jordan disconnected the call. I walked across the bedroom and started rummaging through my dresser, trying to find something decent enough to be seen in public without looking like I was on the prowl. I opted for a pair of skinny jeans and an oversized hoodie with my combat boots. Comfortable, with the casual air of having put no thought into the evening.

As I finished getting dressed, my stomach churned. Jack hadn't set any rules about whether I was allowed to go out with friends, but, for some reason, it didn't feel right going out without him knowing. But what would it say if I texted him to get permission, and that wasn't something he expected of me? Every time I felt like I had a firm grasp on how relationships like this worked, something came up that threw me into a tailspin.

I heard the front door open and my heart leaped. For a second, I thought maybe Jack had taken the night off work so we could spend time together, and I wouldn't be subjected to the inquisition from Jordan. When my best friend's form appeared in the hall outside my bedroom, my shoulders slumped forward. I really shouldn't be upset about spending the night with him, but dammit, I missed my Daddy.

"While that's certainly a look, I think you'd be more comfortable if you were wearing both boots," Jordan quipped. I looked down at my feet and realized that, yes, I was only wearing one boot. Fuck. I really needed to get my shit together. Jordan quickly crossed the room, grabbing me by my shoulders, and leading me over to the bed. "What's wrong, Slade?"

"You'll think I'm stupid," I muttered.

"I promise, I won't. You can talk to me about anything, you know that." I nodded, because Jordan has always been the one person who I could say anything to without worrying about his reaction. And it wasn't like I had to worry that he'd think my relationship with Jack was perverted or disgusting.

"I'm old enough that I should know how these things work."

"What things would those be?" Jordan asked as he sat next to me at the end of the bed. He draped an arm over my shoulder, and I leaned into his side. He used to be the more tactile of the two of us, but ever since that first night with Jack, I found myself craving a physical connection.

"Relationships," I clarified.

"Well, even if you understood how normal relationships worked, I'm pretty sure that's not what you and Jack have, is it?" I shook my head. "So why don't you tell me what it is that has you upset, and, if I can, I'll help you work through it. I'm not an expert by any means, but I've gotten to know Jack a bit, and I do know two other demanding Daddies."

"He set these rules for me," I explained. "And they help, but sometimes they confuse me, too."

"What sort of rules?" I could hear the amusement in Jordan's voice.

"Not those kinds of rules, you freak," I teased him. I sagged deeper into Jordan's embrace. "Honestly, I think it'd be easier for me to deal with if he'd told me I had to wear a cock cage every damn day. Instead, he tells me shit like he expects me to eat real food, get a good night of sleep, and other boring shit. The worst part is, I dig it. I never understood it before, but I'm starting to see why you like it when Doug and Eli take charge."

"Nope," Jordan scolded me. "You're not changing the subject on me now. What exactly is it that has you pale and staring at your phone like it's going to explode in your hand?"

"I never used to give a shit what anyone thought, and I liked not having to answer to anyone. But, as I was getting ready, I wondered if I'm supposed to text Jack to let him know I'm going out." My cheeks burned, and, even though I knew Jordan would understand, I couldn't bring myself to look at him. I'd have given anything for this to not be so fucking complicated. "Do I need to ask him if it's okay?"

"Well, I suppose it depends on if that's something you want from him," Jordan responded. "I mean, it's not something that's for everyone, but there's also nothing wrong if you want to give him that sort of control."

"But I've never been the type to ask permission," I reminded him.

"Just because you haven't in the past doesn't mean you can't in the future. Tell me this, would it make you feel better if you texted Jack to ask him if you could hang out with me tonight?" He waited a few beats before adding, "I promise, I won't think any less of you if you say yes."

I shrugged, considering my answer. Hell, Jordan was here tonight because one of his Daddies suggested to him that we hang out. It wouldn't really be that much different if I texted Jack to see if he was okay with me going out to the bar tonight.

"I mean, sort of," I finally admitted. "Is it wrong that part of me wants him to say I can't go to certain bars anymore?"

"I'm starting to understand what this is all about." Jordan gave my shoulder a squeeze. "It's not about the band, is it?"

I shook my head. "I haven't done this relationship thing before, Jordan." It sucked to admit that, even to my best friend. "What if I go into The Ginger and everything is like it used to be?"

"The fact you're even thinking like that, tells me you have nothing to worry about, Slade."

"How can you be so sure?"

Jordan placed a hand over my chest. "Because as much as you try to hide from everyone else, I know you. You have an amazing heart. In fact, I think that's why you always shied away from relationships."

I bent forward at the waist, wringing my hands through my hair. God, what was it with everyone thinking they knew what I thought and felt?

Jordan started rubbing my back. "Relax, Slade. You put up all these walls to try and keep everybody out because you think it's easier that way. The man who stood on that stage, flirting with bars full of people, wasn't the real you."

"Then who in the hell am I?" Everything I thought I'd known about myself had vanished over the past few months, and now Jordan was implying that wasn't me at all. That was a hard pill to swallow.

"Don't you think it's about time you find out?" Jordan and I might have been the same age, but sometimes it seemed like he was much older and wiser than I was. Maybe that was the result of him not being emotionally stunted, despite the string of failed relationships he had before he finally found one that worked for him.

"How am I supposed to do that?"

"For starters, we're going down to The Dandy Ginger, no matter how much you think it's a bad idea," Jordan informed me. "You're going to take a seat at the bar, and you'll see Rusty. That much is inevitable. But if I know you half as well as I think I do, you aren't even going to be tempted to flirt with him. You know damn well that you've got a good thing going with Jack. Hiding from the rest of the world isn't going to help you preserve that relationship. The only thing you can do is go out there and pass every test you face."

"Fine, but if I start doing anything stupid, you have to promise me you'll yank me out of there."

Jordan gathered my hair, twisting it around his hand. I winced when he gave it a playful, sharp yank. My scalp was still tender from last night, when Jack used my hair as leverage while he fucked my face. "You don't even have to ask. I've been keeping you from getting into trouble since we were kids. And, seeing as you're dating a guy who's like family to me, you can bet I won't let you screw up."

I leaned my head on Jordan's shoulder. "Thanks, man. I probably don't say it as often as I should, but I appreciate you."

"No thanks needed." Jordan picked up my phone and handed it to me. "Text him. The only way he's ever going to know what you need is if you show him."

"And you promise it doesn't make me pathetic to ask him permission to go out for the night?"

"Hell no! I love it when Doug and Eli boss me around. I think you do, too."

"No, Eli telling me what to do is annoying as hell," I quipped. Jordan rolled his eyes. "Fine, maybe I get what you're saying."

I tapped out a quick message to Jack.

Jordan wants to head down to The Dandy Ginger for a drink. Is that okay with you?

I stared at the phone while I waited for Jack's response. What would I do if he had left the phone in his office and he was busy dealing with something at work? Now that I had asked him for permission, it didn't seem right to leave my apartment without his blessing. The minutes dragged by and I grew uneasy. What if he wasn't responding because he didn't want this level of control over me? What if our power exchange was something he preferred to keep confined to private spaces?

That's fine, Princess.

I couldn't help but smile when his response finally came through. Jordan leaned over, trying to see Jack's response, and I turned the display away from him. I didn't want him knowing that I allowed Jack to call me Princess, when I would have kicked the shit out of anyone else for doing the same. Then, another text message came through.

I want you to make sure you limit yourself to three drinks.

Before I could even read his response, two more appeared.

And I expect you to be home and in bed by midnight.

I shouldn't have to stay here too late. Will you be a good boy for me?

And now I was supposed to head out for the night with my dick pressing against the front of my jeans. It would be wrong to ask Jordan to give me a few minutes so I could rub one out quick, right? Right.

Besides, Jack hadn't given me permission to touch myself, so there was nothing for me to do but hope and pray this erection wouldn't last the entire night. We were almost to the front door when I realized I had never responded to Jack's last message. As we walked down to Jordan's car, I pulled my phone out of my pocket and tapped out a quick message.

I'm always a good boy, Daddy. It just depends on if you catch me or not.

I stowed my phone after that, committed to giving Jordan my attention tonight.

There was so much the two of us needed to catch up on. It seemed like ever since I'd started working at Club 83, we hadn't spent much time outside of work together. There wasn't the same need to connect with him because we saw one another several nights a week, but, at the same time, we couldn't hang out while we were on the clock.

"Things still going well with the three of you?" I asked as Jordan maneuvered his way through remnants of rush hour. For some reason, traffic never seemed to die down until after eight o'clock at night, probably because so many people commuted from Annandale into the city.

"Yeah," Jordan responded with a dopey grin on his face. "I know you don't understand it, but the three of us are good together. It's not something I ever would've imagined for myself, but now that I have the two of them, I can't imagine my life any other way. Part of me thinks the reason my past relationships failed was that I was never meant to be with just one person."

"No, your other relationships failed because you have horrible taste in men," I teased him.

With the exception of Tyson, who wasn't a complete dickhead, Jordan had a tendency to fall for all the wrong guys. It had been hard for me to be a good friend and keep my mouth shut when yet another bag of dicks walked out of his life. Even with Tyson, I had known long before either of them had, that it wasn't going to last. The two of them were completely different and deserved to be happy, which wouldn't have happened if they had stayed together.

"Not always," Jordan protested.

"You're right. A few of them weren't total losers," I conceded. "And you did pretty damn good by yourself in the end. Speaking of, have you heard from Tyson at all?"

The last boyfriend he had packed up all of his shit and moved to the mountains for some sort of crunchy granola research project. The dude was a total nerd. But I knew Jordan had wanted to stay friends with him, even though they couldn't make it work as lovers. This was me trying to be a supportive friend.

"Yeah, he's doing pretty good now. He might be coming back in a few months."

"And how do you feel about that?"

"Now who's the one playing armchair therapist?" Jordan

asked. I cocked my head to the side and lifted an eyebrow. "I feel fine about it. Sometimes, it feels like being with him was this whole other life. He's solidly in my past. Doug and Eli are the only men I want to be with now."

"Good. I'm glad to hear that."

"And what about you?" I knew it was too much to hope that we would keep talking about his relationship. "Are things with you and Jack getting serious now?"

I shrugged. Honestly, it felt serious as hell to me, but I wasn't exactly a good judge of things like that. And Jack was almost too careful about not rushing me into putting a label on our relationship. Either that, or he was just as scared as I was that what we shared was a fling that couldn't stand the test of time.

"I like him, Jordan," I admitted. I swallowed around the lump in my throat. This was my chance. I'd been bemoaning the distance with my friend, and I could bridge that gap now. I trusted him; he wouldn't run home and share everything we talked about with his men. I blew out a long breath, working up the courage to ask the question that had been bothering me. "How do you know when you are falling in love with someone?"

"That's one of those questions that I don't think has a right answer. Being in love is different for everyone. And even falling in love with one person isn't necessarily the same as falling in love with someone else. Believe me, I've had enough experience with thinking I was in love to know it's always thrilling and terrifying at the same time. Do you really think you might be in love with him?"

"Don't know. I don't exactly have the best role models in my life, you know?"

"I get it, man." Jordan reached across the console and

squeezed my knee. "But just because your parents were bitter and felt stuck with one another, doesn't mean every relationship winds up that way. They're idiots to stay together because both of them want the other one to bail first. It's like watching a game of chicken; you know it's going to suck at the end, but they're too damn stubborn to spare themselves."

"But how do I know the same won't happen with Jack and me?"

"Listen, you might not have shining examples of what a good relationship is supposed to look like, but you know better than a lot of people what a shady one looks like. I have faith you will get out before it gets that far."

I was glad one of us did. I already felt so dependent on Jack, I wondered if it would be possible for me to walk away from him, or if I would stay just so I wouldn't have to go back to the lonely, miserable existence I had before he dragged my drunk ass home that first night.

Jordan parked down the street from the bar, and the two of us bypassed the line. Maybe we shouldn't have, because it wasn't exactly a busy night, but if I could still get away with a quick handshake for the bouncer and not have to sit out here in the freezing cold, I'd be an idiot to wait with everyone else.

My ass had barely hit the stool when I noticed Rusty making a beeline for us. I stiffened when he threw his arms around me. "Good to see ya, Slade. I was afraid we'd seen the last of you when you hightailed it outta here."

"Yeah, sorry about that." The rest of the band had wanted to close down the bar for old time's sake, but I hadn't been in a mood for reminiscing. Everyone else was moving on with their lives, and, at the time, the only thing I had felt was anger and bitterness because they were all going home to these great lives that they were building, and I had, once again, been cast aside.

"You don't ever need to apologize, Slade," he told me. "Just promise me you aren't going to pull another Houdini on me. Hasn't been anyone around trying to inflate an old man's ego since you left."

"I hate to break it to you, Rusty, but..." I eased myself out of his embrace. Jordan was right. I had zero desire to flirt with Rusty. It wasn't that I found him any less attractive than I had in the past, but who needed him when I had Daddy waiting until the end of his shift so he could come over and make sure I hadn't disobeyed him.

"Holy shit! Are you seriously saying you finally found someone willing to tame your needy ass?" Rusty's arms dropped to his sides as he took a step back. His gaze traveled over my body and he chewed on the corner of his bottom lip.

My hole clenched as I remembered all the ways Jack had tamed me over the past month. My ass was definitely not deprived of attention. And, with any luck, in a few hours, I'd be able to bare my hole for him again as I begged him to fill me.

"Guess I'll have to find me a new boy to treat me like I'm the rock star."

"Don't worry, Rusty," Jordan said. "Just because Slade's finally settling down doesn't mean there aren't plenty of single boys waiting for you to notice them."

"That's kind of you to say, but we both know it's a lie." Rusty's shoulders slumped forward, and I couldn't help but wonder if I'd misread the cues from him during the years I'd spent playing weekend gigs here. Maybe he had wanted me to keep goading him until he caved. "No one wants a grumpy old man who's already married to his work."

Peace settled over me when I realized it didn't matter if Rusty's intention had been for me to keep working at him until he gave in. If I had ever pursued anything with him, beyond some shameless flirting at the bar, I might not have been available when my path crossed with Jack's. And I wouldn't trade him for anything.

With that knowledge in the back my mind, I settled onto my stool and flagged down the bartender while Jordan and Rusty bantered back-and-forth. For almost as long as I had been trying to get in Rusty's pants, Rusty had been trying to get Jordan to leave Club 83 and work the bar at The Dandy Ginger. My friend was something of a big deal in the local bartending circles. He would deny it, but the bar owners all wished he'd work for them because customers would follow.

A few minutes later, Jordan took the stool next to mine. He gave my shoulder a quick squeeze. "See, I told you there was nothing to worry about."

"You were right." I took a long draw off the bottled beer I was nursing. If I was only allowed three drinks, I needed to pace myself. "Is it wrong that part of me wants to go home now and wait for Jack to get done with work?"

"Not at all," Jordan reassured me. "Because as soon I know the two of us have hung out long enough that Eli won't lecture me, I plan on heading home so my Daddies can reward me for being a good boy, too."

I chuckled and shook my head. Who would've thought this is where the two of us would have wound up? Now, I just needed to touch base with Jack and make sure he and I were on the same page, because I didn't want him for just a month or two. As much as it scared the ever-living shit out of me, I wanted to be Jack's boy for as long as he'd have me. Maybe even forever.

17

JACK

"So, when are you going to bring that boy down here so we can warn him all about you?" William teased as we worked to set up for tonight's exhibition. He hadn't given me many details about it, other than to say it had to do with the renovations Sam was spearheading. This was all part of his initiative to make me ease up on the reins, but he still swore he wasn't interested in officially working for me. Over the past week or two, I'd started understanding a few of his motivations, but I wasn't going to call him out on it just yet. "Hell, you could give him a call and tell him to get his cute little ass down here tonight. You never know, this might be right up his alley."

"He's working," I told him. I was so damn proud of Slade for how much effort he was putting in at Club 83. Had I known he was that hard of a worker, I might have suggested he come to work for me instead. But, at the time, I'd been worried it would be awkward if things between us didn't work out. Now, he was doing a great job working for my brother-in-law, and it would be a dick move to try and poach him.

"And even if he wasn't, I'm not sure he'd be comfortable here. He can be a bit cagey at times." Skittish was more like it. He wasn't as bad as he used to be, but, from what I'd gathered, it seemed his self-esteem had taken one hell of a hit when the band split up. He'd gone from a man who confidently stepped onto a stage every weekend, to a pile of shattered remnants worried about what everyone thought of him.

"And what?" William handed me two boxes before pointing toward the opposite side of the room. "The Jack I know loves nothing more than nudging boys out of their comfort zones."

That was true, but, no matter how many nights I spent in Slade's uncomfortable bed, I couldn't bring myself to change what we were doing. Things were working for us. As long as I didn't force him into anything, I didn't have to worry about him taking off.

"Oh, hell no," William spat out. "Do not tell me you're going soft because of this boy."

"It's not like that," I argued.

.   .   .

"OH REALLY? Then call him and tell him to get his ass down here once he's done with work. What does he do, anyway?" William crouched to start unpacking a stack of boxes. I took a step back and watched as he created mini scenes around the room. This was genius. I still wasn't sure how many would show up, but he was doing a damn good job to show that age play was more than diapers and binkies. Hell, maybe there could be something here for Slade. I still wasn't convinced he wouldn't find peace in a bit of regression. The boy had bratty Middle written all over him.

"He's working for Eli. He and Jordan are good friends, and Jordan helped him get the job there." It felt important to me to explain that, before William could jump to any conclusions about me trying to keep distance between my relationship and my business.

"BETTER YET. You know damn well that if you call Eli, he'll let the boy off."

"HIS NAME IS SLADE," I ground out. I didn't like anyone referring to him by such a generic term. He wasn't some nameless, faceless plaything. He was the center of my universe. "And I'm not going to meddle. It's important for him to prove that he can make it on his own."

I THOUGHT back to that first morning, when he had gotten pissed off at me for ordering groceries when I realized he didn't have any. I admired his determination to hold onto his independence. In some ways, it made his submission that much sweeter.

. . .

WILLIAM THREW the books he was unpacking into a sloppy pile and rounded on me. "This is what I'm talking about, Jack. You're going to sit there and get all worked up about me not calling him by his name, but you haven't bothered to bring him around so the rest of us can meet him. Sure, I might've joked around about wanting to warn him about you, but it's more than that. If this thing is real, and it must be if you're this twitchy, you need to bring him down here. Let your friends meet the man who's brought you back to life."

"BOTH OF US ARE BUSY," I offered as a weak excuse.

HE'S NOT, the voice in my head pointed out. *He sits home every night he isn't scheduled and you're here. It'd be easy for you to ask him to come down and see you.*

"WHEN WAS the last time the two of you went out and did something?" William asked as he went back to sorting the picture books. "This is exactly the type of shit that got you in trouble with Colin. We all stood by then, but I'll be damned if I'm going to watch you destroy what has the potential to be a very good thing because you're married to this place."

"THAT'S NOT WHAT WE DO." I swallowed around the lump in my throat. I wanted to be pissed at William for being so blunt, but that's just who he was; he wouldn't tell me what I wanted to hear. "And this isn't like Colin at all. We spend every Monday together, sometimes Tuesdays, too. And most nights, we try and make time for each other. I promise I'm not ignoring him."

"So, what do you do when you're spending all this quality time with him?"

"We mostly hang out at his place," I explained. "When I have to work late, I'll head over once I leave. He gave me a key to his place because I hated the idea of waking him up."

Among other reasons...

"That's not a relationship, Jack. That's a fucking booty call and you know it." I scrunched my nose, and then my stomach turned because William had gotten too close to the truth. Not that Slade was someone for me to call when I wanted to get laid, but that was how I was treating him.

"I really hate you sometimes."

"No, you don't." William groaned as he stood. "You love me because you know I'll never blow sunshine up your ass. I'm probably one of the few people who isn't afraid to call you out on your bullshit, other than Eli. Does that mean you're going to bring him down here?"

. . .

I SHOOK MY HEAD. Part of me was trying to shelter him. A lot of the boys who hung out here were shallow, jealous little shits, and I didn't want him subjected to their cattiness when they found out he had something they couldn't.

WILLIAM NOTICED MY DISCOMFORT, and added, "Otherwise, you could invite a few friends over to your place if you think that would be easier for him."

"No, you're right. I think about bringing him down here a lot, but I keep telling myself he might get turned off by the scene."

"AND IS that because he's close-minded, or because it's an easy excuse so you can keep your life in neat little boxes?" William challenged.

"NOT ANSWERING THAT," I grumbled. I left William to finish setting up for tonight's exhibition and wandered through the bar.

COREY HAD everything under control there. He was busy unpacking snacks and drinks that, to anyone unfamiliar with what was going on here, would seem out of place.

"HEY BOSS," Corey greeted me when he noticed me leaning

against the end of the bar. "Things are crazy around here, huh?"

"No crazier than usual," I remarked. "I'm excited to see everything starting to come together. Do you think many will come out tonight?"

Corey was the eyes and ears of The Lodge. Nothing happened that he didn't know about. If anyone had been making negative comments about the changes we had in the works, he'd be the first to hear it. No, they wouldn't come directly to him to complain, but he had a knack for picking up on any conversation that directly impacted business.

"Hard to tell," he hedged. "A lot of the people who are interested in stuff like this, aren't the same ones to hang out here every week. I think we can definitely draw them in, but it's going to take effort."

While he made a valid point, it concerned me. I would've been much happier had he given me a resounding yes.

"Don't get me wrong, I think it's awesome what you're trying to do. We need more places we can be ourselves." He dipped is face away from me, likely just realizing what he had divulged.

· · ·

WE? Well, that was certainly a surprise.

COREY MUST HAVE NOTICED my failed attempt to school my features. "I get it, boss man. You don't exactly look at someone like me and think I'd be into any of that." He waved a hand toward the other side of the room. "But, maybe, that's exactly why what you're doing is so important. Most clubs claim to be accepting and open. You hear it everywhere you go—no kink-shaming, your kink isn't my kink and that's okay—all the catchphrases. But then, someone like me walks into a kink club and I don't see anyone I can relate to. All of the more popular kinks are hot enough to look at, but they're nothing that really speaks to me. What you're doing does."

"AND IS that why you made a run to the store to change up what we're carrying at the bar?"

Corey's chin dipped again, and his shoulders curled forward as if he was in trouble. "Hey, I'm not scolding you. I'm just curious about these new additions."

I PICKED up the juice boxes, noticing they were name brand and organic. Good. If we were going to do this, I wanted us to be all-in. I'd done some research after my first conversation with Sam, and nothing like our play place existed within two hundred miles.

"OH." He brightened a bit, nearly bouncing on the balls of

his feet as he continued stocking the chip rack with an assortment of cookies, animal crackers, and even those little fish-shaped snacks that seem to be a hit with toddlers. "Yeah. I talked to Sam about it a little bit. He said it would be okay."

"WHY DIDN'T YOU ASK WILLIAM?" It wasn't like Corey to circumvent anyone, so I wasn't worried he'd gone to Sam, instead of me, because he feared I would mock him or deny his request. But tonight's event wasn't part of the renovations, it was an exhibition just like we did almost every weekend.

COREY JUST SHOOK HIS HEAD. It seemed my observations a while back, about there being bad blood of some sort between them, hadn't been my imagination. At some point, one of them needed to explain to me what was going on, because I couldn't have my head bartender and the friend I'd put in charge of community education, at odds.

I HELD up my hands in surrender. "Okay. Not going to push you to talk to me. But you know you can, right?"

"YEAH, BOSS." His mood seemed to brighten enough, I felt comfortable leaving him to his work.

"GOOD." I rapped my knuckles on the edge of the bar a couple of times, ready to go check in with Sam.

. . .

"HEY BOSS," Corey called out before I made it three steps away from the bar. I turned back to him. "You know, the same goes. I don't think you need it or anything, because you've been really happy lately, but if you ever need someone to talk to, I'm here."

"THAT'S A VERY KIND OFFER, COREY." One I wouldn't take him up on because I would always try to maintain a separation between my business life and what was going on in my personal life. It wasn't right for me to unload on one of my employees. That's what I had William for. And since he'd made it abundantly clear he never wanted to be on the payroll, I didn't have to worry about losing my confidant.

"AND, you know, if you ever wanted to bring someone down here, we'd all have his back," Corey added when I tried to step away again before things got awkward. "I mean, if he needed that. Not saying there is anyone, but you've seemed happier lately, so I thought maybe..."

"ARE YOU FISHING FOR GOSSIP, COREY?" I teased, and he quickly shook his head. "I'll remember that. And maybe I will invite him to visit sometime."

SOMETIME WOUND UP being less than an hour later, when my phone lit up with a new text message from Slade.

. . .

Slow night. Eli's cutting me early.

I wasn't sure I believed in fate or anything like that, but I couldn't deny I was curious how Slade would react if he was exposed to more kinks. Knowing him, he'd probably walk around making mental notes about various things he wanted me to try on him.

Not that there would be a damn thing wrong with that. I wanted to share everything with him. If there was something he was curious about, I wanted to be the one to show him.

Before I could second-guess myself, I tapped out a quick reply.

We have a little event taking place tonight. Want to come down and see it?

Depends on what it is, Slade replied.

Even though I didn't think he'd be repulsed, I couldn't bring myself to lay it all on the table. This was one of those things he needed to see to understand.

I promise it's not anything scandalous. Humor me?

. . .

I TAPPED my foot impatiently as I waited for Slade's response to appear on my screen. I wasn't sure if it was better or worse that he didn't have the same model phone I had, because I couldn't tell if he read the message, if he was tapping out a reply, or if he was simply doing something else and I needed to be patient.

CAN JORDAN COME, too? It might be easier for me to have someone I know with me the first time I come down to your place. No offense, but it's a little intimidating knowing what you do for a living. That's a lot of pressure on a guy.

LEAVE it to Slade to compose an essay, instead of simply asking permission. He probably thought I was more likely to say yes if he laid on a bit of guilt.

HE COULDN'T' have known this was a request I couldn't grant. It wasn't because I didn't want him spending time with his friends, but I wasn't about to give him permission to bring Jordan down here.

DOUG AND ELI had never brought their boy into the club, and I wasn't going to be the reason he made his first visit without them. I walked down the hall to my office, leaning back in my office chair before scrolling to find my brother's phone number. This wasn't how I wanted to officially tell him about me and Slade.

. . .

PART of me hoped Doug wouldn't answer, so I wouldn't have to answer questions about how long Slade and I had been seeing one another, and why I hadn't told him sooner. Now that William had brought it to my attention, I felt like I had done wrong, not only by Slade, but by everyone in my life who simply wanted me to be as happy as they were.

OF COURSE, this was the time Doug answered on the first ring.

"HEY MAN, WHAT'S UP?" I heard music in the background, meaning Doug was upstairs working in his studio. While I hadn't understood his obsession when he first started trying to learn everything he could about pottery, I couldn't deny that my brother was talented. And he was taking a completely different path to creating a better life for himself, having recently left his boring accounting job to create art full time.

"DID I catch you at a bad time?" Saying yes wouldn't be a bad thing, I added to myself. There was still time to not have this conversation over the phone.

"NOT AT ALL," he assured me. "I was just putting everything away for the night. Eli texted to let me know they're dead downstairs, so he and Jordan are coming home early."

. . .

GREAT. Now, not only was I going to have to deal with Doug, Eli would be there too, if they were on board with my idea. These were the lengths I went to in order to keep Slade happy. That should tell me something about my feelings for him.

I SCRUBBED a hand over my jaw, taking a few steady breaths before jumping into things with Doug.

"AWESOME," I responded, trying to muster up some enthusiasm. "So, I have a bit of an odd request for you."

"NAME IT," Doug responded without hesitation. That was the kind of guy he was. He didn't care what anyone needed, if they reached out to him, he would do just about anything as long as it wouldn't land him in jail or dead.

"So, UM," I stammered. I was a grown man. It shouldn't be this difficult for me to tell my younger brother that I was seeing someone.

BUT IT'S NOT JUST someone, it's his boy's best friend.

"SPIT IT OUT ALREADY," Doug grumbled. "Once Eli gets home, I can't guarantee I'm going to be as eager to help out with whatever's bugging you. If I take too long, the two of them will start without me."

. . .

"Did not need to know that," I complained. Man, we were polar opposites when it came to our relationships. He was an open book—sometimes too open—and I was hiding shit from him. But it was time to step out of the shadows. "So, I probably should have said something about this sooner, but I've been seeing Slade for a little over a month."

"It's about damn time you told me," was his only response. Not what I'd expected.

"You knew?"

"Of course, I knew. I'm pretty sure everyone figured it out within the first week. Your boy isn't exactly discreet."

"I don't expect him to be," I shot back. One of the few things I had promised Slade, was that he wasn't my dirty little secret.

And then you kept everything about the two of you hidden behind closed doors.

It wasn't done on purpose, but that didn't make the outcome any different. Part of me wanted to ask Doug what he'd heard, and why he hadn't called me on my secrecy sooner, but all that could wait.

"Sorry, it's been a rough day," I apologized. "First William busted my balls, and now you. I get it; I screwed up. Anyway, I invited Slade to come down and see me at work tonight."

"Damn," Doug interrupted. "Things must be getting serious if you want him down there with you."

"I'm not sure about that, but William took me to task earlier because I haven't brought him down. And we have that age play information session tonight. Nothing too kinky, but Sam wanted to start running some events so we could drum up interest for when the renovations are complete." I'd checked out the progress earlier, and I couldn't figure out what he thought still needed to be done before the big reveal.

"I think that's a great idea," Doug agreed. "But what does that have to do with me?"

"He wants to bring Jordan with him," I informed my brother. "He said he'd be more comfortable if he knew someone, and I can understand that, but I don't want to step on any toes."

· · ·

"So, you were hoping that I would escort them down there?" Doug finished. Pushy bastard couldn't give me a second to breathe.

"Yeah, something like that." Doug didn't seem as eager to agree, now that he knew what I wanted his help with. This was a horrible idea.

"Let me talk to Eli, but I don't think it'll be a problem. I know he's been wanting to get down there, but he's been worried about Jordan getting the wrong idea." It didn't take a psychic to know Eli had valid concerns. Before Jordan, he'd tried hiding his own desires by playing the role of a hyper-masculine Dom. He was good at it, but those of us who knew him could see it was a facade.

"Man, aren't we quite the pair?" I let out a sigh.

"No one ever said relationships were easy, Jack. I just happened to get myself tangled up with a boy who's new to the scene and one who still can't admit what he truly needs. But now, Eli—"

"I'm going to stop you right there," I interrupted him. "I don't know how that sentence ended, but I'm pretty sure you were about two seconds away from sharing far more with me than Eli would be comfortable with. Let me know what

Eli says. I need to get back out there and make sure everything's set up."

"IF WE COME DOWN, are you going to give us a sneak peek at what's been going on in the new area?"

"OF COURSE. In fact, I'd like to get your opinion on a few things." Doug had played a bit with a few Littles, so he might be able to tell us what we'd all overlooked.

"YOU GOT IT." A door slammed shut and I heard Eli's rumbling voice in the background.

"GO TALK to them and let me know what's going on."

"SOUNDS GOOD." The sound of Doug's breathing filled the line. After a few long beats, he said,
    "And I think I can safely speak for all of us when I say we're happy for you, Jack. I get why you were a bit gun shy after Collin left, but it's good to see you happy again."

"THANKS. I AM HAPPY." I'd said those words countless times over the years but hadn't meant them. Not like I did now.

"YOU SAY THAT NOW," Doug scoffed. "We'll see if you're

ready to tear your hair out a few months down the road. I get the impression Slade is a handful."

"And I wouldn't have it any other way." We disconnected the call, and I leaned back in the chair while I gave my racing heart a chance to slow down. Having Slade here for the night was exactly what I wanted, even if I hadn't realized it yet. Now, I just had to hope all of the moving pieces fit together.

18

SLADE

"Have you ever been here before?" I whispered as Doug drove us to The Lodge.

I was a bit unsettled, having my boyfriend's brother drive me to a kink club, even if I understood that it was easier if we all rode together. And Jack should be proud of me for accepting a ride with them. The alternative would've been taking a ride-sharing service, and, in his mind, that would've been wasted money. Because of his nagging, I finally had a little bit more of a buffer in the bank. I would probably always worry about waking up some morning and seeing all zeros or a negative balance but, for now, I could breathe again.

Jordan shook his head. "Nope. I've asked a few times, but Eli's always been a bit cagey. No matter what I say, he's still worried I'll get freaked out and think I want him to do whatever I see there. Doug glanced into the rearview mirror and Jordan's cheeks turned pink. It was adorable to see how he blushed so easily now.

"Even now, he worries about that?" I kept my voice low so the men in the front seat hopefully wouldn't hear us. The last thing I needed was Eli adding in his two cents. He was a great guy but opinionated as hell. "Doesn't he understand by now that you have no problem telling him if you're not interested in something?"

"Everyone has their hang-ups," Jordan replied. "This happens to be one of his. And I'm not going to get into it, but there are other reasons he feels that way. It all makes more sense if you understand how he really is."

"But those other reasons are some sort of secret?" Jordan and I didn't do secrets. We shared everything. Well, except a bit there at the beginning of our respective relationships when we didn't tell one another about the kinkier aspects, but that didn't count.

"I'm not saying that." Jordan sighed and shook his head. "You wouldn't want me telling them things you hadn't shared, would you?"

"I suppose not." Did Jack feel the same way as Eli? Was that why he hadn't invited me to see the business he was so proud of sooner? Well, I was going to go out of my way tonight to prove to him that I wasn't going to be scared off. I trusted Jack to understand there was more of the kink lifestyle I could never picture myself trying than there was that interested me.

When we arrived at the club, it was nothing like I had expected. It wasn't a dark, seedy place with all the warmth of a medieval dungeon. It felt more like an upscale cigar bar. Somehow, it seemed like exactly the type of place Jack would create.

Eli turned around, crossing his arms tightly over his chest, while Doug checked us in at the front desk. "A few things before we head in."

I fought the urge to roll my eyes. Eli wasn't my Daddy, and I didn't have to listen just because he started throwing rules around. Hell, it was hard enough for me to not talk back when Jack added new items on his list of things for me to either do or avoid.

"I'm serious, Slade," Eli said sternly. Oops. Apparently, I hadn't hidden my annoyance as well as I thought. "The club can be overwhelming for anyone, if they haven't been here before. You're going to see things that you don't understand. Don't stare. This isn't a circus freak show and the men inside aren't here to be on display."

"But some of them might be," Doug pointed out, and Jordan slapped a hand over his mouth to stifle his laughter.

Eli glared at Doug, then at Jordan, then narrowed his eyes at me, as if daring me to laugh as well. I held up my hands in surrender. "I'm listening, Eli. But I'm pretty sure Doug is right. There are probably at least a few guys in there who would love nothing more than for Jordan and me to watch what they're doing. You act like we're kids. We're not. Just because we haven't been in kink clubs before, doesn't mean we lack basic courtesy. Now, is there anything else or can I go find Jack?"

It was a bit strange to not have to carefully avoid talking about Jack anymore. I liked the fact that he had reached out to Doug and invited all of them to come down here tonight. Even though I wasn't particularly close with Doug and Eli, now that we were here, I understood why Jack hadn't immediately agreed to Jordan accompanying me without them. They needed to be here for him.

"He's probably back in his office," Doug informed me. "He spends more time back there than anywhere else."

"Why?" I had imagined Jack as the type of business owner who sauntered around the room, chatting up his regulars and greeting everyone who he had never seen in there before.

"That's for you to take up with him," Eli responded curtly, then glared at Doug again. It was strange. When we were all at Club 83, or the few times I had hung out with Jordan at their apartment, I got the impression that Doug was the top dog, so to speak, but here, Eli seemed more in his element and definitely in charge. He jerked his head toward the door leading from the reception area into the main club.

"I feel seriously overdressed," I muttered to Jordan as I took in the plethora of naked torsos. There were even a few guys here wearing little more than a jock.

"Same," Jordan responded. "Next time, we definitely need to plan ahead. They like to coddle me, but this is really cool. I think it could be fun to try and shock Eli. Do you think Jack would help me with that?"

"I don't know, but you should definitely ask him." We hadn't talked about much when it came to all of this, but I got the impression Jordan was far more adventurous than either of his men thought.

I caught a glimpse of broad shoulders and salt-and-pepper hair, covered in a navy pinstripe jacket. There was only one man who'd be in a place like this dressed like that. "I'll catch up with you in a bit. I'm going to go let Jack know I'm here."

The bartender's eyes widened, and he did a double-take as I eased my way through the crowd toward Jack. I paid him no attention as I wrapped my arms around Jack's waist from behind. He stiffened, and I thought I'd just made a huge mistake. Then, he spun around, his mouth open, ready to lecture me. He flashed me a wide smile before hugging me just as tightly and kissing the top of my head.

"Hey baby," he greeted me. "It's good to see you here."

He reached for my hand and grabbed the elastic around

my wrist. It was funny to see how much Jack liked grooming me. And, unless he was in a certain mood, he always tied my hair back for me when it was hanging loose. He said it was because he wanted easy access to my neck but wasn't a fan of a mouthful of hair. I could live with that logic.

"Nice place you got here, Daddy." My heart skipped a beat when I realized what I had just called him. That was a name that had, until now, been reserved for the privacy of my apartment. Would he have a problem with me sinking into that role here?

"I'm glad you think so." Jack chuckled, releasing me from his embrace but keeping one arm curled around my back. "It's not too stuffy for you?"

So, there was part of the problem. I was used to dive bars, and Jack worried I'd judge him for how posh this place seemed. I cringed, realizing I had brought that on myself. I was the one who made a big deal about our differences when we first got together. He had never treated me like I was less than him, but I had certainly made assumptions based on the way he looked and what he drove. Maybe I wasn't the only one dealing with insecurities.

"No, I really like it. It's not what I imagined it would be," I admitted. When Jack's brow furrowed, I quickly added, "I mean that in a good way. You hear about places like this, and you think they're going to be dark with hard leather benches, chains, and guys crying in pain."

"Oh, all of that definitely happens," Jack promised. "Tonight's a pretty relaxed one for us. We have a bit of a special event going on that I wanted you to see."

"Okay." My heart raced and my palms began to sweat. "Don't worry, it's nothing extreme. There will be no whips, chains, broken skin, or anything else."

"Darn," I responded playfully. "I was sort of hoping for all of the above."

"You were?"

I pressed a hand to Jack's chest. "No. Haven't you learned by now I am a sarcastic shit most of the time?"

"I just wanted to make sure," he told me. "Come on. There's someone who's been dying to meet you."

He led me to the perimeter of the room where a burly man, who had to be about Jack's age, was talking to a much slighter guy with sandy brown hair. He barely looked old enough to be in here, but it was obvious, even from a distance, that the older man deferred to him.

"That's Sam," Jack told me. "He's my right-hand man around here."

"The big guy?"

Jack chuckled. "No, sweetheart. The younger guy. I think you'd really like him. The other is William."

They were still far enough away there was no chance he'd heard Jack say his name, but William glanced over his shoulder, his eyes going wide when he noticed me. He quickly turned back to say something to Sam, then moved toward us.

"I didn't think you were going to drag him down here right away," William quipped. I glanced up at Jack. His lips were drawn into a tight pucker, like he was resisting the urge to say something, and his body went stiff next to mine. There was something unspoken between the two of them. Whatever it was, I started to question Jack's motivations for inviting me to the club. Had he been goaded into it by this guy? Would he have made the invitation otherwise? William held out a hand. "William Andrews."

"Slade Roberts," I offered in return, shaking his hand. No matter how insecure I felt with Jack's sudden discomfort,

I held my shoulders square and my back straight. He was the only one who got to see my vulnerability.

"Sweetheart, William is the lead instructor here," Jack informed me.

"Also, one of his best friends since high school," William added.

"So, the two of you work together?"

"He could only get so lucky," William quipped. "He keeps trying to put me on the payroll, but I do much better on a volunteer basis."

It must be rough. Here I was, busting my ass trying to make ends meet, and this guy volunteered his time working at the club? It made no sense. People didn't do that out of the goodness of their hearts—decades of friendship or not.

William quickly excused himself, saying he had to finish talking to Sam about something. I turned toward Jack, wanting to clear the air before I got lost in my own head. "What did he mean about you dragging me down here? If you don't want me to be here, tell me. I can go home and wait for you, just like every other night."

Jack curled his hand around the back my neck, dragging me close enough that he could press his forehead against mine. "Sometimes I have a tendency to get stuck in my own ways," Jack admitted. "There are a host of reasons why I had been reluctant to bring you down here, but please don't ever think any of them had to do with you. William's known me long enough that he figured out what I was doing, and he called me on my bullshit."

"It's always good to have a friend like that." Jordan was that person for me, and I felt better knowing Jack had someone like that in his life. "So, what bullshit did he get on your case about?"

"He was giving me a hard time because we don't go out

and do anything," Jack admitted. "He told me that if I really love you, I have to stop treating you like a booty call."

My heart might have stopped beating right then and there. It was way too soon to be throwing around words like that.

"Hey, easy, sweetheart," Jack whispered when he noticed I was on the verge of a panic attack. "I'm not saying that's where things are between us just yet, but he made a very valid point. I can't treat you like this is casual if it's anything but. You wormed your way into my heart, now it's time for me to show you the rest of my life. That way, you can make an informed decision on if you want to stick around or if it's all too much."

"I wouldn't care if you worked here, having sex for money," I insisted. "How I feel about you has nothing to do with what you do for a living. I don't give a shit that you have more money than I do, or that you're surrounded by naked men all night. And what we do behind closed doors is enough. If it wasn't, I would've said something."

"Are you sure?"

"Positive," I responded competently. "I know I made a big deal about you having money when we first met, but I've gotten over that. I see now that you're not the type to flash your wealth around. We might still have a lot to learn about one another, but I've already figured out that you're a pretty private guy. I figured that was why we didn't go out and do a lot of stuff in public."

"I am," he confirmed. "But that's no excuse. I'm still trying to wrap my head around everything between us." He pressed his lips to my forehead. "Promise you'll be patient with me and always speak up if you're uncomfortable with something?"

"That was part of the original deal," I reminded him. "That hasn't changed, and it won't."

Things had definitely gotten heavier than I think either of us had intended.

Luckily, right about then, Jordan came rushing over to me. "Dude! You gotta see this!"

He clamped his hand around my wrist and started dragging me across the room. I looked back at Jack, needing his reassurance that we were good. He nodded, shooing me away.

"Go, I want to check on a few more things and chat with Doug and Eli." He followed, catching up to us quickly with his long strides. He cupped my cheek and planted a chaste kiss on my lips. "We'll talk about this later, baby. Okay?"

"Yeah." I let out a deep breath and, along with it, the tension I hadn't realized had been collecting in my shoulders.

"You sure you aren't upset?" I wanted to reach up and smooth the creases from Jack's brow. Even if I had momentarily questioned why he asked me here, I was cool now.

"I am," I reassured him. "Now that I know you want me here, there's nothing to worry about. I'll go see what's got Jordan so excited, then I will come and find you, okay?"

"Sounds like a good plan." Jack kissed me once more, this time cupping my ass as he forced his tongue into my mouth. Maybe I was mistaken, but it sure as hell felt like he was staking his claim on me in front of everyone who had wandered into the bar so far that night.

As we crossed the room, Jordan still holding on to me as if worried I would flee, I noticed a few critical glances and one guy who barely concealed his distaste. The old me would have flipped him off. I didn't have time for judgmental assholes in my life. I didn't even know this guy, what the hell was his problem?

"Looks to me like someone's jealous," Jordan surmised. I glanced over at him, and he nodded toward the guy who looked like he'd just swallowed something sour. "Man, you should've seen it. As soon as Jack kissed you, that dude went from nearly bouncing on his seat to..." He waved his hand around at nothing in particular. "That."

"I hadn't even thought about that," I admitted. There were so many things I hadn't considered when it came to visiting Jack at work. I knew he'd never really fooled around with guys here at the club. He confessed to me one night, that it was hard for him to find somebody because it was difficult to discern who wanted him and who wanted to brag that they'd had him. Still, what would happen if these guys stopped coming in once they realized he was off the market? It was sort of like the whole theory in that movie about the girls bartending in New York City. Places like this worked if you appeared single but weren't available to anyone.

Jordan smacked my shoulder. "Whatever you're thinking, stop it. That man is crazy about you."

"Yeah, but that doesn't mean it's a good idea for me to hang out here," I argued.

"They'll get over it." I startled at the sound of Eli's voice nearby, then offered him a smile of thanks. He joined us, standing to the other side of Jordan as he continued. "If you ask me, you are exactly what Jack needs in this place. Since he and Colin broke up, he's been hiding out in his office because of fools like that. They aren't always the best at taking subtle hints, and he's too professional to be rude to them and tell them to back the fuck off."

"But what if they stop coming in?" I asked him.

Eli simply shook his head, rolling his eyes as if it was

ludicrous to think my presence could cost him business. "The customers around here are even more loyal than anyone we get at my place. Where our customers have their choice of bars, there aren't many kink clubs around. And there's sure as hell no other place within a fifty-mile radius that does everything Jack and his crew have introduced here. The people who come in here, they're looking for a unique connection. Whether that's someone to hurt them, humiliate them, tie them up, or tell them they're a pretty boy —people know this is where they can find it. If those boys shy away because one man is off the market, they have nowhere else to go to meet people.

"So, essentially, you're saying Jack has a monopoly?" Jordan asked.

Eli chuckled and kissed the side of his head. "No, sweetheart. What I'm saying is, he has built what others have tried and failed. That's why people keep coming back here. And once the new room is open, I think he's going to see even more business."

"You've got to see this!" Jordan dragged me into a room that was a night and day difference to the rest of the establishment. The walls were bright and cheery, with a huge mural along the back wall. It was interesting to see the clear delineation between various setups.

I crinkled my nose when I noticed the oversized playpen, soft toys, and blocks at the far end of the room. Definitely not something I wanted to try, but as I scanned the entire room, I noticed a progression.

Next to that, there was a low bookcase filled with picture books, different blocks, what appeared to be a train set, and a huge bin of crayons. Then, next to that, was a completely different variety of toys. And closest to us, the space was a muted blue with two bean bag chairs on the floor and an entertainment system against the wall. My eyes widened as I took in the assortment of gaming systems there. "What in the world is this?"

"It's a special room for Littles!" Jordan responded, already on his way to the entertainment center.

"Is that something you're into?" I wasn't going to judge him if he was, but I didn't understand it.

"I don't need the stuff that's down that way, but this is freaking awesome." He tossed a controller to me, and we flopped onto one of the bean bags.

The tightness in my chest eased as an old school game loaded up. I pushed the jealous little twit from earlier out of my mind and stopped thinking about the pressure of being Jack's partner when we were here, as Jordan talked shit about how he was going to kick my ass.

"In your dreams," I retorted. "We've been playing this since we were little, and I can't remember a single time you've won."

"Yeah, well maybe I've been practicing," he shot back, and I quirked an eyebrow. "What? It could happen."

"No, it couldn't," I responded. "I love you, J, but you suck at video games."

"Boys," Eli admonished us. Why in the hell did that get my dick hard? I shook my head. No way was I going to get turned on by my boss. "Play nice or we're turning it off."

"Sorry, Daddy," Jordan mumbled.

Eli bent down and pressed a kiss to the top of Jordan's head again. Before Jack, it weirded me out a little to see how Doug and Eli doted on Jordan, but now it made sense. Being their boy didn't have anything to do with any of the perverted reasons people came up with about relationships like theirs. The way I settled whenever Jack pushed me to be my best, wasn't because of lingering daddy issues or anything like that. It was simply another way to feel good.

And maybe it was okay for Eli to make me feel good too. Not in a sexual way because... I paused the game when a bizarre thought popped in my head.

"So, if Doug is your Daddy and Jack is my Daddy does that make us cousins?" Jordan's face scrunched up, and he waved a finger around in the air as he tried to figure out what the hell I was talking about. "And does that mean Eli would be my uncle and Doug is my uncle because they're my Daddy's brother and his partner? Eww, gross, but then you're their partner too, so does that mean you're my uncle? This is all confusing."

I sunk deeper into the bean bag, shielding my face with my forearm.

"What in the hell are you talking about?" Jordan shook his head. "Is this really the type of thing you sit up and think of at night?"

"You act like you don't know me at all," I scoffed. "Of course, I think about these things. Now answer the question. I need to know if I'm supposed to call Eli something other than Eli, because I don't want to screw this up."

Jordan puffed out his cheeks then blew out a harsh breath. He dropped his controller and flipped onto his stomach. "Daddy, Slade has a question for you."

Eli approached, crouching down in front of us. I was so going to kill Jordan when I got the chance. Or, at least put him in a headlock and give him a noogie. "What's up, Slade?"

"Nothing," I mumbled.

"No, now you have to ask him," Jordan said, chewing on his bottom lip. "Now that you got me thinking about it, I'm going to obsess about it until we get answers. You have to ask."

"It's stupid," I insisted.

"Well, yeah," Jordan scoffed. "But you're the one who said it, so now you have to ask Daddy Eli. Or is that..."

I tackled Jordan, clamping a hand over his mouth.

"Don't say it," I hissed. "I'm begging you, Jordan."

"I don't see why it's that big of a deal," he shot back, and we wrestled around a bit more on the floor. I couldn't tell you the last time I felt this light and happy. It was fun tussling with my friend.

Then, just like when we were younger, a pair of long legs appeared in front of us. We stilled, looking up to see Eli scowling down at us. "Are you boys about through?"

We both nodded.

"Either of you care to tell me what it was that was so important you called me over here?" I pursed my lips and glared at Jordan. He shook his head, and I did the same.

"It was nothing, really," I reassured them. "I was just being stupid, and Jordan thought I was serious."

Eli ruffled my hair. "I highly doubt that. Anyway, do you think the two of you can keep from breaking anything long enough for me to go out and see what Jack and Doug are up to?"

We nodded in unison, then I gave Jordan a playful shove. "Thanks, jerk face."

"What did I do?" Jordan picked up both controllers and tossed mine back to me. "It wasn't really a bad question."

"No, but it's embarrassing as hell. Just because I wanted to talk to you about it, doesn't mean I wanted you blabbing to Eli about it."

"Don't you mean *Uncle* Eli?" he teased, and I flipped him off.

We started playing the game, working our way through the levels to try and rescue the princess. I was filled with a lightness I hadn't felt in forever. Even when I was a kid, I couldn't remember feeling this carefree. I wondered what it would take to stay like this forever.

19

JACK

"Tell me one thing," Eli demanded as he approached the bar where Doug and I were catching up over a glass of whiskey. He grabbed Doug's and drained it.

"What's up?" I lifted my glass to take another sip. Luckily, that was as far as I got before Eli could pose his question.

"Tell me you're not renovating the bar because you found a Middle to spoil."

"What?" I asked in disbelief. "Even if I did have someone who was into age play, do you really think I'd go out of my way to give him a playroom if it wasn't a sound business investment?"

"I hate to break it to you," Eli responded, hitching a thumb over his shoulder, "But you're an idiot if you don't realize that that's exactly what you have on your hands."

"How so?"

Eli gaped at me like I was the village idiot.

"Come here, you need to see this." I stood to follow, and Doug was close behind me. The three of us filled the doorway to the new playroom, watching as Slade and

Jordan played video games, clowning around like they were teenagers. When Slade smiled, his entire face lit up. Everything we had done together, all the reassurances I'd given him, and not once had I seen his face look that brilliantly alive.

"Just because he likes playing video games doesn't mean he's into age play," I protested.

Eli shuffled to the side, then motioned for me to follow him around the corner where we could still spy on the boys without disturbing them. "Don't be an idiot, Jack. Let's think about this logically for a second. Maybe he hasn't come out and told you he is, but, I'm telling you, it fits. Since the first time you met him, you've been correcting his disruptive behavior, and even when he pushes back, he complies. That's because he wants you to be proud of him. When you suggested he talk to me about a job, he did, even though he'd refused every time Jordan suggested it. "And look at them, Jack." He peeked around the corner and I did the same. "I swear, as soon as he flopped onto that bean bag, it was like a switch flipped in him. He's finally in his element."

"So, are you saying Jordan is a Middle, too?" Because, how could he claim that one of them was and the other wasn't, when they were in there playing together?

"No. I think he's enjoying spending time with his friend. He took it really hard when Slade started sinking into depression after the band split up. In his mind, he has his friend back. He probably doesn't even understand why Slade is so much more comfortable tonight."

I leaned against the doorway and watched them a little longer. The way Slade reached over, knocking the controller out of Jordan's hands when Jordan was beating him, the easy way they bantered back-and-forth. And, as I stood there, I considered everything I knew about Slade. How he thrived when I imposed rules on him. The way he seemed to crave someone else to take control of the day-to-day decisions for him.

"Son of a—"

"Just now figuring it out?" Eli asked with a laugh, then clamped a hand on my shoulder. "For what it's worth, I was just giving you a hard time earlier about doing all of this for him. I know you wouldn't have done that, but now it seems like maybe there's a reason you agreed to this project right after the two of you got together."

"And what would that be?"

"He's only working for me a few nights a week. Don't you think there are better places for him to be on the nights he's off, rather than sitting at home waiting for you? Maybe this is one of those cases of everything happens for a reason?"

I'd always struggled with that belief. I couldn't wrap my head around all of the bad shit happening just to get to the good stuff. In Slade's case, I didn't want to think that his band had split up, and he'd found himself on a dangerous downward spiral, just so we could eventually wind up here. Even if there was some truth to that, I refused to be grateful for the misery I saw in his eyes the first time he turned on me outside Doug's apartment.

"It's not a horrible idea," Doug added. "You need someone to monitor the playroom, but I think it would be easier for everyone if things felt more organic, you know?"

"Organic, how?"

"When you're busy working, he can hang out here," Doug explained. "He could be the room monitor, but you can give him a fun title. He could be the babysitter or something. He'd probably love the hell out of that. He could watch over the littler Littles and help them out. He could keep an eye on the little ones when their Daddies needed to run to the bathroom or to get them something to snack on."

"Shit." I pinched the bridge of my nose. For someone who had good business sense, I'd certainly overlooked these details. And they were right. This would be the perfect job for Slade.

"And, as a bonus, you could stop in and check on him whenever you wanted. It would be the best of both worlds. He'd feel useful, and you'd have your boy close by."

That really did sound perfect.

"Let me talk to Sam about it," I insisted. "This is his brainchild." Eli gaped at me. "Yes, even a complete control freak like me can let someone else take the lead every once in a while."

"You're just making all sorts of changes, aren't you?" Eli quipped.

"It's about damn time," Doug added. I flipped them off and my brother just laughed. "Seriously man, it's good to see you happy again. We were both worried about you after Collin took off."

"Gee, I had no clue," I said, glaring at Eli. Where my brother had been silently supportive, his partner hadn't been nearly as quiet about his own concerns. For a while, it'd been hard to spend time with the two of them, because every time we were together, Eli pushed me to try and get back into the game.

I continued watching Slade, a slow smile creeping onto my face. If I didn't know them better, I'd have thought they had been working behind the scenes to fix me up with their boy's friend. He certainly ticked all of my boxes.

I couldn't wait to start exploring some of my darker fantasies with him. In an odd way, I was grateful I hadn't figured out Slade might be a Middle sooner. If I had, I'm not sure I would have broached some of the darker topics with him. I needed to make sure he understood the two were very different kinks, and both could coexist with one another.

"Jack, I hate to bug you." I turned, noticing Corey sheepishly approaching me.

"Is everything okay?" I reached out to give his arm a comforting squeeze. Corey felt like a walking time bomb.

I wasn't sure what had happened between him and William, but, whatever it was, it affected him on a cellular level. If I wasn't so levelheaded, I'd kick the shit out of my friend and ask questions later. The guys who worked for me were family, and I didn't want to see any of them hurt. The only thing worse than that was knowing one of them might have hurt another, even if it'd been unintentional.

"I was just wondering..." His gaze drifted toward the new playroom. "Sam hasn't let me see what he's been working on. Is it okay if I go in, now that Slade and his friend are in there? It would really help me be able to explain to the customers what we're doing, if I had a better idea myself."

I pursed my lips, amused by his weak excuse. If I wasn't worried that he was about to crack, I would have given him a hard time, asking him how long it had taken him to come up with that line.

"Absolutely." I ushered him into the room with a smile. "What do you think?"

His eyes grew wide, and his gaze darted all over the room, as if he didn't know what to look at first. "This is great! It's going to be a huge hit. Sam thought of everything."

"What do you say Doug and I keep an eye on the bar for a few minutes, and you can let him play," Eli suggested quietly. Corey had definitely perked up as soon he entered the playroom. "Maybe a few minutes to decompress would be good for him."

"I think that's a great idea," I agreed. "And I'm going to test another one of your theories at the same time."

Doug and Eli made their way to the bar and I went to the middle space, crouching down between Jordan and Slade. "Hey boys, are you having a good time?"

"This is really awesome, Jack," Jordan responded, never taking his eyes off the game. Slade, on the other hand, simply nodded. He was completely captivated by the animated images on the screen. I began rubbing his back and he leaned into the touch, sighing softly.

"Baby, I need to get some work done," I told him. "Do you think you can keep an eye on Corey for me?"

I felt bad when Slade's focus was broken, and his character crashed to his death. He turned to me, worry creasing his forehead. "Is he okay?"

I pointed toward the other side of the room where Corey was cautiously pulling toys off the low bookshelf. Interesting. I'd expected him to want to play with Slade and Jordan, but he seemed content coloring at a low table. "He's fine, sweetheart. But I'd still like you to keep an eye on him."

"Okay, Daddy." He sat up a bit straighter. "I can do that for you. Anything else?"

The boy was such a natural at this, I wondered why I hadn't realized it sooner. "No, sweetheart. I'll be back as soon as I can."

I placed a chaste kiss to his lips. Anything deeper than that felt wrong when he was in this headspace, and I wasn't about to do anything that might jeopardize the serenity he'd found.

I made a mental note to pick up some of the same gaming systems for my own place, and maybe see what else interested Slade. If this was what it took to help my boy find peace, I was going to go all out. What was the point of having money if you couldn't spend it on the people you loved?

Shit. Did I love him?

Yeah, I did. I think that had been a foregone conclusion since the moment we met. Maybe even before, if things like fate, and everything else Eli talked about, actually existed. But I wouldn't tell him just yet, not after the way he'd nearly bolted when I let the word slip earlier.

"Are they all settled in there?" Eli asked as I slid onto the stool next to Doug's. I nodded, lifting the now watered-down drink to my lips. "Are you still going to tell me I was imagining things?"

"No," I grumbled. "I'm just pissed at myself that I didn't realize it sooner. How could I have not known?"

"Because your judgment was clouded by including sex in the mix." Eli grabbed a bar towel and started wiping down every horizontal surface he could find. He did the same when we were relaxing at my house. I was pretty sure it was a habit he didn't even realize he had. "I've seen the evolution of Slade. I knew him as a regular in the bar, chasing his next orgasm. He never found what he was looking for, because it wasn't getting off that he needed. Then, I knew him as Jordan's best friend. I listened to Jordan worry about him after the band split up, and he started to withdraw from everyone, including Jordan. He was in a really dark place, but then you came along. And you were able to take care of his needs, even if neither of you realized right away what those were."

"You're a pretty smart guy, you know that?" Eli rolled his eyes. It wasn't often that I complimented my brother's partner, but I realized then that I hadn't given him credit for his observation skills. You'd think I would've learned that about him in the past decade and a half that we'd known one another.

Eli quickly poured three fresh glasses of whiskey. I held up a hand, trying to pass.

"Hell no," Doug protested. "If I'm drinking, so are you."

"I still have to work tonight," I reminded them.

"Take the night off," Eli suggested. "Show your staff that you trust them to keep things under control and hang out with your brother and me. If it's easier for you, we don't even have to stay here. We can head back to your place."

"Inviting yourself over?" I was only teasing him, but I was nervous about the prospect of inviting Slade to my house for the first time when we wouldn't be alone. This felt like a step that should be taken with just the two of us.

"I figured you'd be more comfortable there," Eli explained. "Plus, if the boys fall asleep watching a movie, we can crash in the guest room. You'd be a hell of a lot more comfortable there than at our place."

"You make a good point," I told him. "But would it be okay if you guys either hang back for a few minutes, or swing by your place and grab clothes if you plan on spending the night?"

Eli eyed me curiously, and a pit formed in my stomach. Was I really going to confess this to them?

Yeah, I was. If nothing else, I knew I could trust Doug and Eli to keep me on the right path when it came to giving Slade whatever he needed. Much like William, they weren't afraid to call me on my bullshit. I needed more people like that my life, otherwise I was doomed to repeat the past at some point.

"I'd prefer the first time Slade sees my house to not be with the three of you hot on our heels," I admitted to them.

Doug's eyes grew wide and Eli simply hung his head, muttering about what an idiot I had been. I didn't dispute him. It wasn't fair to Slade that I had never invited him to my place when he so freely opened his house to me. But tonight was the night everything changed. I couldn't go back and correct the mistakes I'd already made, but I could do everything in my power to make sure he knew how much I cared about him.

"Yeah, whatever you need." Doug rested his hand on my shoulder. "Don't beat yourself up. I know none of this has been easy on you. And, believe it or not, even you aren't perfect. You were bound to screw up at some point."

"Gee, thanks for that reminder," I muttered. "Now, what do you say we go get our boys and get out of here?"

Doug turned my body away from the playroom when I went to retrieve Slade. "No. We will go tell the boys it's time to leave. You need to let everyone know you're taking the night off. And tell them not to call you for a few days, unless it's an emergency."

"Little bit bossy, aren't you?"

"You might be older, but if you need someone to keep you in check, I'm more than man enough to take on that role. It's time for you to open up your life to him."

SLADE WAS WAITING for me at the bar when I finished talking to Sam and William. They'd both been shocked when I told them I was taking a few days off and not to call me before Thursday unless it was an absolute emergency. My skin itched, realizing that they would listen to me. I couldn't remember the last time I had been completely out of touch with the club.

Now that Eli and Doug had left with Jordan in tow,

Corey was back behind the bar. The sad, haunted look was gone from his eyes, and he was back to his bubbly self. He was right. I never would have imagined age play to be his kink, but maybe if I had spent more time getting to know him, it wouldn't have come as such a shock. At some point, I would let him know that he was welcome to go back there any time he needed to reset.

"You ready, baby?" I asked Slade, wrapping an arm around his waist. He hugged me tightly, burying his face against my chest. "In case I didn't say it earlier, thank you for inviting me down here."

"You don't need to thank me, baby. I'm sorry it took me so long to get my head out of my ass."

"Lucky for you, I can be patient." I snorted out a laugh. There were many adjectives I could use to describe Slade, but patient would never be among them. "Come on, brat. Let's get out of here so Corey can get back to work."

"What are we doing?" Slade asked as I led him to the back entrance. "Doug and Eli were all quiet when I asked them. They said I needed to ask you."

"The three of us decided we'd rather spend a quiet night with our boys than be at the club," I informed him. "It's probably going to take me a while before I can fully relax with you there. I know you're more than capable of taking care of yourself, but I don't ever want anyone being rude to you. If they are, I want you to tell me."

Slade spun around, pressing a hand to my chest. "I'm a big boy, Daddy. If I need your help, I'll ask for it, but I'm more than capable of taking care of myself."

Oh my God, the brat in him was definitely out in full force tonight. All that was missing was him pouting and stomping his foot.

"I know you are, sweetheart." I cupped his cheek. Slade

didn't hesitate before leaning in to kiss me. I buried my hands in his back pockets, kneading his ass as he deepened the kiss. He ground against me. "You know what you really need to go with that playroom?"

"What's that, sweetheart?"

"Bedrooms. I know you have the private playrooms, but have you ever thought about the fact that you need some other places, too?"

"Bedrooms, huh? And why would that be?" I pursed my lips to keep from laughing. Slade seemed adamant that this was absolutely necessary to complete the renovations.

"Sometimes kids get tired," he explained. "They might need nap time, and nap time isn't any good if people are being loud. And for the littler ones, they're going to want to play if they see other friends playing."

Either he had given this an insane amount of thought in the past hour, or this wasn't the first time he'd considered age play. This was definitely something we would be exploring more at home.

"You make a very convincing argument, baby. Would you like to talk to Sam about that?"

His face twisted in confusion. "Why would I talk to him?"

"Because it was your idea," I explained. "And I like the idea of you having a say in things around here."

I stopped myself from saying anything more. I needed to remember that everything with Slade and me was still new, and he would be skittish for a long time to come. Tipping my hand wouldn't do either of us any good.

"Come on, brat. Let's go home," I said before he could get worked up. I helped him into the car, leaning in to buckle his seatbelt. When he opened his mouth to protest, I pressed a finger to his lips. "Humor an old man. I want to do this for you."

He settled back into the seat. "Okay, Daddy."

Slade was quiet the entire way home.

"You do realize this is the first time I'm seeing where you live?" he asked as I wound through the neighborhood. It wasn't an accusation or meant to make me feel guilty, it was a simple statement.

"And I'm sorry for that, sweetheart." If I explained why I had been reluctant to bring him home, would he understand? Would he even believe me?

"What changed your mind?"

"I want to do right by you," I explained. "No matter what, I always want you to know I want you wherever I am. You've seen me at work, now I want to see you in my home. Someday, I'd love nothing more than to discuss you getting rid of that shit hole apartment you live in."

"I thought you said it wasn't a shit hole," Slade protested.

"I lied. I didn't want to make you feel bad. It's horrible."

"Yeah, tell me about it. You say the word and I'll go and pack my shit."

"The word." It was corny as hell, but now that I knew Slade was open to the idea, I wasn't wasting any time.

"That was horrible." It was, but he was laughing, so that was good. I stared at him, waiting for an answer, then he gaped at me. "Are you fucking serious right now?"

"As a heart attack," I responded. Slade's expression fell, leaving me to wonder what I'd done wrong. "Baby, what happened just then?"

"I just... You'll probably think it's stupid," he hedged.

"I swear, if you don't quit saying that, I'm going to beat it out of you," I warned him. It'd been weeks since I'd heard

Slade get down on himself like that. I thought he'd broken himself of the habit. "Now tell me."

"I told you the night we met that my head is a mess. I know you were just joking about the heart attack thing, but I don't like thinking about something happening to you," he admitted. The organ in question clenched with a deep ache for this amazing man.

"Then we'd better make sure you keep me young." I lifted his hand to my mouth, placing tender kisses on each finger. "Now, if you were serious about being willing to move in with me, let's go so I can give you the grand tour."

"Yeah, let's." Hand-in-hand, we walked up the driveway to the front door. I stopped myself from doing anything too corny, like carrying him over the threshold—there would be time for that later.

20

SLADE

I t was a damn good thing Jack had invited me to move in with him last night. It was reckless and possibly one of the stupidest ideas I'd ever had, but after one night curled in his arms in the most comfortable bed I'd ever slept in, there was no way in hell I could return to my dingy apartment. I had felt all sorts of grown-up hanging out with Jordan and his Daddies. We'd gone from being a couple, hiding away from the real world, to socializing, and it felt good. I loved the way Jack sought me out, no matter where I was, always ready with a quick hug or kiss.

I even relaxed enough that I sunk into the role of host. I was still trying to figure out where everything was, but Jordan helped me whenever our Daddies needed something. Eventually, they told us to head down to the rec room and relax for a while. There had been a few tense moments when I felt like they were trying to cast us aside, but Jack quickly soothed my frayed nerves, telling me he wanted me to make myself at home.

The basement had been amazing. There was a huge TV mounted on one wall over a fireplace, a pool table, and even a couple of old school arcade games. It was possibly the first glimpse I'd had that Jack did know how to have fun. After playing all of the games, Jordan and I had curled up on one of the oversized couches and watched movies until both of us fell asleep. At some point, Jack had come down to carry me to bed. No shit, he actually scooped me up and urged me to wrap my arms around his neck. I did. It felt amazing, and I wanted to stay like that forever.

"It's still early," Jack pointed out. His voice was raspy, his words still slurred a bit from sleep.

"Why don't you go back to sleep for a bit, baby?"

"That's the weird thing," I admitted. "I feel like I've gotten plenty of sleep. Now I have all this pent-up energy, and I want to do something."

Usually, it was Jack trying to urge me into action, not the other way around.

Jack curled his arms tighter around my waist. "We have all day, sweetheart. Let me savor this a little bit longer."

Well, when he put it that way, how could I refuse? I flipped over so I could rest my head against his chest. I laid there quietly, waiting to see if Jack's breathing would even out as he drifted back to sleep. It didn't. Part of me felt bad about that, because Jack probably wanted to relax on his day off.

The good news was, he didn't have to get up and drive across town, so the two of us could spend the day together.

Jack let out an exaggerated sigh. "What are you so busy thinking about, sweetheart?"

"Can I ask you a question?" I propped myself on my elbows, bending down to kiss my way across Jack's collarbones.

"If the question is whether or not I'll let you suck me as

a thank you for last night, then by all means," he teased, giving my arm a playful tug.

"No, that's not what I was going to ask." I playfully swatted his chest, and Jack quirked an eyebrow. "I mean, I'm definitely up for that, but I'm trying to be serious here."

"Well, that's an interesting turn of events," Jack teased. He pushed himself upright and leaned against the headboard. When he lifted an arm, I wasted no time pressing my body against his side. "What is it, sweetheart?"

"Is it weird that I felt peaceful last night?"

"You'll have to be a little more specific, Slade." I closed my eyes as Jack continued combing his fingers through my hair. He slowed when he reached a tangled knot, carefully separating the strands before continuing.

"I mean, at the club," I explained. "I can't even explain what it was like, but as soon as Jordan and I went into the playroom, it was like something started to settle inside of me."

"And what do you think that means?" I let out a frustrated huff. He was bad as a therapist. That's what I was trying to figure out, and he was the one who was supposed to have all the answers. "Sweetheart, I have my own assumptions, but I want to hear it from you, first."

"I don't know," I ground out, pounding my fist against the mattress. "That's why I needed to talk to you about it. I'm not stupid, I have heard of age play before, and I know that's what that room was built for."

"Okay, and is that something you want to explore together?"

I shook my head quickly. "No, I didn't care for some of that stuff. I mean, if other people are into it, cool, but that's not me. But then there was other stuff that I wanted to sit down and play with, so what does that say?"

"You're talking in circles, Slade," Jack pointed out. "Why don't we focus more on what you did like, than what you didn't."

"Okay." That I could do. "Jordan and I used to hang out at my place playing video games, but it felt different when we were there," I admitted. "Why?"

"I think that's something that only you can answer, sweetheart." He traced lazy circles on my chest. I arched my back when he got close to my nipple, and he withdrew. "Nope, we're going to break the habit of using sex as a diversion tactic."

"Aren't you supposed to have all the answers," I grumbled. "And, for your information, sex isn't a diversion this time, but when you play like that and I know you still have morning wood, I'm going to take advantage if you let me."

"I'll keep that in mind but we're going to discuss this first. Do you want to hear my thoughts?" I nodded. "And you promise you'll hear me out before you interrupt me to tell me how wrong I am?"

I pursed my lips together. "I'll try." Both of us knew, damn well, I sucked at being patient.

Jack pulled me onto his lap, so my legs were draped to one side and my head was near Jack's shoulder. I curled myself into a ball so I could rest my head and close my eyes as Jack gave me his expert opinion. Okay, so it wasn't like he'd gone to school for this or anything, but he had a hell of a lot more experience in the lifestyle than I had.

"Based on what I saw last night, and a few other observations, I think you may be what they call a Middle."

"A Middle?" That was a phrase I had never heard before. Jack flicked my shoulder.

Oh, right. I had promised I wouldn't interrupt him. "Sorry, Daddy. But that really doesn't count as an interruption since I wanted you to explain something to me, does it?"

Jack chuckled. "No, sweetheart, I guess it doesn't. Anyway, a Middle is someone who regresses, but not necessarily as far as other Littles do."

"Okay, I'm listening," I told him. "And you think that's what I am? Why?"

This time, he pinched my side, making me squirm. "Sorry."

"It's okay." He brushed the hair away from my face and offered me a chaste kiss. "I like knowing that you're curious about this. Part of me worried you wouldn't be receptive if I tried talking to you about it."

"Well, it is a bit weird," I admitted. "Then again, you've already shown me a lot of other things I never knew turned me on, so why should this be any different?"

Flashes of the past month appeared in my mind. The way I couldn't help but obey when he left me a list of chores that first day. I'd tried. Damn, how I'd tried. But then I imagined his disapproval, and the threat of him never coming back scared the hell out of me. He had slowly crafted routines for me, checking in without being overbearing. When I'd struggled with his radio silence a few nights in a row, he'd changed his own behaviors. He encouraged me to keep after my art, even when I'd proclaimed it a lost cause.

I paused before turning to look at Jack. "Have you known this the whole time?"

"No, sweetheart. But, looking back, I realize I must have been blind to not see it sooner," he admitted.

"Okay, so what signs did you miss?" I teased him. I felt a little bit better knowing that this turn of events had taken him by surprise as well.

"You don't want to be in control," he explained. "Even

with the simplest tasks, you have handed over that authority to me."

"Maybe that's just because being an adult sucks sometimes," I pointed out. Jack glared at me, and I hitched up my shoulders. "What? It's the truth. Oh wait, is that part of why you think I might be a Middle?"

"That's definitely part of it," he confirmed. "And with Middles, sometimes it's harder to see the regression. But last night really clinched it for me."

"How so?"

"Do you even realize how beautiful you were when you were sitting there playing video games with Jordan?" I scrunched up my nose. It was still difficult for me to accept compliments, but I couldn't remember a time anybody had ever called me beautiful—and certainly not because of how I played a game.

"Don't look at me like that," he scolded. "As soon as you two sat down to play, this sense of peace washed over you. Part of it, I'm assuming, was the space you were in. Your mind knew you were in a safe place, where you didn't have to worry about everything that weighs you down out in the real world."

"Okay, but maybe I was just excited to finally see you at work," I countered. "And do you know how hard it is to come by some of those old school games? Seriously, you need to give Sam a raise, because it was a genius move on his part to include gaming systems from when we were kids."

Jack shook his head and let out a sigh. "Are you going to contradict me on everything I say? Do I need to put you in a timeout?"

He completely ignored everything I'd said about how awesome the playroom was. A spanking sounded like a hell of a lot more fun, but I didn't say that. I might be clueless about all of this Middle stuff he was talking about, but I was pretty sure talking back would earn me consequences, and not the kinky fun type.

"Sorry, Daddy." I rested my head on his shoulder and closed my eyes. "Please, go on."

Jack tightened his arms around me. "Maybe part of it was that we were together, somewhere other than inside your apartment, but I think even more of it was that you were given a no-pressure way to let your Middle out to play. Seriously, it was like watching what you and Jordan would've been like when you were preteens."

I stiffened, a sarcastic quip about maturity on the tip of my tongue. I somehow managed to bite it back.

"Good boy," Jack praised me. "As I said, most of this is just a hunch, but I'm not the only one who thinks this might be exactly what you need."

A low groan rumbled through my body. I didn't want other people knowing my personal business. And it didn't take three guesses to know who else had figured out the secret even I hadn't known existed. "Let me guess, Eli?"

"And Doug," he added. "But don't worry, sweetheart. Just because this is how you are, doesn't mean anyone else is going to treat you any differently, unless you want that. For now, it can be something only the two of us share. To the rest of the world, you'll be the same guy you've always been, just without the hard edge you've honed to keep everyone at a distance."

"But how would that work if we're out with other people?" He made it sound like this was something I could turn on or off as I wanted. If that was the case, was this just a form of play-acting?

"I'm more than happy to follow your lead. If you don't

feel comfortable showing that sort of vulnerability, then everyone else will see us as the equals we are. But, eventually, I think you will learn to enjoy being yourself around our closest friends and family."

My body nearly melted. *Our* family and friends. Not his or mine, but a combined family. I liked the sound of that, and I didn't want to hold back in front of them. Since even Jack said that the differences between grown-up me and Middle me were subtle, I could just be me, and not have to worry about what they thought of me because they already knew. "Can we test this theory of yours a little more?"

"What do you have in mind?" I let out a frustrated huff. I didn't want to make these decisions. Like he said, I hated being the one in control. Wasn't it enough that I asked him this time? He should know how to move forward from here.

"I don't know." I fisted my hands in my hair, twisting it around my knuckles. Jack reached up, coaxing my fingers free before I hurt myself. "This is all crazy. I don't know what I'm supposed to be asking you to get what I want."

Jack shifted beneath me. As comfortable as his mattress was, it couldn't be good for him to be slouched back against the headboard with my weight on top of him. I sat up, and Jack lifted me up and turned me. I took the hint and straddled his legs. Like this, I was towering over him. I rested my chin on the top of his head. "I want to try this, but I don't know what that means. Maybe it would be easier if I was a real Little. That way you could change my clothes and pull out my toys, and I'd just know it was time to play."

"Just because you identify differently than some other Littles, doesn't mean you're any less real than they are." Jack traced patterns over my back. "Why don't we get dressed and meet in the kitchen," he suggested. "I'll make us breakfast, and we can figure out what we want to do next. The great thing about relationships—even kinky ones—is there isn't a set of rules to follow. I can't tell you what we're supposed to do next, because we're not following some preprinted checklist. So, we're going to figure this out together."

He gripped my chin tightly when I sat back, forcing me down until our lips crashed together. His tongue invaded my mouth as his fingers dug into the flesh of my ass.

This was quickly turning into a very hot diversion. And he dared to accuse me of being the one who tried to turn things sexual? Yeah, well it seemed I might be learning from the master.

"Daddy," I complained on a long whine when we came up for air. My dick was hard and leaking against his stomach. I twisted my hips, seeking out more friction. It wouldn't take long for me to get off, then I could slide down his legs and give him that thank you he'd suggested earlier.

"Nuh-uh," he scolded me, then lifted me up as if I weighed nothing and sat me down next to him on the bed. "Sorry, baby. That was mean of me."

The jerk didn't even look ashamed of himself. He wasn't sorry at all. In fact, the way he was biting down on his lip as he glanced at the problematic erection I was sporting, almost seemed as if he was pretty damn pleased with himself.

"You started it," I quipped. "Aren't you the one who tells me to finish what I start? I think the same should apply to you."

"You're absolutely right, sweetheart." He gave my hip a playful swat. "Why don't you go get dressed? And remember the rules."

I groaned as I dropped my feet to the floor. He seriously sucked, and not in a good way. I didn't bother asking which rule he was talking about. Well, he was going to have to deal with me coming to the breakfast table with a massive boner, because it wasn't gonna go down without some relief.

I kept my back turned as we both got dressed. Seeing his toned, naked ass wasn't going to do anything but drive me crazy. I stomped out of the bedroom, ignoring him when he called out my name. If he wanted a glimpse of preteen me, he was going to get it. It was totally normal for a preteen boy to throw a temper tantrum when he couldn't get off, right?

As I shut the bedroom door behind me, I swore I heard him chuckling at me. Jerk.

Somehow, he looked completely unaffected when I joined him in the kitchen. Like every other morning we had spent together, he was busy chopping vegetables. Today, I could also smell the breakfast sausage cooking in a pan on the stove. That was a new and pleasant surprise.

"What's for breakfast?" I asked, wrapping my arms around his waist from behind.

"Oh, now you're talking to me?"

"I can't be held responsible for my actions when I'm sex deprived and cranky," I warned him.

"I'll take that into consideration." Jack chuckled. After he set down the knife, he turned around and leaned against the counter. He noticed that I had already pulled my hair back, and his eyes lit up. I tipped my head to the side, knowing there was no way he could resist that invitation. I instantly regretted the impulsive move when he began sucking on the side of my neck. He held me firmly so I couldn't inch closer to him. He pulled back, licking his lips. "You're bound and determined to test your limits, aren't you?"

"Isn't that what I'm supposed to do?"

"It is, but remember, there are consequences for bad

behavior and rewards for being a good boy." Rewards. I like the sound of that a hell of a lot more than punishments.

"What sort of rewards?" Maybe knowing what I was working toward would help me when I was tempted to act out.

"We'll figure those out when we have some food in us." He pulled out a single coffee mug and filled it. When I tried skirting behind him to grab a mug of my own, he stopped me by wrapping his hand around my wrist.

"Not this morning, sweetheart," he informed me. "There's orange juice and milk in the fridge."

"You seriously expect me to function without coffee?"

"Let's call it a challenge. If you'd like, you can also take it as a simple test." This time, he drew me close in his arms, cupping the back my head, and pressing my face against his chest. "Boys shouldn't drink coffee. You've heard what they say."

"That is dangerous to tell a man he can't have his coffee," I quipped.

"No sweetheart, it'll stunt your growth."

I opened my mouth to point out that I had quit growing years ago, and then it dawned on me what he was doing. And, damn, if my dick didn't get on board with that. So did the rest of me. I sagged against Jack's body as the tension in my muscles released.

"Yes, Daddy," I agreed. I was the one who told him I wanted to explore regression a bit more, so, really, he was only giving me what I had asked for. "Anything else I should know?"

"Not yet. Would you mind setting the table? The plates are up there, and the silverware is right here," he told me, pointing to the drawer at his hip.

I quickly moved to pull two plates out of the cupboard in

the corner, then reached for the silverware. He shifted to the side, his fingers ghosting down my arm. I shivered at the casual touch.

As I allowed myself to relax, I became aware of a sensation I hadn't felt in a hell of a long time. I was happy. Not the fake happy I showed the rest of the world, but truly content. And it was because I was here with Jack, and he had asked me to move in with him.

Stupid. Reckless. Perfect.

I silently watched him finish making breakfast for us. While he worked, I pulled out my phone and did a quick search, wanting to find out everything I could about being a Middle. I still didn't want to jump into anything, but the more I thought about doing this, the more excited I became.

I stumbled over a forum and scrolled through the posts. It wasn't ideal, because it was geared for Daddies and little girls, not boys, but it was better than nothing, and it was a hell of a lot easier to read about others' real-life experiences, rather than work up the stones to ask Corey about it. My face flamed red as I realized why he'd offered for me to stop by and chat with him anytime if I had questions. Last night was starting to feel like an impromptu coming out of adult time party, with me as the guest of honor. I was horrified to think everyone who was there now knew about me.

I shook my head, preferring to focus on what I'd set out to do. As I read the questions and answers, something became clear to me: no one seemed able to put together a list of what makes a person a Middle, as opposed to a Little or even just Daddy's boy (or girl). That made me feel a bit better, since some of these people had been living this way for years.

Then, I saw a girl talking about how her Daddy helped her reclaim a hobby she'd given up because of an ex. I got emotional while reading her post about how this jerk in her past had told her she'd never amount to anything. While I hadn't suffered that, it sure as shit fit how I felt when my bandmates walked away.

I missed playing. Maybe my Daddy could help me get over my insecurity? It probably wouldn't ever be a career at this point, but I could still play for me.

"Daddy?"

Jack stopped what he was doing and glanced up. "Yes, sweetheart."

"I'm reading about Middles. I know we were going to wait until after breakfast to talk, and this probably sounds stupid, but I didn't want to wait to ask you about it."

Jack set down the spatula and took the stool next to mine. "Nothing you ask is stupid," he reassured me. "What is it?"

"Okay, maybe this doesn't even fall into what we're talking about, but I figured I'd ask anyway."

"Spit it out, already."

"Do you think it would be okay for you to give me rules about practicing my guitar?" The way Jack's face brightened it was obvious I had made a good decision. "And maybe we could set aside time for me to write, too. I know I said I couldn't sit down and write, but if I don't try, I'll never know if I could have something decent inside of me."

"I think that's a wonderful idea, sweetheart. Do you need someone to make sure you don't forget how important music is to you?"

I nodded, sucking my bottom lip between my teeth.

"Then that will definitely be one of your rules," he promised me. "Anything else you've seen that interests you?"

"Not so far," I responded. "I'm going to keep reading

while you finish up breakfast. I might come up with some-thing while we're talking."

"There's no hurry, sweetheart." He carried the pan of eggs to the table, scooping some onto each of our plates. Instead of sitting at one of the chairs, Jack crouched in front of me. "I'm proud of you for telling me what you want. As long as you promise you'll keep doing that, the sky's the limit."

I didn't believe in much, but as Jack rested his head on my knee, I thanked whatever higher power might be out there. This crazy, wonderful man had pulled me from the depths of rock bottom, and he'd offered me the world on a platter. I'd try every day to be worthy of his love.

THIS IS ONLY the beginning for Jack and Slade. They'll continue to explore kinks Slade can only dream of as The Lodge series continues with Corey and William's story in *Looks Can Be Deceiving.*

If you missed the introduction to the coolest kink club in Annandale, you'll want to check out Frankie's story as Calvin teaches him there are legal ways to surrender in *Exploration.*

Matteo and Levi can't wait for the new playroom to open! If you're in the mood for age play, you can read their story (and find out how Teo compares sex to pizza) in *Discovery.*

Jordan has been a constant through the entire Annan-dale series. Learn more about the club where he found love starting with *Kiss Me, Daddy.*

Annandale is quickly earning a reputation as the kinkiest city on the coast. Find out what happens when

Chase's secret comes out and his roommate won't let him hide his little side in *Rooming Together*.

NEVER MISS a new release announcement when you sign up for Quinn's newsletter. And as a thank you, you'll receive the short story where we first saw Theron. You're going to want to meet the man who will know how to take care of Sam!

A NOTE FROM QUINN

If you enjoyed *Rules to Live By*, I would love it if you let your friends know so they can experience the relationship of Jack and Slade as well! As with all of my books, I have enabled lending on all platforms in which it is allowed to make it easy to share with a friend. If you leave a review for *Rules to Live By* on the site from which you purchased the book, Goodreads or your own blog, I would love to read it! Email me the link at **quinn@quinnwardwrites.com**

You can stay up-to-date on upcoming releases and sales by joining my newsletter or readers' group.
Newsletter: http://bit.ly/QuinnWardWrites
Reader Group: http://bit.ly/Quinntessential

WELCOME TO ANNANDALE!

I hope you enjoyed this glimpse of the fictional town of Annandale. I've loved spending the past few years of my writing career building a kinky little city full of inter-connected characters. So far, you can visit:

Marino's - Mama was definitely shocked to learn all of her sons were kinky in one way or another, but she's proud of the men who are running the family restaurant.

Club 83 - Eli's worked hard to build a welcoming bar for the LGBTQ+ community. These daddies and boys will work their way into your kinky little heart.

The Lodge - As Jayden so astutely pointed out, The Lodge is like a mullet: it's innocent (enough) in the front, but the party is most definitely in the rear. So far, we've only seen the sweeter side, but there will definitely be a trip to The Back Deck in the future.

Talbert Hall - Coming very soon, you'll get your first glimpse of the kinkiest residence hall on campus. It's a known fact that those who thrive in Talbert don't fit in well other places. Be sure to join Quinn-tessential Readers if you'd like a sneak peek!

ABOUT QUINN WARD

Quinn Ward is a zamboni-driving, hockey-loving parent of two kids who are pretty okay most of the time.

When Quinn was three, their parents received a call from the principal asking them to pick them up from school. Apparently, if you aren't enrolled, you can't attend classes, even in Kindergarten. The next week, they were in preschool and started plotting their first story soon after.

Later in life, their parents needed to do something to help the socially awkward, uncoordinated child come out of their shell and figured there was no better place than a bar on Wednesday nights. It's a good thing they did because this is where Quinn found their love of reading and writing. Who needs socialization when you can sit alone in your bedroom with a good book?

Quinn's been kicked out of the PTA in three school districts and is no longer asked to help with fundraisers because they've been known get lost in a good book and forget they have somewhere to be.

ALSO BY QUINN WARD

Kinky in the City: Marino's

Exploration

Challenge

Discovery

Adventure

Club 83

Kiss Me, Daddy

Use Me, Daddy

Show Me, Daddy

Made in the USA
Coppell, TX
06 January 2021

47401421R00164

RSjAN2)